DANCES

DANCES

A Novel

Nicole Cuffy

ONE WORLD

NEW YORK

Published in the United States by One World, an imprint of Random House, a division of Penguin Random House LLC, New York.

ONE WORLD and colophon are registered trademarks of Penguin Random House LLC.

Hardback ISBN 978-0-593-49815-6
Ebook ISBN 978-0-593-49816-3

Printed in the United States of America on acid-free paper

oneworldlit.com
randomhousebooks.com

2 4 6 8 9 7 5 3 1

FIRST EDITION

Book design by Dana Leigh Blanchette

For all the little dancers

I

ENTRÉE

[barre]

The princess has shed some of her earlier shyness and learned to trust her suitors. Her smile is as confident and bright as a new coin; gone is her earlier hesitation. There is plain, fresh-faced gratitude as she accepts a rose from each of her suitors. The roses are bright, white, scentless. She throws them, not cruelly but joyfully, almost ecstatically. It has been some fresh miracle, learning to trust these four princes, a dawning. No one has hurt her yet. She has not been hurt a day in her life, in fact, never so much as pricked her finger. She suspects that there is no such thing as suffering. She understands suffering in the abstract—it is what made her shy of her suitors at first, but that they have not caused her pain makes its possibility even more remote. No one has let her down yet. She can almost believe there is no such thing.

I am the princess.

My reality is dual: I am Aurora, the white princess, just turned sixteen, who knows no suffering, and I am also Cece, the Black dancer of twenty-two, whose toes are screaming from being en pointe for so long, who is sweating like a slave, and whose ankle is throbbing distantly from a slow-healing sprain. I am counting as I dance—there is little room in my head for much else, though for a flash I do wonder if I feel up to holding that last balance for a couple of extra beats. I step forward, taking my suitor's hand as I rise en pointe in attitude derrière, ready for the first promenade. I am turned 360 degrees like a figurine, pivoting on the toes of my pointed foot, ankle protesting just outside the gates of my attention. I won't hold the balance too long, but I'll make sure to get my leg up nice and high in the arabesque to make up for it.

My second suitor approaches, and I steady myself, signaling the first suitor with a quick squeeze when I am ready for him to let go of my hand. For a brief moment, I am unsupported—or rather, I support myself—balanced on one leg. I bring both arms overhead in fifth position, the space between them an imaginary crown, and then I bring my arm back down, give my hand to the second suitor. Second promenade. I do this four times in total, ending with my high, unsupported arabesque. The music is swelling, the orchestra creating a big inhale. I tease the conductor a little bit by making the last supported pirouette a triple—he controls the music to match me. I smile mischievously at an audience I can't see beyond the lights. The music thuds to its dramatic conclusion as I flourish my arms in third position. *Oh Tchaikovsky,* I think.

At the barre, I drown out the clunky, repetitive accompaniment by playing Tchaikovsky's violin concerto in my mind. Tchaikovsky and Shostakovich—those were Paul's favorites. Demi-plié and then grand plié, butt low to the ground, knees reaching over the second toes. Tendus, foot caressing the floor and then pointing: *front, front, front fifth, front fifth, side, side, side fifth, side fifth, back, back, back fourth, back fourth, temps liés.* And then dégagés, slow and fast, the foot caresses and then flies—*front, side, back, side, side, back, side, front.* Rond de jambe, the foot sweeping graceful half circles into the floor, and fondus and développés, the legs growing long now, delicious bloom in the hips and the inner thighs. Frappes, the legs loose at the knees, the feet playful. And finally, grand battements, lifting high, throwing the leg front, side, back, side. Company class is both repetitive and vital.

Alison is one of my favorite ballet mistresses at the company. She is perpetually in a good mood, her combinations are thoughtful, her corrections precise and gentle. She is in the middle of the room now, humming to herself and doing a kind of half dancing, sketching. I barely have to listen as she sets the next steps. I have been taking class with Alison since my student days at the School of American Ballet. The New York City Ballet does not hold open auditions; it pulls its dancers from SAB. Every class was a battle raged against imperfection. I remember the desperate thrill of it, the hunger. I stood out because of my Blackness, and I was determined then to obliterate it, to render my Blackness irrelevant with perfection.

Kaz, NYCB's artistic director, took an interest in me early. He would slip into a class of young dancers, study us with his trademark stare. And he'd stop in front of me, watching me up close, very rarely offering a correction—only looking. To have Kaz's eye on you was like an anointment, his very gaze material, an investiture. His fascination with me was unnerving, terrifying. His visits to classes were unpredictable. I never knew when he would be watching me, and so I had to constantly be perfect, beautiful. I was the only Black face in a sea of white and tan; I could not be anything but visible.

The pressure was enormous. I couldn't have a bad turn day, or a fat day, when, no matter which clothes I wore, which mirror I checked, which angle I viewed myself from, all I saw was my body taking up too much space. When my knee started to ache, I couldn't sit out for the big jumps at the end of class. I was a brick-brown kid from Brooklyn. There were people around me—students and faculty alike—waiting for proof that I couldn't be graceful, that I was too heavy, too muscular, that my feet were too big, too flat, that I wasn't classical. Ballet has always been about the body. The white body, specifically. So they watched my Black body, waited for it to confirm their prejudices, grew ever more anxious as it failed to do so, again and again.

I mark the little flourishes, the movement phases with my hands and feet, and then my body knows what to do. This has always been a skill of mine, remembering. I have been doing this routine—or variations thereof—every day for seventeen years. It is as ingrained in me as the movements required for tying my ribbons. I don't have to think about it. Instead, I return to a favorite daydream of mine: I see the curtains rising, and the violin concerto is inflating, an orchestral bubble, and I can never work out whether it is I who appears first or my brother. Dwelling on Paul is a precious and carefully rationed indulgence. I just want him to see me now.

Préparation

Paul's arrival in the world came ten years before my own. I remember the bony press of my brother's lanky thigh against my knobby knee. There was, as there so often was, a record playing—Paganini, I think. In my small lap, I held the book Paul had brought home for me—an illustrated book about a ballerina, which neither of us could read because it was in Italian, but the last page of the book was a large watercolor of a girl in the middle of a grand pirouette en arabesque, pink-satin-clothed foot perfectly pointed. *That'll be you one day,* Paul told me. I ran a finger along the dancer's slender leg, reverent.

I tried to picture myself in the sparkling pink costume from the picture, spinning en pointe. I could almost feel it in my little body—the weight of the sequins and tulle, the weightlessness of the dance, the hard floor underneath my toes.

The dancer in the book had skin the color of a cloud in sunrise and straight yellow hair. My mother straightened my hair with chemicals over our kitchen sink, but given the thick grease she moisturized my scalp with and my utter disinterest in keeping my hair dry at all costs, it did not swing sensuously from my head but rather hung stiffly, like our homemade taffeta curtains. I couldn't picture that beautiful costume against my dark skin.

On the couch next to me, my brother was working with his

charcoals. Over the music, we could both hear our mother speaking sharply into the phone, and then Paganini's violin stuttered as she walked into the room. It was our mother's habit to walk around the apartment so heavily that she'd make my brother's records skip (Paul preferred the sound of vinyl to anything else).

That was your father, she told us. She spat the word *father* out like an accusation, like poison. I could never tell how my mother was going to feel about my father on any given moment. Now, she seemed angry. But the night before, I'd heard her crying in her bath. I'd opened the door and crept in, kneeling beside the tub. Her body was wavy under the water, transformed, her head leaning against the back of the tub, her eyes slightly wary. She'd crossed her arms over her stomach.

What's wrong, Mama? I'd asked.

She'd splashed water on her face, disguising the tears. *Nothing.* She'd sounded small. I'd noticed for the first time what a slight woman my mother was.

Now, she glanced down at my ballerina book and shook her head disapprovingly. *That what you want to look like? Is that why you like that ballet so much? Trying to dance your way out of being Black?*

Christ, Ma, said Paul. *Don't take you and Dad out on her.*

Don't encourage her. Celine, that *is not what we Black women look like. And it's not all we can do, dancing for the white folks.*

She can do what she wants. Isn't that the point? Let her be.

Who are you to reprimand me, boy? Can't even see straight, can you?

I looked between them, confused. Neither of them was looking at the other anymore. Or me. Or anything.

I think your tummy is pretty, I said to my mother, trying to be helpful.

But she only laughed an unhappy laugh. *You're just like your fa-*ther, *the both of you. Only difference is you two still got a chance to grow up.*

She left the room, the record punctured with staccato stutters.

She'll take him back again, Paul said. *They always do this.*

I looked up at him, not quite knowing what he meant but not wanting to reveal my ignorance. I didn't want him thinking I was a baby. *Mama's always mad at him,* I said.

Paul scoffed. *Can't really blame her.* He glanced at me and shook his head. *But it's never enough, is it? She just takes it out on us.* He checked that our mother was really gone and then fished something out of his pocket. He turned away from me, first bending all the way forward and then tilting his head back. When he turned back around, his nostrils flared and he smiled at my curious face. *You'll understand when you're older,* he said. *Hey, you haven't drawn me a picture in a while.*

Eagerly, I put my book away and got construction paper and crayons from my side of our room. When I came back, it looked like Paul had been crying, his eyes glassy and his hand absently rubbing his nose. I wanted to make something beautiful for him, but I kept stealing glances at him as he worked—the tip of his tongue kept peeking out at the corner of his mouth, there was a little crease between his eyebrows. His hands on the paper moved so beautifully, more graceful by far than my own clunky coloring. I tried to copy him. I saw him smile.

You trying to be like me?

I grinned and nodded.

He made some mistake I couldn't discern and threw down his charcoal, brought a hand to his forehead, smearing black there. *Shit,* he said.

My mouth opened in shock.

Sorry, he told me. *Whatever you do, Cece, do it pretty. They're always watching.*

I didn't know what he meant until I fell in love with dance, until I became used to the constant visibility.

[center]

My mother's birthday was Sunday, but I was busy dancing the matinee for *The Sleeping Beauty,* and I completely forgot to call her. For four days. We don't do gifts or cards, but I try to at least call her and wish her a happy birthday if I can't get out to Brooklyn to visit her. Sheepishly, I call her as I'm laid out on my back in the living room, doing my morning stretches. It's early, but I know she has her criminal law class at Brooklyn College this morning, so she will be awake. Ryn is boiling eggs, and their sulfuric stink leaks from our kitchen.

My mother takes a long time to answer, and when she does, she sounds slightly out of breath, like she's had to run to answer her phone.

"Happy belated birthday," I say.

"Happy birthday!" Ryn calls from the kitchen.

"Well, thank you," says my mother. "And thank you to Kathryn."

Kathryn shortened her name to Ryn when we got our apprenticeships with the company to sound more intriguing, but my mother never calls her Ryn.

"How's it going?" my mother asks. "What are you having for breakfast?"

"Ryn is making eggs," I say.

My mother and I generally keep our conversations at the surface level, but she is convinced that I must be anorexic because I'm a dancer. Asking about my meals is her way of checking in. It's not nearly as subtle as she seems to think it is, and I find it irritating. I pull my right knee into my chest, feel the sharp ridge of my patella against my palm. My ribs kiss my thigh as I take a deep breath.

"You know who I ran into the other day?" my mother asks.

"Who?"

"Señora Sandy."

Señora Sandy—Señora Ochoa-Famosa y Sandoval—was a small, freckled woman with an unruly halo of unnaturally red hair. She was a defector from the Ballet Nacional de Cuba, a fact she was fond of mentioning frequently to her students. Beginning when I was five, I took ballet classes from her in what would have been the living room of her cluttered Fort Greene brownstone, which seemed unbelievably lavish to me compared to the small Bed-Stuy apartment I shared with my mother and my brother and, intermittently, my father. Paul used to walk me to classes. He paid for them himself when my mother decided she didn't like how invested I was getting in ballet.

"I haven't seen her in forever," I say. "How is she?"

"She's walking with a cane now."

My mother says this in a faintly moralizing tone, as though this is what you get when you put your body through a career of ballet. I bite the inside of my cheek. I straighten my right leg, grabbing my heel and pushing my toes down somewhere above my head, a supine split. If my mother had ever had any use for dance, I believe her calling would have been African dance or contemporary—the two often bear a striking resemblance. She has the presence for it.

My mother is a latent Garveyite who keeps a framed map of

Africa over the dining table, and who, for the past two years, has been enrolled at Brooklyn College majoring in sociology and minoring in criminal justice so she can quit her job as a home-health aide and work for the NAACP. This accounts for at least some of her apathy toward my career. She is heavy in every sense of the word but the physical. She does everything with the full force of herself. It can be unbearable—most of all, I suspect, for her. She would have made a brilliant dancer, a heavy-footed modernist, consuming Katherine Dunham. If she'd had any use for dance.

But I resist heaviness, my presence is soft. It is ballet that chose me. But I chose it back, and I sometimes wonder if it wasn't, in part, a small act of rebellion. African dance is a pulse. It is thick, wise, and wild. Clamorous and uncanny. African dance says, *I am here.* Ballet says, *I am there.*

"She asked about you," my mother says.

"Oh?" I say, trying to picture what Señora Sandy would look like now, after so many years.

Señora Sandy was the first person to tell me I was a dancer. She was also the first person to tell me I couldn't dance with the New York City Ballet. *The life of a dancer is difficult,* she'd said. *A classical ballerina—a Balanchine ballerina—must have a certain body type. Long limbs, long neck, a small head, big eyes. Very lean and feminine. You, Cece, are not going to be that. You are athletic—powerful, thick muscles, you understand? Your butt sticks out, your chest is already budding, your mouth is not small like a doll's. There is a reason there have been very few Black ballerinas.*

She'd told me to set my sights on Alvin Ailey or Philadanco instead.

Dreams are for children, mami, she'd said. *You are a dancer.*

I'd left her studio when I was eleven, and got myself a scholarship to a prestigious school on the Upper East Side, owned by Luca Esposito and Galina Zaretsky. I paid for pointe shoes with my babysitting money. By this time, my brother had lost his scholarship to the School of Visual Arts after only a year. I knew it bothered him, but he tried to pretend it didn't. He said the teachers didn't get him, and all his classmates were older than him anyway. He was working as a line cook and producing frightening sketches—full of lines drawn so furiously they tore through the page—in a dark apartment that smelled of liquor and stale sweat. I was on my own.

I wonder what Señora Sandy makes of me now.

"Anyway," my mother is saying, "I have class in twenty minutes. Tell Kathryn I say hello and have a good time at dance." A note of condescension.

We hang up and I toss my phone onto the couch and switch legs, pulling my left knee into my chest. I can feel my heartbeat against my quadriceps, faintly, like a whisper. Ryn walks in, chewing something. She is wearing a tank top and dance briefs. Her legs don't have a scrap of fat on them—all sharply defined muscle and bone. I pull my knee into my chest harder, watch my thigh spread as it is pressed between my calf and my breast.

"Want an egg?" Ryn asks.

"Yeah," I say.

I get up and follow her into the kitchen. I douse my boiled egg in salt, and shove most of it into my mouth in one vicious bite.

My brother made it bearable to live with my mother. I adored him. It was he, not my mother, who constantly encouraged my love of ballet, even if it meant he had to do bad things to afford it. On a late fall day as he was walking me to class, I saw for the first time that there was a side of Paul he kept from me. A side I didn't know. We didn't exactly walk together—he was tall, and one of his strides could easily fit two of mine. I walked a little behind

him, trying to place my feet exactly in his footsteps. In order to
accomplish this, I had to do what was nearly a grand jeté, and
then that became more fun than finding my brother's footprints,
so I jetéd down Gates Avenue behind him. Paul was in one of his
bad moods—he walked without glancing back at me, listening to
Vivaldi on his old Discman. I knew it was Vivaldi because he had
been playing it so loudly when he came to pick me up that I could
feel the manic strings. He was not looking at me. I leapt bigger,
hoping to catch his attention, but I was rewarded with not so
much as a glance.

"Paul," I said. "Paul, watch me." But he couldn't hear me.

"Paul," said a much bigger, louder voice. This, my brother did
hear.

He took his headphones off and turned. I turned too. There
was a very large man coming toward us, one hand raised in a
wave. He was dressed entirely in baggy denim, the cuffs of his
jeans tucked into the whitest pair of sneakers I'd ever seen.

"What's good, cuz?" the man said. "I've been looking for
you—I got twenty."

Paul scowled at him. "The fuck you want, homeboy? You see I
got my little sister with me."

I frowned at the change in Paul's voice—it wasn't that he'd
cursed but that his entire voice, his entire accent had changed.
Our mother didn't like us to talk that way; she insisted we speak
"proper English."

The man held up his hands. "My bad, man," he said. "I ain't
realize she was with you." He smiled down at me. One of his front
teeth was gold. "How you doing?"

My brother cut in before I could say anything. "Holla at me
later—I got you then."

It was a dismissal, and the man seemed to understand it as

such. Once he'd walked out of earshot, I asked my brother, "Who was that?"

Paul turned his scowl on me. "Stop playing around back there and keep up. You want to be late?"

He put his headphones back on and began walking again at an even faster pace. I had to just about jog to keep up with him, so that by the time we reached Señora Sandy's brownstone, I was sweaty under my jacket.

I hesitated at the bottom of the stoop, hoping my brother would come out of his funk and say something nice to me. I thought I must have done something to annoy him, but I couldn't think what it was and I didn't know how to fix it. I tried so hard not to be an annoying little sister, but Paul's bad moods always felt like they were my fault.

"Well?" he snapped. I noticed that he was sweating too—it glimmered subtly at his hairline. And he was fidgeting with his oversized watch, shaking his knee back and forth. I wondered if he had to pee. "You going in or what? Because otherwise, what'd I walk you all the way over here for?"

I didn't move. I wanted my brother to say something kind, to undo the unpleasant aftertaste his mood had left on the day. But I was sure anything I said would be the wrong thing.

He sighed impatiently, rolled his eyes. He checked his watch, ran a hand over his face. His movements were jerky, like there was something inhuman possessing his body, and it hadn't yet figured out how to control the muscles smoothly.

"I can't keep walking you to and from class, you know. I'm busy—I'm working, I'm in college. You need to tell Ma that. You're big enough now."

I panicked. If Paul couldn't walk me to class anymore, then soon he wouldn't pay for my classes anymore either. And without him paying, I was certain our mother would decide I was done with ballet once and for all. I began to cry.

"Jesus, Cece," Paul said. He placed one large hand on top of my head, reluctantly comforting. "Come on, stop it. People are going to think I hit you or something."

"Good," I cried. "I hope they put you in jail."

"You do? Why?"

I could hear a little amusement in his voice and it soothed me slightly. He was reemerging, my brother.

"Because you're mean," I said.

He nudged at my carefully pinned bun and I ducked my head away from him.

"Look," he said, "you don't have to worry about the money, okay? I'll still pay. You're going to be a famous ballerina one day, right?"

I nodded, my tears slowing.

"Then you need your classes." He nodded at Señora Sandy's front door. "Go in."

I went up the stoop, drying my face with my sleeve. Now that I wasn't crying anymore, I was angry. I never asked Paul to walk me to class. That was our mother—he could save his bad mood for her. And he'd messed up my bun. Straightening it, I walked in. I began to stretch like I saw the older girls do. Class would begin soon. The same exercises, my body settling into a comfortable pattern. Barre and then center; little jumps, big jumps. Ballet made it so that I felt nothing but music. Ballet would take it all away.

I am beginning the ritual of putting on pointe shoes. Center is my favorite part of class. Alison is giving us a moment to catch our breath, drink water. I bend my shoes over the barre to warm up the shank. I've broken in these pointe shoes already so they mold to me, but they're still a little stiff. I tape my second toes because they're longer than my big toes and tend to lose the nail if I'm not careful. I slip on my toe pads—I usually stick with good, old-fashioned lamb's wool so I can feel the floor, but I'm being careful with my ankle, so I use the gel pads today.

I slip my feet into the shoes, lace the ribbons up and around my ankles, make a small knot and tuck it in so it won't dig into my Achilles tendon once I start dancing. And now, the sweetest part of class: I stand, come up onto my toes, listen to the whispered creak of my shoes yielding to me, bending, moving through the shapes my feet can make. Their life is short. Jasper puts his hand on my back and I wince. Not at his touch, but because I'm sweaty from barre and I'm worried that, upon touching my sweaty back, he'll be repulsed. But he only grins at me. I grin back.

"Love you, kiddo," he says.

We begin with adagio. I am growing up toward the ceiling like new, green life—développé to the side, arabesque, promenade in attitude, passé, pirouette attitude en dedans. I spin with my leg behind me, bent at the knee, arms stretched overhead. I catch a glimpse of my feet in the mirrors—I remember when I had to point with all my might to get them into the right shape. It is less effort now.

Jasper smiles at me as I finish the combination. He is handsome, flirtatious. I still get a fizzy feeling in my chest when I have his attention. His eyes leave me quickly. He is examining himself in the mirror now, and the feeling in my chest goes away. I try to lengthen my spine, mark the next combination with my hands. When I look in the mirror, all I can see is myself. I go into character, let my vision lose its focus. I pretend that the only thing before my eyes is the black void of audience. I perform a series of turns across the studio floor with three of the other female soloists—Ryn, Sylvia, and Anya. Ryn has the most beautiful balance, Sylvia is a long-legged waif, and Anya is always calculated perfection.

I don't know when Kaz entered the room, but I see him now, watching me thoughtfully. I run to the corner to take a swig from my water bottle. Jasper passes by and playfully spiders his fingers up my spine. I turn and frown at him—I don't like him to act this way when we're at work. But he only chuckles and takes his turn to spin across the room. Jasper and I have been together for four years. Everyone in the company knows we're a couple. But to the public, we're a dream pairing. Critics gush about our natural chemistry. We get compared to Mikhail Baryshnikov and Gelsey Kirkland. This only works in our favor if we keep our personal life personal.

I glance at Kaz before beginning the next steps. *And* croisé fondu to the front, croisé fondu to the back, plié—use the floor—passé, and développé à la seconde, arabesque, into retiré and rond, double rond with plié, sous-sus, pas de bourrée into fifth, and pirouette, and again—go for double—and soutenu, other side. I watch myself in the mirror. Point harder, reach through the toes; stay on your leg; get your shoulders down; lift up more; higher, higher. Over my shoulder, I can see Kaz watching me too as he taps Ryn between the shoulder blades, a reminder to lift her chest, use her upper back. His look is intense, inscrutable.

Turns now: We travel across the floor. We venture out together in groups of five. I turn with Jasper—we have a way of turning in unison without really trying. I'm going for triples and, mostly, I make them. After I finish in a particularly dramatic arabesque, Jasper laughs and wraps an arm around my waist. I can't help but laugh too. He keeps his arm around me as we move to the right-hand corner to prepare for the same steps, other side. Kaz has coerced our accompanist into making room for him on the piano bench. Every time I glance at him, his eyes are resolutely on me.

Petit allegro—we start with sautés, jetés, assemblés, sissonnes. Then échappé to coupé back, échappé coupé, chassé front fifth, and chassé effacé, assemblé croisé, and one, two, three, four, entrechat entrechat entrechat, hold. And on to the bigger jumps. The company flies across the floor. Sissonne side, *and* sissonne side, *and* tombé, pas de bourrée, glissade, pas de chat, relevé, entrechat six, relevé, tour jeté, *and* chassé développé croisé ta-ta-ta jeté croisé ta-ta-ta assemblé croisé, finish beautifully. The men try for a double saut de basque to finish.

At the end of class, as I'm peeling off my wet tights and shimmying into my warm-ups, Kaz approaches.

"Come to my office, darling," he says. "I want to talk to you."

From a few feet away, Jasper raises his eyebrows at me. I scowl at him.

Kaz defected from Soviet Russia in the early '70s, when Russian defectors were in high demand in the ballet world. He will tell anyone who listens that he defected out of love for his art and not out of disdain for the USSR. He still denounces decadence and capitalism. His office is spare and dark, the walls bare but for a portrait of Balanchine, the polished mahogany desk empty except for his thick old Mac and a lamp.

As I sit down Kaz smiles at me, and his eyes crinkle at the corners. I didn't notice how tense I was until just now; his smile relaxes me. I don't have much by way of family—my mother seems to think I'm a different species, my father was never consistently around, and I haven't seen or heard from my brother since I first got my apprenticeship at NYCB when I was sixteen. For me, Kaz and the company are it. Sometimes this feels rather precarious.

"How are you feeling, darling?" Kaz asks.

"Good," I answer.

He raises an eyebrow. "How is your ankle?"

It is throbbing distantly from class, but it's not the sharp, stabbing pain of a few days earlier.

"Better," I say.

Kaz sniffs. "Make sure you take very careful care of yourself," he says. "The body is precious. Yours is beautiful, an art. You cannot be careless with it."

I nod.

"Mi Yeong has done something terrible to her low back," he tells me. "I don't think she'll be able to do Saturday's show." He tsks.

Mi Yeong is first-cast for *The Sleeping Beauty*. She has been a principal for so long that the role kind of belongs to her. The Saturday-night show is our last performance for the spring season. I can't imagine Mi Yeong being out for it.

"*You* will dance Aurora Saturday evening," Kaz says.

I meet his eyes. His gaze is steady, uncanny. He is waiting for me to respond, and I can't think of what to say. All I can think of is how disappointed the audience and the critics will be to see a soloist take over a principal's role in the last performance. How I will have to be perfect. How this must mean something—Kaz is testing me either because he believes in me or because he wants me to finally, spectacularly fail.

"You are speechless?" Kaz asks. He is Russian, but his accent has always sounded faintly British to me. It has a way of making everything he says sound gentle yet full of gravitas.

"I—what about Mi Yeong's understudy?"

Kaz shakes his head. "You."

"Will Jasper dance Désiré?"

Kaz rolls his eyes. "As you wish."

Kaz holds an inexplicable contempt toward Jasper. *Jewels* was the first ballet I performed as a soloist. It is a Balanchine classic in three parts: "Emeralds," "Rubies," and "Diamonds." I danced the second ballerina role in "Emeralds" and got a rave review in *The New York Times* after that performance. *Celine Cordell,* they said, *surpasses her eighteen years in maturity and grace. She dances with her entire body with a suppleness that suggests that her bones are made not of collagen and calcium but of honey.* This sounded kind of horrible to me, like a debilitating disease. I tried to downplay the review, but it must've gotten Jasper's attention. He asked to partner me soon after that. Kaz has been absolutely evil toward him ever since.

I inhale deeply, relieved. Even though I have partnered with Rohan—Mi Yeong's Désiré—before, I'll feel much more secure with Jasper. "Thank you."

Kaz waves a hand.

I am dismissed. I get up and nearly run out to tell Jasper the news.

[adage]

Jasper walks in on me as I'm contorting myself in his mirror. It's a habit I picked up when I was a kid, soon after Señora Sandy told me I'd never be lean or feminine enough to be a classical ballerina. Before that, my body had meant almost nothing to me. That is, it did what I wanted and that was enough. I didn't know to care about how it looked, how long it was, how thin it was. I began to study my naked body in mirrors. And then I grew to distrust what the mirrors showed me.

Jasper has a full-length mirror in his bedroom, but I no longer trust it. I am suspicious of all mirrors. I test them by looking at my feet: If they seem smaller in the mirror than they do to my naked eye, then I walk away. This is not an exact science. But I believe the mirror in Jasper's bedroom to be slimming, so I am standing on his vanity and bending over so that I can get a good look at myself. Jasper rolls his eyes.

"It's too early for this," he grumbles.

We celebrated our Saturday casting last night, and I stayed at his apartment. I spend approximately half my time here; it is a second home. I lost my virginity here, to Jasper. We were rehearsing the *Barber Violin Concerto*—the first show we danced together—and he had this way of holding me. He wasn't really my type, but he's one of those people who's objectively beautiful—coppery brown hair, hazel eyes, tall, and a tremendous dancer. And he was so in control—he made us both look good. When he invited me to his place after work, I knew what it meant. He cooked me dinner—some kind of pasta. From there it was all very theatrical. He carried me in a ballet lift to his bedroom. He took his time undressing me, but he was assertive, his hands warm and strong. At one point, I almost felt like performing a pas de bourrée couru away from him and then letting him catch me, spin me, virginal swan princess. I didn't let the pain show in my face—I was used to that. I wasn't sure whether or not he could feel that he was deflowering me, but in case he couldn't, I wasn't going to give it away. I emoted for him just as I would in a role. And after he was done, he said that he guessed it was true that the darker the berry, the sweeter the juice, and I vowed to never let him touch me again.

Jasper grabs a handful of my ass on his way to the toilet. He pisses without lifting the seat. My ass smarts where he grabbed it; he was too rough.

"I don't know why you're still doing this," he says. "I have a scale. You don't have to guesstimate."

"I don't want to weigh myself," I tell him.

"Why not?"

He asks this as though we haven't had this conversation a dozen times.

"You *know* why," I say irritably.

He gestures toward his high-tech scale. Apparently, it can calculate your BMI and monitor your lean mass, bone mass, and water weight.

"You can't argue with empirical data," he says. "You're either where you want to be or you're not."

"That isn't the point," I grind out. "I don't want to fixate on the number."

"But you're fixating either way."

I shake my head. "You don't get it. It can be difficult for us girls. Last year, when that critic called Fran doughy, she wouldn't eat more than six hundred calories a day. Kaz made her take a break."

"You wouldn't do that."

"You don't get it," I repeat.

"You're like one of these chicks that complains about 'unrealistic beauty standards' and never thinks to just go to the gym."

I gesture to my body. "Are you complaining?"

"Obviously not."

"Then leave me alone." I bend over and pull my torso away from my legs, trying to see my thighs as other people might. Do they look as monstrous as I think they do, or is it a matter of perspective? I look into the mirror, bending and straightening my legs, watching the muscles work. When I squeeze my glutes, I see not only muscle but also the faint dimpling of cellulite. I frown, thinking back to that goddamn bread bowl at dinner last night.

Jasper wraps his arms around me, lifts me down from the vanity. He stoops to bury his face in my neck, a conciliatory gesture. "How many times do I have to tell you how beautiful you are?"

I want to argue, I want to talk about the cellulite.

"But you'll never believe me." He kisses me behind my ear. "I just wish you trusted me more."

I pause. This catches me off guard. "I trust you," I say.

"You never listen to me."

"I do. I listen to you."

"It kinda sucks, babe."

I look up at him, wrap my arms around his waist. "I'm sorry. I do trust you."

He half smiles, shrugs. "Let's get ready for work."

He leaves me alone in the bathroom again. I hold up a hand in the mirror. I try to gauge whether my hand's reflection is the same size as the hand itself. I try to gauge whether this mirror is distorting me or not. I stretch my arms out to the side, watch my skin stretch taut against my sternum, the bone rippling at the center of my chest like lake water. Or that is just a trick of light and shadow. I can never be sure of my own eyes.

I am at attention. I take my place and bourrée toward Gwen, who is dancing the Lilac Fairy. I use her for balance as I go into an arabesque penché, reaching with my whole body toward Jasper, an enchanted Désiré. He wants me, but Lilac stands between me and him. I am only a vision. He has not earned me yet.

We are interrupted: "*Stop.*"

Cecilia is rehearsing us for *The Sleeping Beauty*—we are going through act two. Cecilia is Kaz's twiggy, Spaniard wife, and she has hated me since I was an apprentice. She is tall, thin in a model way more than in a dancer way. She has an olive complexion and blond hair, and she has this long nose that somehow makes her face more interesting. Not quite pretty but interesting. She towers over me. She must've been difficult to partner when she was still dancing.

"Try not to manhandle Gwen, Celine, eh? Or can you not do an unsupported penché? Again."

I nod resolutely, and we start over again. This time I make it through the two penchés. I bourrée toward Jasper twice and spin out of his reach at the last minute. I pretend I'm onstage, feel my audience, my critics, watching. Cecilia slips out of the forefront of my mind. But then I bourrée up behind Jasper, place a hand on his shoulder and lift my back leg. He walks around in a circle, rotating me, a promenade en dehors. I lose my balance and begin to wobble, my back leg dropping slightly. I am not having a good balance day. I bite my tongue in frustration as I flop out of pointe.

"Stop," Cecilia says again, unnecessarily.

Sweat drips into my eyes, and I all but slap it away. Jasper places a hand on my lower back but I shake him off.

"Celine," Cecilia says, but she says it in the French way—*Céline*—which she does when she's about to say something particularly passive-aggressive. "Maybe you will not be ready for Saturday. You hurt your ankle, didn't you?"

Gwen rolls her eyes at me from behind Cecilia's back.

"It's better," I say.

She harrumphs, turns her back, and waves a hand.

We begin again.

Jasper holds me at the waist, and I développé. I exaggerate the extension, pushing my leg toward my ear, my foot toward the ceiling, and then it opens into a penché.

"Watch your arms," Cecilia says over the piano. "This isn't *Swan Lake*." But she doesn't stop us.

Passé, fouetté, *and* développé. I run through a line of dancers—the corps—once again evading Jasper's grasp. My practice tutu scrapes their spare waists. Again, Lilac steps in to keep Désiré away. Still, he has not earned me. I am running, pausing occasionally for seductive arabesques. I am definitely more of an adagio dancer, even if my balance is sometimes questionable. All this quick-footed running winds me.

"Do you not have turnout?" Cecilia calls. "You are dancing, not running a marathon. Fix your feet."

Yes, yes, I think. My feet. I don't have flat turnout *and* I don't have a super-pronounced instep *and* my balance is sometimes off *and* I have trouble turning left *and* I have that patch of cellulite on my ass *and* my tits are a monstrous B cup. Cecilia can't say anything I haven't already said about myself.

Jasper catches me at the waist again and I lift my right leg in attitude and lift up into développé, and renversé back into penché, and pirouette, ending chest to chest with Jasper, and I peel my torso away, with a backbend toward the audience. I arabesque, and Jasper lifts me overhead, a press lift, my arms in fifth as we rotate. Back down into an arabesque. He reaches out a hand to me, and I take it. I lose my balance again in attitude derrière, and I see Cecilia narrow her eyes. Pirouette into penché, and then a supported grand jeté off the "stage"—for now, we press ourselves against the side wall of the studio.

Jasper puts me down. I am panting, my leotard clinging wetly to my abs. Even the backs of my hands are slick with sweat. Jasper is sweating too, but not like this, and Gwen is pristine. I resist the urge to double over, instead looking at myself in the mirror. No one here is as drenched as I am. The corps does their dance and I get only a moment's respite. Then I'm back at the center of the room. Small hops for a rotating arabesque, fouetté, en dedans, and again, and again, then the chaînés out of Jasper's way.

The music is more playful now, the steps faster. There is more contact between Aurora and Désiré. My pirouettes wobble like the spinning of a dreidel, I am off my leg in penché. I can feel my jaw tightening. Obviously, it isn't like I've never danced Aurora, but the role suddenly feels brand-new to me. I am going to botch Saturday's show, Mi Yeong's show. The critics will gut me, like when they called Rohan a flat-footed trucker. Sauté, and run away. I run to the corner of the studio. The piano stops and Cecilia rises from her chair like an oversized cat. Jasper, Gwen, and I wait for notes. I am panting, my belly expanding with every intake of breath. I suck in my stomach.

There is a film of mucus at the back of my throat as Cecilia more or less tells Jasper and Gwen that they were perfect.

"And you," she says to me. "My husband is trusting you with the last show this season."

I nod mutely.

. . .

It's been a while since I visited Luca and Galina. He is Italian, from some village in the north I'd never heard of until I met him. She is Ukrainian, named after Galina Ulanova, who was Russian. Both had danced for the Kirov, or, as she would patiently but infallibly correct, the Mariinsky. They have been married for something like forty years. I'd found them in an article in *Dance Magazine* when I was eleven. Some intensive Google research revealed to me that many of their students went on to dance at American Ballet Theatre, Pacific Northwest Ballet, Joffrey Ballet, Houston Ballet, Boston Ballet, and, yes, even NYCB. They were who I turned to when I'd outgrown Señora Sandy.

There is some crazy construction going on in the subway, so I take an Uber to the Upper East Side. I remember taking the subway here from my house, a trip that generally lasted more than an hour, and slipping into a world of privileged white kids—I was the only student of color, the only one on scholarship. Luca and Galina fully took me under their wing for three years—they made little ballets on me, helped me win competitions; *The Village Voice* had done a piece about me playing Marie in their version of *The Nutcracker.* And when I was fourteen, they proudly sent me off to audition for the School of American Ballet, unsurprised when I got in. They were my first stable family.

I walk inside the building through the unmarked door to the left of the vegan café downstairs, past the disinterested doorman. I take the elevator to the second floor; I remember that, the first time I came here, I wasn't sure what I'd see once the elevator doors opened, and I'd tried to appear unbothered in case the doorman was watching me on a security camera. I follow the dim, carpeted hallway, which has always smelled like the inside of a dance bag, past the domed, industrial window and around a corner, where the studio's waiting room suddenly appears: white chairs against a brick wall, a pile of dance magazines on a low table.

Music is coming from one of the studios—Luca on his violin. Faintly, I can hear Galina's sharp voice offering acerbic corrections. I smile at the three perfumed dance moms in the waiting room who are eyeing me curiously. I check my phone. Class should be over in a few minutes. I settle myself into one of the chairs. On the wall across from me is one of Paul's charcoal drawings, his *Little Dancer* series, after Degas. I, twelve or thirteen, am standing casually en pointe, my form emerging from a furious mass of black lines—Paul's signature style. Something aches deep inside. I remember Paul shyly presenting the piece to Luca and Galina, thanking them for giving me a scholarship. They didn't want to take it for free, but his wound, his fragility was plain in his eyes.

The studio door opens and preteen dancers stalk out, their grace underdeveloped, awkward. A couple of them glance at me, and then look back with a more lingering gaze. I wonder if they recognize me, or if I am simply strange to them. The dance moms gather their cygnets and leave, and after a few moments, I hear the piano start up, the violin accompanying. It will be Luca, of course, on the violin, and Galina on the piano. I stand, begin to walk quietly to the open door.

The only treat better than seeing them play together was seeing them dance together. I remember the first time I saw it; they did the pas de deux from *Giselle:* I watched Galina's face. Only she wasn't Galina; she was an innocent peasant girl with a weak heart, falling in love for the first time. It was all there in her face, in her feet, her supple arms. Her torso was a limb too—it moved with as much grace, as much flexibility and fluidity as her arms. And even though they had both aged out of their dancing careers, I could see the aching, hungry need for dance still in them. I recognized it. I was almost brought to tears.

I stand in the doorway, watching Luca sway on his feet as he coaxes something melancholy and sweet from his violin, Galina improvising accompaniment. I recognize it: Bach's Chaconne. They have not noticed me yet, so I kick off my sneakers and bourrée into the studio in my socks. I can hear it in the music when they see me, though they don't stop—the music only grows, it gathers more heat, more energy. The piece is for solo violin, but Galina's piano sweetens the music.

I make it up as I go: pirouette to plié, again, pop up to arabesque, promenade, kick up into développé, renversé, penché. I walk slowly across the floor in demi-pointe, my arms melting slowly from fifth down to my sides. I am constantly improvising, choreographing in my head, wherever there's music. I let their music move me, they let me move their music. It is more fluid than thinking, more intimate than collaboration. The dance is the music and the music is the dance. We understand each other so naturally. Not for the first time, and not without guilt, I wish Luca and Galina were my parents, that our connection extended even to blood.

When I'd first come to Luca and Galina's studio, Paul was already beginning to disappear. My mother had kicked him out because, as I later found out, he was a drug addict. He'd gone to live with our father and hated it, and my mother had let him move back home. But he was never the same. He began gradually fading from my life. I mourned him, even when I still saw him every day. In him, I saw that that thing in us—that thing that made him love art, and me ballet—could devour us whole if we didn't maintain control over it. By eleven, I was more independent, more mature, than I should've been. The first time I traveled to the Upper East Side to this studio, I was struck by how different a world it was.

It was Luca I met first. I'd been prepared for them to be skeptical of me, dismissive. I had a script ready, had practiced emulat-
ing a confidence I didn't feel.

"I want to be a dancer," I'd told him. "I want to come to school
here, with you and Madame Esposito."

He looked bemused but intrigued, and there was something
hard, exacting there as well. "Have you been taking ballet?"

I nodded. "Since I was five."

"Have you started pointe?"

"Last month."

He crossed his arms. "What is your name?"

"Celine."

"Many little girls want to become dancers, Celine. Few ever do.
Most will never be ballerinas. Do you know what it takes?"

"Lots of hard work. And discipline."

"That's right. Dedication. Our serious girls take classes here
five days a week."

"I'm ready."

He looked me over, assessing. "I believe you, little one. Bring
your mother tomorrow. We will all talk."

I shook my head. This was going to be the hard part, convinc-
ing him that I didn't need my mother, that this decision could be
mine alone. "My mother doesn't understand. I didn't tell her I
was coming here—she thinks ballet isn't 'useful.'" I used air
quotes. "But," I added quickly, "I can pay. I babysit; it's how I've
been paying for my dance classes. And my brother can help. He's
twenty-one. I mean, I haven't asked him, but I know he would."

Luca lifted one eyebrow, hesitated. He looked me over again,
bit his lower lip. "Why don't you dance for me?" he said.

This, I had been expecting. I set down my dance bag, took off
my jacket and jeans. I sat down to put on my slippers, hoping I
was warm enough. I did a few quick stretches on the floor, aware

of Luca watching me, evaluating. I stood, feeling self-conscious even as my muscles, knowing what was to come, yearned to move, to leap and stretch.

"What do you want me to do?" I asked.

He shrugged, with a little impatient flourish of his fingers. "Dance."

"Whatever I want?"

"Whatever you want."

I gave a brief, obedient nod of my head. I had been prepared for this too. I made my way to the far corner of the room. Stage right. I did not announce the variation I intended to perform; I only prepared, lengthening, my whole body humming in anticipation. I began to count—one, and two, and three, and four, *and*—playing the music in my head. At the time, the score was familiar to me, but still novel, still enchanting, not rote as it is now, as mundane and repugnant as the screech of the C train on its tracks. I had a DVD of the Bolshoi's Nutcracker at home, and it was this Sugar Plum Fairy that I channeled, because it was the most beautiful interpretation I'd ever seen.

I smiled at Luca as I danced, no longer Celine Cordell but magical royalty. Though in slippers—I was not confident enough yet in my toe shoes—I danced as though I were en pointe, long, light. By the time I reached the lightning-fast turns at the end I was ecstatic, transported, scarcely aware of what my body was doing except that it was doing it effortlessly. I'd reached a sweet spot. I was flying. I ended without wobbling, sweating and panting, one leg extended in front of the other, toes pointing into the floor, arms in fourth. I was still smiling, but I wasn't looking at Luca anymore. I couldn't. I looked down my nose, my vision still blurred from thirty-two counts of spinning.

"What is this you do?"

The voice was not Luca's. Though I couldn't see her at the

studio door behind me, I knew it was Galina. Her Ukrainian accent was much thicker than her husband's Italian one. I relaxed back into myself, releasing the pose, and turned to face her.

"It was the Sugar Plum Fairy," I said.

"Sugar Plum Fairy," she scoffed. "Sugar Plum Fairy, she is regal, playful—da da da *dum* dum—but in control always. Your arms are sloppy in manèges, your butt stick out in piqué. Go to barre."

I obeyed, held on to the barre as she lifted my leg to my ear, told me to point my foot and then flex it. She nestled her arm against the small of my back and had me bend backward over it. She prodded my ribs, my chest, my hip bones with firm, almost rough fingers. I noticed that she had perfect, strangely youthful hands. She stretched my arms out to the sides and seemed to measure them with her eyes. She knelt down and examined my knees, knocked at my shins, dug her smooth fingers into my thighs until she could feel my femurs. She told me to come into first position, and she studied my turnout.

"So, you want to be dancer?" she asked.

"Yes."

She stood up straight. She was a very small woman, only a few inches taller than me. "Play for us, dorogoy," she said to Luca. And to me, "Do this: arabesque penché, promenade, attitude, prépare, sissonne, pas de bourrée, pas de chat, piqué, piqué, piqué, and chaînés to finish, yes?" She gave the directions rapidly, sketching the movements as she went.

I nodded. I knew she was testing me. I could already feel the combination, my body itched to perform the movements. As Luca began to play, I leaned forward in a balance, brought my back leg up as high as it could go behind me, toes longing for the ceiling. In this position, using the strength of my balancing leg and the bouncing of my foot, I turned myself in a circle, wobbling as I fought to maintain balance. I came up, crossing my back leg in front of me and pausing there, just for a beat. The arch of my balancing foot was beginning to ache and I was glad when I brought my other foot down to prépare. I did the first jump, a relatively small one, my legs sweeping away from each other in the air, and then a little side step followed by traveling little jumps on the diagonal, my toes brushing the insides of my thighs as I hopped. Then the turns, continuing my diagonal line with three spins, one foot coming up to the inside of my thigh, and then rapid spinning on two feet until I reached the opposite corner of the room.

I did not hold my finish, but turned to Galina, waiting for criticism with the same eagerness with which one examines a wound as soon as it's been made.

"You are late," she said. "You know how to count, yes? Again. *And* . . . "

I did it again. Sweat beaded on the bridge of my nose, but there was no time to wipe it off. I spun faster at the end, hoping to whisk it away.

"Now arms are sloppy again. They are like noodles in wind. You are tired? How you dance whole ballet if you are tired after only one little combination? Again. *And* . . . "

This time, I nearly fell out of the arabesque as I fought to keep my extended leg from shaking. My eyes suffered the pressure of coming tears by the time I finished the turns. I pushed them back. I had been arrogant, delusional. I was nothing to these Mariinsky veterans. I was a child, a joke.

"Don't be upset," Galina said. "How can you learn if you get upset?" She snapped her fingers at me. "Dancers do not cry. Again. *And* . . . "

I took a deep breath and did it again. I didn't think about anything this time—not the sweat picking its way down my back, not

Galina's bright blue gaze on me, not the steps. My body knew what to do, understood without the leash of consciousness. The only thing I paid attention to was the music, Luca's haunting violin. He was playing a song I had recognized slowly—Sugar Plum Fairy music, in fact, but altered, slowed down and sweetened so that it became almost mournful. I was sorry when he stopped playing. I finished with a dainty port de bras, my arms reaching for the ghost of the music.

"Aha," Galina said, as though I'd solved her riddle.

She and Luca began to speak to each other in French. I only knew some words in French, and with their accents, I couldn't understand anything. Though I didn't exactly try to understand; I didn't want to know what they were saying. Despite my sweating, I felt chilled. I hugged myself, looking down at my feet in my ballet slippers. I heard Luca say my name and Galina repeat it, but they weren't talking to me. I was just a kid, I thought. Just a stupid, regular kid.

"Come here, little one," said Luca.

I didn't look at either one of their faces as I approached. I looked at Luca's violin, at the piano in the corner of the room, at Galina's shining pink fingernails.

"Feet are straight," said Galina, and my heart sank lower than I thought it could. "Face looks startled, like Kewpie doll. Port de bras is chaotic, fifth position is lazy, balance is like baby horse. And why you stick butt out in plié?"

I was, again, dangerously close to tears. I wanted to run out of the studio. I already knew by now that I wasn't good enough, that I was unteachable. Why did Galina have to torture me? Why pick apart every little thing that made me not a dancer?

"But," she said, "beautiful turns, beautiful jumps. Good ballon. And very good memory for little girl."

"You are very musical, Celine," said Luca.

I looked up. Luca was smiling at me, and Galina was not smiling, but there was a softness in her blue eyes, around her mouth.

"Yes," she said. "We make dancer out of you. We teach in the way of Vaganova here—you know Vaganova? You learn American style later, if necessary. You want?"

I nodded so hard that my head swam. I felt as though I'd been held over a flame and then pulled away at the last second.

"Good," said Galina.

"This is a commitment, Celine," said Luca. "We will expect you to be serious. And babysitting will not cover the cost."

My heart sank all over again, and my vision clouded with wetness.

"You are talented," Luca continued. "We want to help you. Every now and then, when we meet a young girl with promise, we offer a scholarship."

I sniffed, shoved the tears back with an almost violent determination. I looked from Luca to Galina and back, astonished, hopeful.

"We are impressed by you, Celine," said Luca. "And we think you would be right for the scholarship."

Now my insides took flight. I was surprised I could stay connected to the floor.

"But there are conditions," Galina said. "You take classes six days a week—every day after school and Saturday mornings. No more babysitting, I think. Private sessions with me four times a week. And you follow rules of school: You show up on time, no skipping, neat attire, hair in bun."

"And we must meet your mother," Luca said. He pressed his hands together as though he were pleading with me. "This is unorthodox enough—we cannot teach you without talking to her. Bring her in tomorrow. You can do it?"

"Yes," I said, though I didn't know yet how I was going to ac-

complish it. My mother went to parent-teacher conferences reli-
giously, but that was about it; no dance recitals or school plays or
even science fairs. *Your report card has everything I need to see,* she'd
say. And I knew she was going to be angry with me for seeking this
studio out on my own. *You think you're grown,* she was going to tell
me, and she wasn't going to want anything to do with it. Getting
her to come was going to be nearly impossible, but somehow, I
had to get it done. "It'll have to be after she gets out of work," I
said.

Luca nodded.

Galina clapped her hands together twice. "Now. You bring
pointe shoes with you? Good. Put them on. We fix those straight
feet, make toes and ankles strong."

I did as I was told, hungrily.

Galina brings a tray of steaming tea, the water boiled on the old
hotplate in her office, and a sleeve of Roshen cookies, which she
brings back in bulk from her annual visits to Ukraine. I used to
never eat these when she offered. As a teenager, I'd held this core,
unarticulated belief that a dancer's joy must come from dance
alone, and all else should be utilitarian. When I looked at pictures
of dancers' spare, sinewy bodies, I thought discipline must be a
single-mindedness, a sacrifice. I, like many young dancers, revered
that form of discipline as one would a god.

I take two cookies and tell them about Saturday night's show.

"Will you come?" I ask.

"Of course we will come," says Luca.

Galina huffs. "Only if you close mouth while dancing," she
says. "And stop thrusting chin. What are you, Osipova?"

"What are you saying?" Luca protests. "Osipova is a beautiful
dancer."

"Osipova is gaping moose with pointe shoes."

"My dear, that is a ridiculous thing to say."

"You are Cecchetti fool."

"I trained at the Vaganova Academy just like you."

"Yes, but you are Italian. All Italians are grotteschi dancers."

"And all Russians are pazzi."

"I am *not* Russian."

"When we go to Kyiv, all I hear is Russian."

"That is not the point. Now, we are making dancer, or we are making moose?"

"We are making a beautiful dancer. Like Natalia Osipova."

I laugh. I have missed their bickering, Galina's insistence that I am still a student of hers, that she is still *making* me.

Galina waves a hand dismissively at her husband. "In any case," she says, "yes, Cece, we come to your show, I think."

"You're dancing for"—Luca snaps his fingers, as though to ignite the spark of memory—"Mi Yeong, yes?"

I nod, and Luca and Galina both raise their eyebrows, exchange a knowing look. I've always admired this, their secret language, as much as it frustrates me to be outside of it. Galina takes a genteel sip of tea, her clear blue eyes meeting my dark ones over the rim of her cup.

"Why you come to see us today?" she asks.

"I missed you."

Galina scoffs and Luca smiles. Both are expressions of affection.

"We wish you would come and visit more often," Luca says. "You are our favorite student."

"You're exaggerating," I say, examining a small snag in my leggings.

"No," Galina says. "We don't exaggerate."

I worry the snag with a fingernail.

"I had the worst rehearsal the other day," I say. "Ever since Kaz told me I was dancing the last show, it's like I don't know how to dance the role anymore."

"Just dance, Cece," says Luca. "You are a dancer. It's in your body already."

"The critics are going to be just waiting to lacerate me. They'll compare me to Mi Yeong, and one time, she held that last balance in the Rose Adagio for, like, a *minute*. I don't know why Kaz is doing this—I feel like a sacrificial lamb."

Galina sets her cup down hard enough that it clanks assertively. "You go fish for compliment? Or you really such a silly girl?"

I don't answer—she doesn't expect me to. I've turned the snag in my leggings into a small hole.

"Don't you know how unheard-of it was for you to audition the way you did? Just a little girl? And for us to give you a scholarship?" Luca flutters his fingers in front of his face. "We saw what a talent you are. We are not the only ones."

"Dorogoy," Galina says, "but it is not about *talent*. Everybody have talent where she is."

"Yes, yes," says Luca. "It's more than that. But—" He sets down his cup and leans forward. "Cece, what do you want?"

He asks me this with such sudden intensity that I am taken aback. Both he and Galina wait, crystal-eyed, for my answer. I think of the ballerina in that little Italian book. I remember the pink of her costume, the bliss on her cartoon face. I remember my brother's hands, his peculiar way of holding the book open with two fingers, its spine resting in his palm. I remember his voice— *you and me, just like Degas and his little dancer*—and the dark moon of his face. The backs of my teeth ache. I push Paul away, hard.

"I want to keep going," I tell Luca and Galina.

They both nod.

"Then don't hide," Galina says. "You know what you are.

Don't pretend you don't know. And when they don't see it, you make them."

"Make them see it on Saturday, Cece," Luca says. "We'll be there."

Now I nod. I bring my mug into my hands, pressing my palms into its side, searching for warmth.

I watch myself in the mirror: black leotard with my tights pulled up on the outside, my hair beginning to rebel against the bun I smoothed it into this morning. It is getting late—this studio is empty but for me. I have been here for twelve hours. I pause to think, and even alone, I stand with one foot in front of the other, knee bent so my legs look good, hands at my sides. My arms look huge today for some reason. I know it's not logical—I thought they looked great yesterday, and I know I didn't gain weight in my arms overnight—but I put my hands on my hips anyway. It's slimming. I tilt my head at myself in the mirror. I wonder if my reflection accurately shows what other people see when they look at me. Whenever I look at myself, I yearn for a perspective other than my own, but I can never have it. I wonder if anyone is watching me right now, from some undetectable vantage point.

Perfection is my goal. I can only try for it and I'll always fall short. But it's the leap itself that makes my art beautiful, not its climax. I watch myself as I dance, correcting myself as I go. Lift the chin, relax the shoulders, soften the elbows, point harder. I execute a pirouette that I'm actually proud of, and I try to remember the sensation of it, every muscle that fired just right, so that I can do it again. I give my reflection a huge stage grin, baring my teeth. I look like an animal.

I am dancing Aurora alone. I've been having trouble with the vision scene I rehearsed with Cecilia the other day. The Rose

Adagio is supposed to be the hard part, but here, Aurora is in between worlds, suspended. She is not innocent anymore—she has
been hurt, cursed—but she has been frozen in time, and so is not
yet a woman, either. In order to break the curse, she has to convince Désiré that she has everything he needs. And yet, this seduction cannot be quite sexual. It must be deeper, spiritual. And it
must all be done from limbo.

Does it hurt, Aurora? I wonder. Are you aware of time having
slipped through your fingers? Are you desperate for Désiré—must
it be him? or will any prince do?—or is your sleep peaceful and
blank? I rise en pointe, arms in fifth. My body is tired, and my
balance is off; I have to fight for control. Right now, it is a losing
battle.

I think of my mother in her best-looking dress and a pair of
scuffed heels, the day she grudgingly went with me to the Upper
East Side to meet Luca and Galina to discuss the scholarship. I
think it was her need to prove that she wasn't whatever she thought
they assumed she was, that she wasn't lazy or negligent, that she
wasn't cruel or dumb, that she wasn't what they believed a Black
single mother was—unemployed, uneducated, on food stamps—
that persuaded her to come with me.

She walked with her back ramrod straight. She held my hand
as we crossed Lexington—something she hadn't done since I was
very small. We'd gotten into a fight, first about the fact that I'd
auditioned without her permission, and then because I refused to
eat the huge plate of pancakes she'd made for breakfast. My
mother was sure I was starving myself, and I was sure she was trying to fatten me up—she valued what she called "stacked" women,
an aesthetic so at odds with classical ballet that I saw it as a kind
of sabotage.

I try to feel that now, the disorientation of finding yourself
somewhere inscrutable, the constant strain of being cloaked in

thorns, both armor and camouflage. Would I want someone slicing through all that, even if it meant I could wake up? Or would
such a prospect terrify me no matter how much I wanted it?

There is lightness now, the ready spring of prey.

An animal, yes. That's what cages make of us. I run from my
imaginary Désiré, keeping myself just out of his reach. This is
part of the seduction, yes, but it is also defensive, part of that prey
struggle. And what do animals do when cornered?

Later that evening, after she'd reluctantly signed her consent,
my mother came into the bathroom as I was brushing my teeth. I
saw her briefly examine herself in the mirror, turning her critical
gaze onto her body in profile. Whatever she thought of her slender frame, it didn't show on her face. She began wrapping her
hair in a ratty satin scarf.

"I don't get this ballet thing," she'd said. "And I don't like you
going behind my back like you're grown, embarrassing me in
front of those people. But, a scholarship's a scholarship, I guess."
She looked at me hard for a moment. "You're not your brother,
are you?" she asked.

I had no idea what she meant. I wasn't sure whether she was
asking if I was going to lose my scholarship like Paul lost his or
whether she was asking if I was going to begin disappearing as
Paul had begun to disappear. Was I going to fail, like Paul? Was I
going to become something shameful, something not to be men-
tioned in front of strangers? I used my foam-filled mouth as an
excuse not to answer her.

"I'd rather take the money and pay for your college, but," she
sighed, "what am I supposed to do?" She rubbed at the space
between her eyebrows. "I'm not even sure what kind of kid you
are sometimes." She stood up straighter, crossed her arms. "Here's
the deal: Your grades cannot drop. At all. If I see anything less
than a B plus on that report card, I'm pulling you out irregardless

of that scholarship. And you need a backup plan. I know you and these . . . these *Russians* think ballet is your whole future, but . . . but it's not the end all, be all, okay? There's other things you can do with yourself."

I spat. "But ballet's all I want to do."

"You're just a kid, Celine. You don't know—anything can happen."

"Like what?"

"I don't know. Anything. I was in school when I got pregnant with your brother. Couldn't graduate. I wanted—" She shook her head, lifted her hands again to fuss with the knot in her head scarf.

"Ballet's all I want to do," I repeated.

She dropped her hands and faced me. "Don't be dramatic. You know what you don't have? Perspective. Lord, I don't know what it is in you kids that makes you not want to listen to me. You both got that from your father." She looked me over and then shook her head. "*Ballet,*" she mumbled. "We'll see." And she left me alone in the bathroom.

My foot, seemingly of its own accord, rolls down from the box of my pointe shoe.

I've lost it now. This is why I try not to let my mother, and especially not Paul, creep into my thoughts when I'm dancing. They push me off my leg. I look at myself in the mirrors, this time not posing. I am panting, sweaty. My legs shake as I stand, the muscles exhausted. My ankle is beginning to ache dully. I am hungry, frustrated. My body is simply rejecting this dance, rebelling. I put my hands on my waist and squeeze until my fingertips touch each other. I begin again.

[allegro]

The studio smells of dust and sweat. The sunlight illuminates slashes of the Marley floor, throws heat onto my shoulders. This part of class, the faster part with the turns and little jumps and then the big jumps, is my least favorite. I am better at adagio, slow, undulous. Everyone is sweating now—not just me—but the energy in the room crackles. The entire company is dancing across the floor in waves—arabesques and pirouettes à la seconde and chaînés. Underneath the music, there's the squeak of shoes on the floor, everyone's panting, our heartbeats ecstatic. Kaz is giving class today, and so everyone, especially everyone who is not a principal, is throwing themselves into the steps.

Kaz gives his corrections with clinical precision, pushing Gwen's shoulders down, lifting Rohan's elbows to correct his port de bras. He stares at Jasper, his mouth pinched, before crouching down to widen his turnout. I spin at double my usual speed. Saturday's show is a yoke, heavy and stiff, getting closer. I feel it in my shoulders. I am sore, my body aches. Kaz stands in front of me, unnervingly close, as I execute a quadruple pirouette en dehors, turning away from my supporting leg.

"Yes," Kaz hisses. "Do it again, Cece."

I'm not sure I can.

I do.

"*Here,*" he says, placing a hand in between my shoulder blades. "Here is perfection." He pinches at the skin between my shoulder blades, tugging it down. I pull my scapulae down more, imagining them slicing through the skin. "Good girl."

My face grows even warmer. Ryn and Jasper beam at me. Now everyone is going for quadruples.

In between turns, Ryn whispers in my ear, "Teacher's pet."

I elbow her gently in the ribs, bone kissing bone. I can only get the occasional triple on my left side, and I try not to let my frustration show. I try not to entertain the envy I feel toward dancers like Anya, who make everything seem so effortless, who look like dancers are supposed to, what they have looked like for far longer than there have been people like me in ballet. I watch as Jasper watches Anya, leggy and ivory, perform a perfectly delicate combination across the studio floor. I take a hurried gulp of water from my bottle, and feel it travel all the way down to my stomach. It sloshes there when I begin dancing again.

I could fuck Kaz, I think. This line of thinking is ridiculous, of course; I'm not attracted to Kaz—he is old, balding, eccentric— and I would never do anything that might jeopardize my career. But if I gave him the slightest hint of a green light, he'd drop Cecilia and pour himself all over me. It's part of why she hates me. But how long would it last? There is something intimate about his command over my body. But it isn't really sexual. Maybe I'd marry him instead. He'd give me security, constant creative stimulation. Only, he'd never allow me to keep Jasper as a lover. And, anyway, men seem to only want what they want until they get it.

Kaz stops Anya after her last piqué turn by cupping his hand over her sharp shoulder. "Don't lose control of the arms," he says, bringing Anya's arms into first position, like she's holding a beach ball in front of her belly. "This is for everyone. Keep the arms in close. Let them creep out and they'll drag you in your turn."

Obediently, Anya does another turn, this time with her arms pulled in closer to her body.

"Lovely," says Kaz.

A few other dancers turn as well, carefully maintaining control over their arms, watching themselves in the mirror. I try for a triple, but don't get it—I manage two turns before I feel myself losing momentum. I frown at my body in the mirror, frustrated. I see myself—a black slash in a line of whippet-thin white—falling short, dancing imperfectly. I start to feel this hunger, this intolerable, cloying anxiety that makes me want to reach out and grab anyone, anything, like I'm clinging to a fraying rope above a void, and hold on so hard, dig in so hard that I feel blood creeping under my fingernails. Jasper brushes his fingers across my knuckles. I look up at him and smile.

I love Jasper. Our relationship has moved at a glacial pace, which, I admit, I have sometimes found frustrating, but I also feel lucky. Our relationship protects me—none of the messy, incestuous entanglements other company members get themselves into. No affairs or casual flings that end in someone catching feelings. I have Jasper. He's one more thing that cements me into the family of this company.

I force the next combination into my body, force myself to feel it, make it inhabit me, take control. I perform the next steps as though possessed.

I have some time between company class and rehearsal, and I should spend it going to physical therapy, or at least getting a massage, but instead, I speed walk over to Fifty-Sixth and Tenth in the gray city rain to a Korean bodega that makes my favorite overstuffed sandwich. I eat it standing under a nearby awning, forgoing most of the bread and focusing instead on the protein, avocado, and kimchi. I should be safe here, but still, I keep my eyes peeled for people from the company, especially any of the principals, or Jasper, or Kaz, or, God forbid, Cecilia.

I can only imagine the field day Cecilia would have if she caught me scarfing down a corner-store sandwich. She'd find a way to weave it into every class she gave, every single rehearsal. She'd tell me she could see it weighing me down when I jumped. She'd tell me I needed to lengthen. She'd get to our fitters, make passive-aggressive remarks about how I'd probably need a little extra space in my costumes. She'd act as though catching a dancer eating were a sign that they lacked discipline, lacked motivation. Not because she believes that—we all know we have to eat to do what we do—but because she's constantly looking for *something* when it comes to me. And she's not the only one.

I am so distracted by thoughts of Cecilia that, despite my wariness, I am caught off guard when I hear my name.

"Celine? *Cece?*"

I look up into a familiar face. Her face has aged slightly, in subtle ways, since we were students at SAB together—it's slightly rounder, not as youthful around the eyes.

"*Irine?*" I squeal. I have the urge to throw my sandwich into a bush, but there are none nearby.

"I can't believe it's you," Irine says. Her accent is somehow both thicker and more refined than I remember.

"I can't believe it's *you*," I say, and we crush each other in a hug. I hold my sandwich away from her body, so I can only hug her with one arm, but still, I feel the muscle, the bone. Irine is much taller than me, bigger boned, but I have always thought her body beautiful, a dancer's body. I don't know why I can't apply this same benevolence to my own body. I don't know why I'm flexing.

"This is crazy," Irine says. "I was just thinking about you. I was just *talking* about you."

I'm so excited it's like I'm drunk. I loved Irine. Ryn and I grieved when she didn't get invited to reenroll at SAB. We'd assumed that, when we fell out of touch, she'd moved back to Israel.

"What have you been up to? Are you still in the city?"

"I am now," Irine says. She wiggles the fingers of her left hand at me, brandishing a comically oversized diamond ring. "I'm married."

She pauses, and I offer the expected congratulations. At twenty-two, marriage is a distant mirage for me; I can barely imagine it.

"I went back home for a while," she says. "But I came back, and—damn it. Listen, I have to run to a meeting. But I really would like to talk and catch up. Could you do lunch soon?"

"Of course," I say. I run through my schedule in my head. "I have some time Friday. Late afternoon."

"Perfect," Irine says. "I'll make it work."

She leans in to hug me again, and this time, she kisses me on both cheeks. Then she is gone, flying with her dancer's grace down Tenth Avenue. It never really goes away, I've noticed, that habit of moving your body as if through a dance. Irine had always been a beautiful dancer. At SAB, she was one-third of the three musketeers, the pas de trois—her, me, and Ryn. We formed a friendship that was intense as only a friendship between adolescent girls can be. The first memory I have of us all together was of splitting a Starbucks doughnut and drinking black coffee, which I hated, and which I suspected the other girls hated as well. I got invited to winter term after only one summer intensive, which was unusual and, along with my complexion, made me a target for suspicion among my peers.

Irine's mother enrolled her in the private Professional Children's School and moved her and her little brother into a lavish apartment overlooking Central Park. And even though Ryn and I went to the Professional Performing Arts School—I was able to get my mother to allow this only because PPAS is a public school—we still had sleepovers at Irine's house every weekend. She and Ryn were my first real girlfriends. Irine's mother, who was gorgeous and spoke precious little English, prepared Middle Eastern feasts for us. We made Irine's little brother partner with us in the wide-open living room. And we talked about our bodies; Irine was the only one of us who had started her period and Ryn had had sex, so I was the only one who wasn't an expert in some aspect of womanhood.

But at the end of our second year at SAB, at her year-end evaluation, Irine was told that at her age, the body could change quickly, unexpectedly, that a beautiful ballet body could become just a beautiful body.

I got my apprenticeship at NYCB at sixteen, only six months before Ryn did, and, around that time, Irine's emails to us became sparser and sparser, until they disappeared altogether. Seeing her has thrown me off-balance in a strange way; I feel like a live wire, buzzing with unstable energy. I wonder what she thought, seeing me; I wonder whether I looked like I deserved to be with the company when she wasn't. I throw the rest of my sandwich into a nearby trash can and begin walking back. I'm on the schedule for this afternoon. Rehearsing *The Sleeping Beauty* again.

No dancer needs to be encouraged to think about her body. We're surrounded all day by wall-to-wall mirrors. We can scarcely escape our reflections. We obsess over things that possibly no one else can see. One person gushes about how long-legged I am, another about my ideal ballerina height (five foot five). But it doesn't keep me from seeing that my torso tapers, that my hips hyperextend, which will probably make them unstable later in my career, and my head is too round, the lines of my legs never straight enough. It doesn't stop me from seeing my skin, which is darker than any other woman's in the company. Flash of black in the walls of mirrors. I can't help but see myself.

That—my Blackness—is a hitch even for me sometimes. I love the culture but feel the ever-present weight of the color in this world that I've chosen. I am not conditioned to see myself as a damsel in distress. I am not conditioned to see myself as fragile, precious. I am not conditioned to see myself as worth saving. No one else is either. I have to work harder, much harder, to be a character like Aurora. To be a character who is innocent, pure, and victimized, and then, finally, swept off her feet and rescued. Perhaps this is where my struggle has been. And maybe this is why I was always so adamant about classical ballet. Not contemporary. Not jazz. A rebellion. An insistence that Black women can be ethereal too. That we don't always have to be drawn in bold lines. Paul never drew me in bold lines. Always thin, intricate strokes, a precise kind of chaos.

I spin, Jasper's hands on my waist, ending in arabesque penché. And then again. The music is exuberant now—the end of the vision scene. I have found it, I think, the limbo. I am not exactly *on*—though both Kaz and Alison are nodding encouragingly—but I am making it happen, my body under my authoritarian control. This is not the goal for Saturday's show. The goal is to do it even better than this. Jasper lifts me into the air. We are so connected that I can feel the strain of his muscles, settling into ease only once I am at my highest point. I throw all of my energy upward, helping. As soon as he sets me down, I run away from him, offstage, a vision fading before Désiré's eyes, leaving him with gaping want. A want that I feel, that we all feel, when we take the great breath in the wings, the moment before dancing onto the stage.

.   .   .

Irine meets me in an overpriced restaurant near Lincoln Center. She is beautiful—her dark hair is swept into a deliberately careless French braid, and she is dressed in crisp white with enormous pearl earrings and gold bangles. I feel as small and dark as a raisin; I'm not even wearing makeup. We kiss hello, and Irine immediately orders a glass of Chablis. I eye it jealously, sipping at my sweating glass of water; it is the middle of my workday. Irine looks at me, her eyes settled on mine, and smiles. There is a small gap between her two front teeth, which has always only added to her beauty.

"Irine," I say, "it's wild seeing you like this."

She laughs. "It's the same for me. Look at you." She shakes her head. "I have been watching you, you know—your career?"

I squirm a bit at this. "How about you?" I ask. "Are you still dancing?"

Irine draws a line through the condensation on her wineglass with a finger. "A lot has happened."

Our waiter returns to ask about our food order. Neither one of us has really looked at the menu, but the place is getting crowded, and our waiter, though polite, holds a bit of strain behind his smile so we make hurried selections: French onion soup for Irine and poached sole for me.

There is a brief, awkward silence when our waiter walks away. I'm not sure whether I've committed some faux pas by asking if Irine's still dancing, if the question brought her back to the pain of being told her body no longer fit into the world she loved. Looking at her now, I can still see the habit of ballet in her posture, in the careful way she holds her head, in the way she gestures with her hands while talking, their movements long, liquid, as though through water.

"A lot has happened," she repeats eventually.

"Tell me everything," I say.

Irine tells me that after she left SAB, she, her mother, and her little brother moved back to Tel Aviv. There, she continued to take dance classes, remaining loyal to ballet even through her two years of military service. Once out of the army, she auditioned for a small regional company in Tel Aviv and was accepted as a corps dancer, but realized quickly—after labral tears in both hips, chronic tendonitis, and a stress fracture—that though she loved ballet, the dancing itself was putting her at odds with her own body.

"But," she says, "by then I had met my husband. He danced with the Royal Ballet, and then freelanced a little here in the States. But when we got together we started talking—what if we made our own company?"

I am taking a sip of ice water when she says this, and an ice cube clunks uncomfortably against my front teeth. I set the glass down. "You *started* a company?"

Irine nods. "We're still growing, but we began touring this year."

Our food arrives and I watch Irine pick the bulk of the cheese off the top of her soup. I want her cheese, but I don't ask for it. Around us there are the sounds of chiming laughter, forks delicately touching ceramic plates, heavy jewelry drumming against the affectedly rustic tabletops.

"I think about you a lot," says Irine, thoughtfully stirring her soup. "My husband will tell you." She sets down her spoon and leans forward. "Do you remember that time in adagio class? You got partnered with that boy with the huge calves, and balletmistress said your makeup was making it look like he'd rolled around in mud?"

Of course I remember this. I very clearly remember the humiliation I felt, the brutal determination it took to keep the heat building in my eyes from welling up and ruining my carefully applied mascara. And my adagio partner—he'd chuckled.

"I thought about that," Irine is saying, "the day they told me my body wasn't right for ballet. I thought about your face. You looked so fierce."

"I was mortified," I say. I say it with a laugh. I load my fork with fish and vegetables.

"You were not just mortified," says Irine. "You were pissed. I thought, that must be the difference between you and me. You could take all their poking and prodding and molding, and still keep your shape. It's good that I didn't get invited back; they would've made me into an automaton, a dancer not even worth watching."

"No," I object. "You belonged there. Maybe even more than me."

Irine nods. "That's what I'm saying. Cece, even when we were just kids anyone could see you had immense talent. Right now, you're caged in the *brand* of City Ballet. But you don't belong in that cage."

This stings. I always dreamed of dancing with NYCB. And I'd made it in, even with everything stacked against me. If I don't belong here, where would I belong?

"What about my company?" Irine says, as though reading my mind. "I know we're more contemporary, but I really think you'd feel at home. You'd *fit*."

My sole is undercooked—in the middle of the filet, the flesh is gelatinous, slick. "My whole career is at City Ballet," I say.

"Cece, I've been watching your career. They're never going to give you roles that let you shine as much as you can. They're only ever going to let you go so far. With us you'd be an individual—you'd be free."

I put a sugar snap pea in my mouth, chewing it down to nearly nothing before I can summon the will to swallow it. I feel its entire journey down. I set my fork on the table.

"I'll admit," Irine says, "part of this is selfish. Having you dance for us—you'd pull more people to our shows. But, Cece, I really think you'd be happier."

I want to tell her that I'm already happy at City Ballet, that the company is my family. But then I remember the shame I feel in class, when I am the first one dripping with sweat, the way Cecilia is always telling me to pull in my butt, how I'd had no one to mentor me in the art of stage makeup. My adagio partner's chuckle.

"I don't know," I say. "I'm really more classical than anything."

"Look, just come to the company one day soon," she says. "Take class with us. I think you'd be surprised."

I make a noncommittal noise and Irine hands me a card— embossed gold—with the address of the company's studios. As the waiter clears our plates, I wonder if Irine has been to any of my shows. What is she seeing in my performances that suggests I don't fit? I consider inviting her to *The Sleeping Beauty* on Saturday, but something inside my chest cramps so I don't mention it. Irine insists on paying the bill. I fight her, but ultimately relent because, actually, it is my turn to go grocery shopping this week—Ryn and I have pledged to start meal prepping for a change.

Irine hails a cab and I begin the walk back to work. I'm suddenly hit with the urge to speak to my mother. I take out my cell and call her. It rings and rings and rings, and she doesn't answer. Her voicemail greeting is the generic, robotic voice that jerkily spells out her phone number and tells me it's not available. I hang up. Family is a fleeting thing. Around me, the city is gray, the air metallic with impending rain. Sometimes I think my brother has the right idea, making his mark through abscondence.

It is the last rehearsal before our Saturday show. Word has leaked that Mi Yeong is out, and Instagram is full of broken-heart emojis and blurry iPhone footage of her last curtain call. Critics have taken to Twitter to speculate on what it means that I will be dancing in her stead. Jasper holds my waist as I try to force myself to stop wobbling while I balance on one leg. I can't find lightness. It feels like I'm fighting for every step. The practice tutu is heavy on my hips.

The music is both sweet and triumphant; the grand wedding pas de deux. Aurora is awake, alive, enamored. Désiré is alight. The wedding pas de deux contains echoes of the Rose Adagio with the four suitors—lots of extensions and balancing en pointe. He reaches for me, I turn my back to Kaz, to the mirrors, my audience: développé front, swivel into attitude derrière, port de bras, port de bras, and arabesque. Sweat trickles in between my shoulder blades. Jasper is himself misty; there is a small wrinkle between his eyebrows. I am frustrating him, I think. The pain in my ankle goes suddenly sharp and I have to come down from pointe. I suck my teeth in frustration. Kaz calls for us to stop. He has insisted on rehearsing us this time, and I am relieved at the break from Cecilia.

"Get out of your head, my beauty, and into Aurora's," he says. "Again, *and* . . ."

We drift away from each other, and then, as though suddenly realizing we're apart and no longer able to bear it, we turn. Désiré runs toward me, drops to one knee, arms reaching. I run to him— arabesque penché—a kiss, our sweaty faces a centimeter apart. We linger there half a beat too long, Jasper squeezing my waist, trying to help me find my center of gravity. Again, we separate and come together again, a force we're helpless to resist. Attitude derrière, promenade and a half; again, my back is to an audience of Kaz and my own reflection. I nearly lose my balance again but I fight it, teeth gritted.

"Watch your face, darling," Kaz says over the music.

I try to put Mi Yeong out of my mind. This role is as much mine as it is hers. It's there for me to claim it even more. Isn't that why Kaz is giving me this chance, this white elephant? I push Mi Yeong, her perfect balance, her beautifully arched feet, her long, slender legs, from my mind through the music's accelerando. A faster promenade, the lines of my body angled down like a magic wand bestowing a spell. Penché to développé stage left, penché to développé stage right; I throw my legs up into the extensions. I try not to think of how effortless Mi Yeong makes it look to catch the pirouette at just the right moment, and then let Désiré support me into a fish dive. Jasper has to take a fraction of a count to put me back on my leg every time.

How would Mi Yeong make this port de bras catch in the audience's chests, here, in this supported arabesque? What would Irine make of my bourrée to stage left, my breasts bouncing painfully with the quick, floating steps? I can't find lightness. Maybe it doesn't come naturally to me. Maybe I am more like my mother than I'd like to think, whose steps are so heavy they echo through the apartment, despite her small stature. Jasper basically spins me like a top through the pirouettes, stopping me when it is time for me to bring my foot down, rallentando. Chaînés to arabesque. I have been told that I am not classical for my whole career. Today, I believe it.

Heavy. Like I'm chained to the earth.

I look into Désiré's face. It's supposed to be loving, but I'm sure I look terrified instead. We bow to each other. Désiré pulls me into an arabesque en pointe. Promenade, three times. I'm so off my leg today Jasper can't let go of my hand—I need him to steady me. He tosses me up and catches me around the waist, sweeps me down into our last fish dive, both our arms spread wide—look Ma, no hands. Again, he has to hold on to me longer than he should, holding me still until I force balance. I end in a very brief arabesque before I wobble off pointe again.

Kaz stands. I'm sure he's going to tell me to just stay home and ice my ankle. That he'd rather Mi Yeong wince her way through the show with her bad back than watch me mangle it.

"Again," he says. "The whole thing. And this time, inhabit it, Cece. Your body already knows. Get your mind in it."

We break for water before beginning again. I am bloated, familiar low ache. I nearly swear aloud. My period is coming. No wonder I'm so heavy. Jasper pinches the base of my neck as I wipe sweat from my face. I don't know if he's trying to soothe me or strangle me. In the mirror, I am strange to my own eyes. Hair mussed, kinking up at the roots, nipples hard through exertion and friction, feet beginning to swell in their pointe shoes. I've been trying for more than an hour to be Aurora. But still, all I see is myself. Jasper and I get ready to start again. I try to find some internal space in which to stuff myself so there's room for something else, something better. *Prépare, and . . .*

Coda

Paul began disappearing when I was eleven, when he moved out. Our mother had kicked him out once before, but that time he'd gone to live with our dad. This time, he'd gotten his own place—small, grimy, with a hallway that smelled like cat piss and something else, something yellowed and ill, like the aftertaste of a bronchitic cough. My mother did not like me to go there without her. At first, Paul seemed better. He was more relaxed now that he wasn't always arguing with our mother. He got a full ride to the School of Visual Arts. He had a job, a routine. He told me he'd started going for long walks through the city at night, walking until he was tired, until his mind could still enough for sleep. He collected wire hangers, wove them into complicated shapes just to have something to do with his hands.

But after his first year, he lost his scholarship. I was old enough by then to know that it was because he liked drugs more than he liked showing up for class, something he tried to hide from me but couldn't. Before he left, he had convinced my mother that I was finally old enough to walk to Señora Sandy's brownstone by myself, but soon after he stopped going to school, he stopped paying for my classes.

One Saturday, after a humiliating conversation with Señora

Sandy after class, I called him. The more his phone rang, the more the heat in my face grew, threatening tears. I didn't think he would pick up, but just before his voicemail kicked in, he answered.

"Hey, little dancer."

I hated his voice when he was high. It was sluggish, thick and filmy like mud.

"What are you doing?" I blurted, the words sharp and with an edge of desperation to them. I wanted to be wrong about his muddy voice. I wanted him to be better.

He let out a disoriented laugh that turned into a sputter and a cough. I wasn't wrong, then. I wiggled my toes under our old, low couch and mercilessly straightened my leg, stretching my instep.

"Señora Sandy says she hasn't been getting the money for my classes. She tried calling you but you didn't answer."

"My bad," Paul slurred.

"I—can you pay? I can't take class if you're not paying, Paul."

"Shit. Sorry. Look, Cece, could you ask Ma to take over for a little while? Just for a bit, while I get my shit together. Okay?"

I switched feet, a masochistic part of me enjoying the pain of the stretch, a pain I could process better than that which my brother was causing me.

"Me and Ma are in a fight," I said.

Again, a sputtering laugh. "Another one?"

"Like you can talk."

"What's her problem this time?"

"Me. She hates me."

"She doesn't hate you, Cece."

"Yeah she does. She's barely talking to me right now—I don't even know what I did. Anyway, she's not going to pay for my classes. She wants me to quit. So, please," I pled, my voice softer now, "can you help?"

"Look, little dancer, I got a lot—" He sighed. "Okay. I'll try, all right?"

If he did try, he failed.

I quickly learned the art of getting things for myself. To pay for ballet, I babysat for every family in our building and most of the families within a three-block radius. Even though I was only a child myself, ballet had given me a poise and polish that made me seem responsible, older than my years to adults.

My mother didn't approve of my busy schedule. "You're too young to be doing all this," she told me.

"Paul won't pay for my ballet classes anymore, and neither will you." Paul had been working full time as a cook at some restaurant instead of making art like he was meant to do. He had staggered into an average life, and because of this he became distant, clinging to things that made the world brighter but him progressively duller.

She shook her head. "All this for *ballet*. Stubborn, just like your father. And your brother. And where did it get either of them?"

I shrugged.

My mother scoffed. "Why do you like ballet so much, anyway? I know you're good at it, but you can be good at lots of things. Something useful. Like science, so you can become a doctor."

"I don't want to be a doctor. I want to dance."

"Art doesn't pay, that's all I'm saying. You go after your art dreams, you end up losing. Look at your brother."

Now I was angry. I knew better than to raise my voice to my mother, but I made sure there was real heat behind my words. "Paul is a great artist."

"No, Paul is a *talented* artist. But it wasn't enough, was it? Now, instead of curing cancer or running a business, he's sweating in some kitchen for minimum wage."

"Why do you hate Paul?" I snapped.

She pointed a finger at me, a warning. "You watch yourself, now. You don't know what you're talking about and you won't until you're grown and have kids of your own. I've always only wanted your brother to do good for himself."

"No you didn't. You're always so mean to him, and that's why I never get to see him anymore."

I still remembered the day she kicked him out of the house. She had come upon him passed out on the couch and tried to nudge him awake with her knee. When he didn't wake, she'd gone into the kitchen and come back with a glass of water that she'd emptied on his face. When he'd startled so badly he'd fallen off the couch, she'd crouched on the floor with him, grabbed his head in her hands, and brought his face right up into hers. Whatever words she'd hissed, I didn't hear, but they seemed to sear him. He'd cried as he packed his things, and our mother locked herself in her room for the rest of the day.

I stood, grabbed my bag, and furiously zipped it closed. I was risking a serious punishment by storming off, but my mother didn't snatch me or demand I come back.

"You don't know *everything*, little girl," she said as I opened the door. She didn't shout it but only spoke it, so that it came to me softly, even though her tone was sharp.

I kicked the door closed and ran down the stairs.

For years I thought about those last words, their softness at odds with their thorns. I wondered what it was I didn't know. It was a long time before I understood that my mother loved me and my brother. I saw it clearly for the first time when she came— grudgingly—to my first performance as a member of the corps. I was only in a couple of scenes, and when I met her after the show, she'd grumbled about barely being able to see me. But I saw her tuck the program carefully into a zippered inner pocket of her purse, which held something else—a crumpled sheet of Bristol paper blackened by chaotic charcoal lines.

She'd closed her purse quickly. *Too late to get anything to eat, either,* she'd complained. *Are all these dance shows so long?*

Tentatively, I'd asked her, *Did you like it?* But it wasn't quite what I wanted to know. I wanted to know if she was proud of me, if she got it now.

She looked me up and down, her lips pressed together firmly. For a while it seemed she didn't know what to say. *You did all right,* she admitted. Then, *Your brother did all right at first too.* She swallowed like there was a nasty taste in her mouth. Her next words seemed to cost her something.

When your brother was little, he used to fight me when I'd dress him in his snowsuit. Fight me so hard he'd make me cry, and your father'd yell at both of us. You were the same way. You'd scream. Didn't matter, me telling you it was freezing out. I used to wonder how you two could be ten years apart and still be like twins. But thank God y'all weren't. By the time you came along, I had ten years of experience. I wasn't crying anymore.

She'd laughed, but I saw it, the shadows of those tears. They were there still, only changed over time, like Paul. Like me. I realized it then—she was terrified of us falling through the world. And that constant terror was like a poison, warping her love into constant disapproval, coldness, anger.

Come on, she said, beginning to walk away from me. *You need to eat something.*

[révérence]

Prince Désiré, with the help of the Lilac Fairy, has found his sleeping beauty, and overcome with love, goes to wake her. For the spell-breaking kiss, Jasper actually sticks his tongue into my mouth. He knows I can't really react without the audience seeing. I sit up, startled and then delighted. I run to my parents, the king and queen, who are also just waking up. I run to the front of the stage, place my hands against my heart, blow a kiss. I do some more delighted running around. And then I see the prince. He declares his love for me, bows to my father, kisses my mother's hand. And then we all hold hands as the music builds to its dramatic finish. I balance in an arabesque and gaze lovingly at the prince while the audience thunders.

Once the curtain goes down, we all let go. We gasp for breath, wipe the sweat out of our eyes. As we hurry, quiet as mice, off-stage, I give Jasper a playful slap on the arm. He smiles down at me.

"We're *on* tonight," he whispers. "Can you feel it?"

I can. Finally. I feel the audience watching, scrutinizing. They wanted Mi Yeong; I am an imposter. Every step I take is a battle to claim this stage, to brand this performance as my own. It is creating this frantic electricity in me. For every step that I make perfectly, I'm all the more afraid I'll screw up the next one. But the big screw-up keeps not coming, and we've almost made it all the way through.

We don't have much time before the third act. Cecilia stalks up to me as a dresser is hooking me into my heavy tutu for the wedding scene. After riding me all week during rehearsals, I wonder if she feels justified or invalidated right now.

"You really need to stay on the music," she says.

"She's always on the music." Jasper comes up behind me, brushes the dresser's hands away, finishes the hooking himself. "It was probably my fault."

Cecilia smiles at him. It looks pained. "I doubt it," she says. She glides off.

"Don't do that," I tell Jasper.

He scoffs. "You're the most musical dancer in the company, and she knows it."

"I can handle her myself," I say. I don't like it when he carries his cavalier routine off the stage, like he's still performing.

"Whatever you say, milady."

He bows, and I don't have time to scold him—we have to go get married. The grand wedding pas de deux. If I'm going to fuck up tonight, it'll be now. I try not to be too careful—the audience, especially the critics, can see that—but I keep pulling my energy upward in pursuit of the lightness that eluded me in our last rehearsal. That frantic electricity is carrying me through the steps, I am aloft; I *feel* it. When I run to Jasper and penché for a kiss, I accidentally slam my face into his. The next time he smiles admiringly at me I can see a pink film of blood on his teeth. I mouth an apology. But the audience can't see it through the panes of stage lighting. Like magic, my balances stick.

By the end, I am exhausted and my ankle is killing me. My feet throb. Jasper is tired too. But we've pulled it off.

We both still have our individual variations to do. I get to rest a bit in the wings and take a sip of water while Prince Désiré leaps around triumphantly. He gets several *Bravos*.

Then it is my turn. It's only been two minutes—I'm still out of breath from the adagio. Even though I am tired, I can feel that I am dancing well. I get a lot of credit for being lyrical, for being a great actress. My brother taught me that—how to listen, how to feel it in your organs. I am lightning fast for the chaînés at the end—I can feel it the way I've been wanting to. I hear people yelling *Brava* as I run offstage so Jasper can do his second solo. As soon as he is done, I run back out to join him, a series of playful, upbeat steps ending with us moving in unison, as one. Then our court, which has been standing still, their muscles cramping this entire time, unfreezes, gathering around us. My smile is more than a stage smile—we've made it. Jasper squeezes my waist, and when we've held our positions for long enough after the curtain drops, he quickly kisses my cheek.

During the curtain calls, both Jasper and I get standing ovations.

Backstage, the energy is high. Ryn runs up to me, still in her cat costume—she played Puss-in-Boots's temperamental girlfriend tonight, as well as one of the Lilac Fairy's attendants.

"Oh my God," she says after kissing my cheek. "You were incredible tonight. We were all trying not to scream from the wings."

Truthfully, Ryn would make a much better Aurora than me. I would love to see her do the Rose Adagio—her balance rivals Viengsay Valdés's. Balance has always been a weak spot of mine, but Ryn makes it look easy.

"*You* were incredible," I say. "You're really funny, Ryn."

Jasper is next to us, bloodied and grinning. I apologize again and he laughs, sloshing water around his mouth and then drinking it, having no place to spit his own metallic blood, diluted. He winks at me. "Who cares?" he says. "School's out for summer, babe." He saunters off.

This was the last performance of the spring season. The company is touring to Paris in June. Kaz let me have a guest artist contract with La Scala, so I will be in Italy then. In July, the company does its short summer season in Saratoga Springs, and I am Hermia, Jasper my Lysander. Then a small group of us—Ryn and Jasper included—are going to Wyoming for the company's annual artists' residency with Dancer's Workshop.

Kaz comes over and puts his arm around my waist, pulls me into his side. He kisses my cheek. Then he gives me his signature stare, a deep, somewhat mischievous look right into the eyes. I never know what to do when he does this. I arrange my face into a mysterious smile, like we both know the secret, and I fight not to let my eyes drop from his. I have no idea what he is about to say, what notes he will give me. I know I've danced well tonight, but I don't know whether it has been enough.

"Well done, my beauty," he says, finally. "Tomorrow will be a big day for you."

"Tomorrow?" I ask, confused. All I plan to do tomorrow is a photo shoot with Ryn and then physical therapy.

"Yes, darling. We'll announce it to the press tomorrow."

Ryn seems to get it before I do. She stands behind Kaz, bouncing and emitting a quiet squeal.

"Announce what?" I ask.

"You know what I'm saying," Kaz murmurs.

And suddenly, I do. He is promoting me. It comes to me in waves: I am going to be a principal. I have made it to the top tier of the company. This is what I've been dreaming of since I was a little girl. *This* has been what tonight was all about.

And then, at last, this: I am now the first Black female principal in the history of the New York City Ballet.

My legs are shaking, the muscles exhausted. Kaz lets go of me and steps away as a flock of dancers who've overheard swarm me. Before they close in, I crane my neck, looking for Jasper. He is nowhere to be seen. Some tenuous feeling spreads in my chest. Cecilia is staring at me, openly glaring. There is clapping and congratulations. All this embarrasses me. Usually, we get promoted in groups—Kaz has made me into a spectacle. My body is hot and tired, and I feel exposed and bloated. I escape to the dressing room that I share with two other dancers; it is mercifully empty. Ryn follows me in and I begin scrubbing my stage makeup off with baby wipes.

"So we're definitely going out tonight to celebrate, and don't give me that crap about being exhausted."

"I *am* exhausted," I say. I wonder if Jasper is still in the theater, if he has heard the news.

"You want a bump?" Ryn asks me, but she doesn't wait for an answer because she knows it is no. Coke fueled Ryn through her years in the corps, when you're busy all the time, doing anywhere from ten to fifteen shows a week. But since she became a soloist a year ago, she only uses when she wants to go out post-performance.

I pop three ibuprofens as Ryn wipes her nose.

"You coming home tonight or are you staying at Jasper's?" she asks.

"Home, I guess. I haven't seen him since curtain call." I try to make that sound breezy, like I don't care one way or the other, like I'm not hoping he walks through the door right now with the congratulatory bouquet of flowers he ran out to get as soon as he heard the news.

"He's a dick, Cece."

"I know. But he's *my* dick." I force a smile.

We both giggle.

"I'll meet you out there," Ryn says, rolling her eyes.

She musses my hair as I pull off my plastic crown, and then practically skips out. I pause, look at myself in the mirror. My costume is a pale pink, darkened now with sweat, with glittering roses at my arms and on my tutu. I stand and hold a hand to my face, comparing the reflection to the real thing. I wonder if there is surveillance in this room, if someone is watching me on a screen somewhere and snickering. I recognize that this thought is crazy, and with the discipline I've honed over my entire life, I do not allow myself to look around for places where a camera might be hidden. I do, however, allow a nervous glance at the open door behind me.

Watching myself—and the doorway—in the mirror, I rise up into an arabesque, my arms in high fifth above my head. My costume is heavy, cooling with the sweat that drenches it. I've managed, in this brief moment, to find perfect balance; it feels nearly weightless, stillness with no effort. The lights in the dressing room are much dimmer than the lights onstage, but I still shimmer pinkly. I see myself—pink satin and black skin. I come out of my pose and bow deeply to my reflection, holding my own eyes until I can't anymore.

Intermezzo

For my fourteenth birthday Luca and Galina gave me a copy of *The Dancer's Way: The New York City Ballet Guide to Mind, Body, and Nutrition.* I packed this along with the Italian book from Paul in my dance bag on the day of my audition for the School of American Ballet's summer intensive. Both Galina and Luca assured me that I was ready, and I wished I had felt as confident about it. I knew I looked good on paper—the Espositos' school was renowned, and I'd won a few competitions over the years. And I had performance experience—*The Nutcracker*, obviously, and *A Midsummer Night's Dream, Swan Lake, Coppélia*, and a bunch of abstractly titled contemporary pieces.

Everything was riding on my SAB audition. I'd called Paul that morning, and was surprised when he picked up. He sounded tired, burned out.

"Got stuck at work until three last night," he said.

A year ago he'd been promoted to station chef at the restaurant where he'd been working since he dropped out of school. I once asked him if he'd decided to become a famous chef instead of a famous artist, and he told me to shut the fuck up. I wasn't trying to be smart, though. Now, I tried not to say anything about his job at all.

"Good luck at your audition today," he said. "Or merde—
that's what you dancers say, right?"

He sounded so far away. No one in my family ever said it plainly
to me, but all the same, I'd come to understand that my brother
was an addict. I didn't yet know what his drug of choice was—
it was more than pot or alcohol—and I couldn't ask anyone. There
was no one thing, nothing in particular that happened to make
me see the truth; rather, it came to me with the same kind of onset
as my own self-awareness. A subconscious thing becoming con-
scious. And I would save him—I knew I could—but he never let
me near him anymore. When he was so far away, I had no oppor-
tunity to step between him and his darkness. I couldn't turn his
head back to his art.

"Do you have time this weekend?" I asked. "We could go see a
movie or something. *The Book of Eli*'s supposed to be good. I won't
even make you pay."

He didn't laugh, so I did it for him.

"Sorry, Cece," he said, and he sounded so weak, so tired. "I've
got work. Maybe some other time."

"That's what you always say. Come on. I haven't seen you in
forever. People don't even think I have a brother."

Paul coughed a smoker's cough. "I know, I know. I'm a pretty
shitty brother, huh? We'll chill real soon."

"When?"

"Soon."

"*When*, Paul?"

"Shit. Look, Cece, I gotta go."

"Don't hang up."

He hung up.

So along with my books and my pointe shoes and my bobby
pins and my nerves, I carried my anger with me to the audition. I
was there alone, and I envied the girls whose mothers hovered

over them, embarrassed them. I envied the girls whose mothers knew how important all this was. I got a lot of stares—some merely curious, and some hostile. I was used to this. I saw only one other Black girl. She was tall and muscular, and her eyes kept flitting to me just as mine kept flitting to her, and we both saw each other looking, and I silently wished her merde.

It was cold that morning—the January air crept into the cracks in the building, so I was careful to warm up well. Despite my anger at him, I couldn't just push Paul from my mind for the sake of the audition. I listened to my iPod Touch as I warmed up— a Christmas present from Paul. He'd loaded it with all of his favorite classical music and then mailed it to me. I didn't actually get to see him for the holidays. The atmosphere around me was tense. Everybody was looking at one another, evaluating, judging. But aside from subtly craning my neck to catch a glimpse of the other Black girl, who I hoped was outstanding, I tried to stay focused on myself. Since I couldn't banish my brother from my mind, I tried to at least banish the anger. If I was going to feel looked at, scrutinized—which I did—then at least I could imagine it was Paul doing the looking.

I warmed up more gracefully and carefully than I normally would. I brought my leg up, flexing and pointing my foot languidly, articulating each movement. I brought my leg around behind me, arching my back as much as I could, opening my chest to the ceiling. All throughout the audition, I conjured Paul's gaze. It quieted my nerves, quieted the anxiety of the other dancers around me. The ballet mistress called out the combinations quickly, testing our attention, our memory. I imagined each of her commands flying across the room like bullets, sinking into my flesh, programming my muscles. I imagined drawing colorful lines in the air with the articulation of my arms and legs as I moved. I was full of magic.

The audition was over quickly—it seemed as though it had been no time at all. When I stepped outside I felt ejected onto the grimy sidewalk, into the blaring of taxis, the roar of traffic, the distant rumble of the subway, smell of exhaust and sugared peanuts and hot dogs and burned soft pretzels, overflowing trash, urine, gray slush. Immediately, I missed the sweat, the clanking piano, the sweet piney scent of rosin. A forbidden city to which I was desperate for admission.

II

ADAGIO

I t is vaguely disappointing, traveling. You get all dazzled at first, but then you start to see that a city is just a city, and people are just people, and the world is just the world. This summer day in New York is not all that different from a summer day in Milan. I am jet-lagged. I wear big cat-eye sunglasses to hide the bags under my eyes. I try to make this look glamorous by adding a dark plum lipstick and a chignon. I no longer feel that I can just walk out barefaced. The gaze is my shadow, larger than ever.

My interviewer is late. I try to remember which publication this is for. *Time? Elle?* No, I've done those already. Danielle, the company's publicist, has been hounding me to hire a manager. I'm close to caving. I wake up to more emails than I can handle. This morning I got one from some filmmakers in LA who want to make a movie about me, and I'm still not convinced it's not a hoax. *New York* magazine, that's it. *New York* magazine, *New York* magazine, *New York* magazine. I repeat this in my head so I don't forget. Maybe they're here already, watching me, observing and taking notes. Here we find Celine in her natural habitat. Look how awkward she really is.

My cellphone buzzes. I look down at the screen—it's Irine. She wants to know if I'm back in the States yet. I haven't gone to one of her company classes, and I've been using Milan as an excuse to avoid her. Even now, even after my promotion, she still doesn't seem convinced that I belong at NYCB, and I don't know why, but it's making me crazy. Either she's right and somebody's going to figure it out, or she's wrong and everything that's happened so far hasn't been enough to show her. Maybe it hasn't been enough to show anybody. I slip my phone into my purse. A passerby does a double take but does not stop. Watch Celine, on edge even in her natural habitat. She is a nervous species, skittish, a prey animal.

Only I'm not in my natural habitat. I'm not sure what my natural habitat is, but it isn't this. I'm used to scrutiny but not celebrity. People recognize me on the street. In Italy, people came up to me after performances, tears in their eyes, took my hands in theirs. I've been on the covers of *Dance Magazine* and *Pointe*. I have interviews scheduled with *The Washington Post*, *USA Today*, *The Telegraph*, *Forbes*, *Rolling Stone*, *Harper's Bazaar*, and *O, The Oprah Magazine*. Not to mention the television appearances. And they all ask me about the same things—diversity in ballet, my diet, Jasper, my inspirational message. And Misty Copeland. They can't help asking me about Misty Copeland. I am in her petite shadow. I never saw this. Hell, I could never even see that pink costume against my skin. I only saw dance.

A tall, thin brunette is approaching my little outside table. I think it must be her, because she is walking with purpose. Quickly, I try to recall the name from the email. Brittany? Tiffany? Katie?

"It's so nice to meet you," she says, extending a hand. "I'm Mandy."

I take her hand and shake it, say, "I'm Celine," and feel instantly ridiculous.

Mandy settles into the seat across from me. She's got a great neck—long and slender. I wonder if, to other people, it looks like *she's* the dancer, and I'm . . . what? The token Black friend? I reach up to take my sunglasses off, but then change my mind.

"Is it okay if I record you?" Mandy asks, setting her iPhone on the table.

I smile and gesture magnanimously.

"Thank you for taking time out of your busy schedule to chat with me," Mandy says. "So, two months ago, at only twenty-two, you became the first Black ballerina at the New York City Ballet. Tell me about that moment."

The answer to this question is far too complicated for words, but words are all I have. I have never been good at sound bites. It's not that I can't produce them, it's that I'm sure I'm coming off as disingenuous as I'm being. I do my best—mostly, I stick to the facts—and Mandy seems satisfied.

"So," Mandy says, "*the* Kazimir Volkov told you personally? Is that right?"

I strive for a self-deprecating laugh. "That's right. That's not usually how it's done, of course, but Kaz has pretty much watched me grow up."

This is the truth, but I am telling a distilled version of the truth. I am letting Mandy believe that Kaz is like a father to me. I'd *like* him to be like a father to me. But Kaz's near-constant gaze is much more complicated than that. And certainly not paternal.

"Tell me what it's like to work for Kazimir Volkov. He's been somewhat controversial since his instatement as artistic director. Some say he's too classical for City Ballet. What's your perspective as one of his dancers?"

One of *his* dancers. I feel strangely protective of Kaz. NYCB purists like to hark on his Russophilia, his predilection for full-length shows. They like to argue that he isn't truly neoclassical. Classical ballets are often full-length productions, with elaborate staging, symmetrical structure, and delicate technique. Neoclassical ballets are abstract, storyless, with minimal staging, and a focus on athleticism. Balanchine, the founder of our company, is the father of neoclassical ballet, so Kaz's love of classical elements is somewhat scandalous.

"Kaz is brilliant," I say, delicately shrugging one shoulder. "I love how he manipulates, and sometimes even discards the horizontal line. And yes, I think he *is* classical in a sense—he values narrative and lyricism. But I do think it's reductive to just call him 'classical.' He plays with gender roles and androgyny in ways that are new and exciting, and he's always looking to make new shapes with the body."

"What's it like to dance one of his works?"

"Exhausting," I say with a laugh. "Kaz isn't a fan of idleness on the stage. He likes us dancing the whole time."

"How would you say he compares to Balanchine?"

This is a loaded question. I need to tread carefully. "Can anyone be compared to Balanchine?" I chuckle airily. "Honestly, they're two completely different artists. Visionaries. Balanchine was all about the body, the woman, the steps. Kaz is about—well, the body too, I guess, but—" I grit my teeth. I sound dumb. I lengthen my spine, an invisible cord traveling through my vertebrae, up through the top of my skull, up beyond the clouds. "Kaz is about plasticity, humanity. Audacity."

I am particularly proud of my use of *audacity*. Such a striking, dramatic word. Mandy must love it.

"Tell me a bit more about how you got here, Celine. When did you start ballet?"

"When I was five."

"What made you fall in love with dance?"

My brother's face shimmers out of a protected corner of my mind. *I got us tickets, my little dancer. That's the stage you'll be on one day.* I push him back in. "It started, for me, with the music. I've always been . . . sensitive to it. My mother would tell you I cried the first time I heard Chopin."

My mother would say nothing of the sort.

But Paul would. *Come in here, Cece. You don't know nothing until you've heard Scarlatti.*

"And you went to the School of American Ballet?"

I nod, and then, remembering the iPhone, say, "I got into SAB's summer course when I was fourteen, and at the end of that summer, I was invited to enroll in winter term."

"Wow," says Mandy. She knows enough to know that this was unusual. "And what was your experience there like?"

I know what she wants me to say. "There weren't many other students who looked like me. I was always aware of that. I felt like I had to work twice as hard as everyone else around me."

Mandy nods sagely. "And what did that feel like?"

This catches me off guard. I had expected that my boilerplate Black ballerina origin story would be enough. "I—it was . . . it could be lonely."

"Lonely how?"

"I mean, I stood out like a sore thumb."

"Wouldn't part of that have been because of your talent? Kazimir Volkov has said that you were a prodigy from early on. Some of your teachers have looked back on you as a wunder-kind."

I blink behind my sunglasses. "I didn't feel that way."

"Why not?"

I wonder if Mandy knows she is getting to me. I wonder if she is *trying* to get to me. But she doesn't know me. She can't know where my uncalloused parts are.

"You have to remember, dancers—we understand ourselves through the spectator's gaze. So the mirror is important, the audience is important, the teacher is important. In the mirror, I could only see that there was nobody like me, and an adolescent girl is bound to interpret that as deficiency. And the notes I got from my teachers only made me believe in my deficiency more."

"How so?"

"Like, I got corrections no one else got. Comments on my body. Someone once told me that my muscles were messing up my lines. Someone else said it was too distracting when I wore red lipstick. Someone called me an Amazon. I'm five foot five."

I did not intend to be so candid. This unvarnished truth has taken me by surprise. As has the lump in my throat. I blink furiously, desperately. I give Mandy a stage smile.

"It makes me even more honored to be where I am today."

Mandy mirrors my smile. "What were your feelings when Misty Copeland congratulated you personally on Twitter?" she asks. "Is she an inspiration for you?"

I consider rolling my eyes but don't. "Of course. I mean, Misty freaking Copeland. She completely changed the ballet world. That tweet meant everything to me. I think I might have it framed."

"And, now, you've been wowing audiences in Italy for the past month. What was dancing with La Scala like? Any major differences?"

I stood out even more among the La Scala dancers. The women were waifish, glamorous. Even the way they smoked cigarettes on their breaks, hands gesturing in that Italian way, detouring occasionally to swipe wisps of hair from their beautiful bare faces—it was all a very specific type of allure, one that I don't think I have access to. And company class there was so slow, but delivered in rapid Italian. Even though I have always considered myself an adagio dancer, my muscles would scream as we moved through poses and their transitions at a far more leisurely pace than what I've grown used to. One of the ballet mistresses clearly believed that my alignment was wrong in every step—she kept scurrying over and kicking my feet into a more acute turnout. Despite all this, they were warm, seemingly happy to have me there.

"A lot of the dancers there were trained in the Cecchetti method, which is this whole different way of learning ballet. Very technical, very beautiful. I learned a lot. But the differences aren't *so* crazy. At the end of the day, everyone is so hardworking and so dedicated and passionate. That's the language all dancers speak."

I've gotten hold of myself now—the varnish is back.

"You and Jasper Campbell have been called *the* ballet partnership of the twenty-first century. Is it just dancing between you two?"

Definitely not. He was so sweet in Europe. We met as frequently as we could either in Milan or in Paris. We had candlelit dinners, we kissed on bridges and held hands on ancient cobblestone streets, we got drunk and made love in medieval alleyways. On his last visit to Milan, he crankily waved away my suggestion that we meet up with some of the La Scala dancers for drinks, and instead pinned me to the bed with its gingham sheets. He held my wrists above my head as he entered me, his forehead resting against mine. He was unusually quiet as we shared a bottle of vinegary red wine in bed afterward. He studied me for a long time. He used his thumb to stroke my ear in a gesture that was unusually tender for him. "You know I love you, right?"

He told me to text him when I landed at JFK, but he never texted back.

Mandy is repeating her question now, and I curse myself. My long silence was basically an admission. The last thing I want is for the public to focus on our personal lives instead of our dancing.

"When you've been dancing with someone for four years, it can't be just dancing. Jasper is great—he's an amazing dancer and he's one of my best friends. We're family."

All true. Just not exactly the whole truth.

"What was your favorite ballet that you've danced with Jasper?"

She wants me to say *Swan Lake*. It's so romantic. I'm not immune to it, either—it's always been my favorite classic. And my Odette/Odile is a crowd-pleaser; people go nuts during the black swan's famous thirty-two fouettés—I try to get in as many as I can, more than thirty-two, spinning at the speed of light. I prefer the full-length production to Balanchine's one-act version.

Or maybe she wants me to say *Agon*, Jasper and I a negative copy of Allegra Kent and Arthur Mitchell.

"*Romeo and Juliet.* I feel like we do the balcony scene differently every time, so it's always fresh for us. We just kind of play off each other."

This is mostly a lie, and I'm not sure why I'm telling it. I've never loved *Romeo and Juliet*—neither the play nor the ballet.

"I have to ask, because everyone wants to know: What do you typically eat, and how do you stay in shape?"

I don't roll my eyes. It is good practice, as a professional dancer, to have a go-to lie in place for when people ask you what you eat. We're trying to dispel those rumors of eating disorders. Here is the truth: A dancer eats either much more or much less than she reports to the public.

"Dance is really the only thing that keeps you in shape for dance, honestly. And during the season, there isn't a lot of time for much else. Off season, I do a lot of yoga and Pilates as well. Gyrotonics. Sometimes I swim. For breakfast, I usually have egg whites, a banana, toast. I don't usually eat lunch because I don't like dancing on a full stomach, but I have little snacks here and there—cheese, almonds, a little yogurt with bee pollen for energy. And dinner is usually pretty simple—sautéed veggies, chicken, or some kind of fish. I love pasta. I don't have much of a sweet tooth."

"What are you most looking forward to for the 2018–2019 season?"

"The dancing," I say.

And that is the whole truth.

I sign a program Mandy's brought—*Swan Lake*. Before she leaves, I notice that her handbag is one of the brands that has been in touch for endorsement deals. I really do need a manager. Maybe if someone else starts handling all this stuff for me, this will start feeling like my life again. I rub at my temple. I don't mean to be so negative, so ungrateful. I'm jet-lagged, I remind myself. I go inside the café and keep my sunglasses on. I duck my head as I order a slice of blueberry pie, warmed and topped with whipped cream. I find a dark, secluded corner where I can eat it.

The human body is not made to do the things dancers make our bodies do. I lift my right leg to my ear, point and flex my foot. I am taking class at Steps on Broadway and as people make their way in, they recognize me but don't make a big deal out of it. I don't feel good. I finally heard from Jasper. This morning, two texted words: *lunch today?* The bastard didn't even bother to capitalize the *L*. I have a week left in New York before I'm due in Saratoga Springs for our summer gala. I bend my left knee to deepen the stretch. There are a few other dancers from the company here this morning—Rohan and Fran and Gwen. They smile at me as they come in, take their places close to me at the barre. I feel safer with them near me.

But then I feel fingertips tapping on my back, and I turn to find

Irine, sleek in a black leotard and silk headscarf. My whole body heats.

"You *are* back," says Irine, grinning.

"I hardly know where I am at all these days," I say, feigning exasperated weariness.

"I bet. You look beautiful," she says, looking me up and down.

I'm already growing hot and we haven't started moving yet. The last thing I need is for Irine to notice my tit sweat before we reach grand battements.

"Thanks. You too. As always."

The teacher enters the room, and so Irine lowers her voice to just above a whisper.

"I'm glad I ran into you. I *really* want you to come to our company class."

I nod as though enthused.

Clearly, I can never take this class again. People are staring. I swear I hear my name whispered. I try taking a deep breath. The next one comes easier.

As soon as the pianist begins her clunking, I turn on. I feel like an intruder, like Irine must be watching my every move. More than once, our eyes meet in one of the mirrors. I am determined to be more classical than ever, though I am a little tender with myself today because my back has been spasming lately. The upside, though, is that my ankle is better. I fight a scowl when something in my hip cracks as I grab my heel and bring my foot up over my head. I'm going to have an adjustment after class. I was supposed to get lunch with Ryn but I rescheduled; I haven't seen Jasper since I've been back. I lean into the pain ricocheting through the muscles in my back, pull my stomach in. Ten minutes into barre, I'm dripping with sweat. This is humiliating—I really do need to look into Botox injections to reduce sweat. I am unbearably hot. The good news about this is that it's making my movements come to me really easily. My feet are pliant, I exaggerate my extensions.

The bad news is that I feel like I have molten lava in my gut. Bile rolls around in my stomach, occasionally bubbles up to the back of my throat. I didn't eat breakfast this morning; I try to remember what I had for dinner last night. A kale salad with radishes and slivered almonds and tofu, a little bit of Ryn's leftover chicken. A fudge brownie I bought on impulse from the Gristedes by our apartment. The brownie, then. Just the thought of it brings on a surge of nausea. I consider making myself throw up after class. I've never actually done this—it feels like cheating, like hitting Undo, and if anyone saw me they'd run to the company nutritionist, and I'd get a gentle talking-to and a lot more scrutiny. I would never do it. But I like to think about it sometimes, like when I stare at a piece of cake or something and repeat *no no no* in my head like a chant until I stop wanting it, and it feels really good, the not wanting it. Except that it hadn't worked with the brownie. I couldn't resist that fucking brownie. I refocus on my breathing and try to connect to my movements. Inhale with each elongation, exhale through the transitions.

I am feeling a bit better by the time we get to center. I watch some of the other people in the class. There are a couple of other professionals, maybe from ABT or Joffrey, which is in New York for the summer doing *La Sylphide*. There are a few students, a couple of whom I can tell are going to make it. They have good bodies, good feet, and they're executing the combinations with a certain hunger, a certain seriousness. There's a crazy guy—he's a big Black guy with a potbelly and a neon headband. He glares at the teacher as she sets the next steps. It is disheartening to note that he is the only one here who's sweating more than I am. He can really turn, though. I do the big jumps with the guys because I want to go high today. I finish the last grand jeté in front of Irine, and I pirouette and bow to her. The room applauds.

At the end of class, Irine pinches my ass on her way out.

"Text me, okay?" she says.

The company's massage therapist, Angela, finds the tight spot in my back and jams her blunt, steely fingers in. My back spasms in protest, a frantic baby-bird struggle. I take deep yoga breaths against the pain. Finally, there is a release. Angela crosses one of my arms over the other and jerks me up off the table until my spine cracks. Then, the reward: a deep, slow massage with lemongrass-scented oil. I leave the table feeling sore, but pleasantly so. I go to sign a pile of my dead pointe shoes. I don't know why people buy these things. I understand they want something personal, but why does it have to be something previously occupied by my stinky, ugly feet? There's something grotesque about it, like they're collecting shrunken heads or scalps.

I start out, heading to meet Jasper for lunch on the Lower East Side. The place is close to his apartment—I am hoping that after lunch, we'll have time for sex. I am starving, more than I should be. Hunger is a type of want I find unsettling. Especially when it's this intense, this much of a threat to my self-control. Maybe it's because of the massage. I bet Irine isn't hungry right now. I bet Gwen is having a Clif Bar for lunch. I feel like I could take down a giraffe and then mount Jasper for dessert. I am an animal.

"Excuse me," someone says.

I turn and find a middle-aged woman I don't recognize. I am taken aback—I almost apologize to her.

"You're Celine Cordell, right? My daughter over there"—she indicates a little girl, about eleven or twelve, who's hanging back shyly—"she's a really big fan. I don't want to bother you, but would you mind taking a picture with her?"

There's a relief, but also mortification, as though this woman could hear what I was just thinking. I am sure I must *look* like an animal. Everyone must be watching. Critics' pens poised.

"Of course," I say. I walk up to the little girl and take her hand. "What's your name?"

"Taylor."

We pose with my arm around her bony shoulders. This kid is a dancer, I can tell. "Are you doing a summer intensive here in the city?" I ask once her mother's taken several shots with her phone.

Taylor nods. "Joffrey," she says.

"That's fantastic. You must be really great."

Taylor blushes and I give her a hug. She's awfully cute.

By now, other people are beginning to recognize me. Some just want to smile, say congratulations, maybe shake my hand. More than one thinks I'm Misty Copeland, even though Misty Copeland and I are shades of brown apart. Some want pictures or autographs. I'm not used to this. After a performance, sure, people want to meet you, take a picture with you, get you to sign something. But never just out on the street. Strangers are telling me that they're proud of me. I feel thwarted, confused. I'm sure they're all missing something. How can I be jaded already? I'm not, I decide. I'm just not sure whether Cece Cordell is as great as Celine Cordell.

Thank you so much, Celine says. *Thank you Thank you Oh that's so sweet Thank you so much.*

What I feel is a niggling disbelief. That people want to see me without the stage and the makeup and the lights. They want to make sure that I am an *inspiration*. That I'm worthy of being an Icon, will one day be a Historical Figure. Part of me thinks that if people knew how hard I've worked and what I've sacrificed, I wouldn't be so impressive. There is no magic. I'm not really the fairy, the princess, or the captivating vision. I'm just another character who's going to die in the end.

The rest of my—I hesitate to even think the word—*fans* dwindle off and I look around to make sure that no one is still watching me, waiting, disapproving. I know I must be late. I check my phone. I *am* late but I don't have any texts or missed calls from Jasper. I resume my walk to the subway. It is a beautiful day. The sunlight is turning the sidewalks a warm silver and the sky is a cerulean blue, which was always my favorite crayon as a kid. My phone dings just as I'm about to descend the grubby stairs to the 1 train. *sorry babe—dr g squeezing me in for my achilles. rain check?*

I try not to feel disappointed. Jasper's Achilles tendon has been bothering him since Paris, and the last thing he wants, that any of us want, is for it to snap.

I text Ryn: *You still free for lunch?*

The first thing Ryn says as I sit down across from her is, "Jasper stand you up?"

"He didn't 'stand me up,'" I say, using air quotes. "He got a last-minute appointment with Dr. Gonzalez, that's all. No big deal."

Ryn pulls her pretty pink lips into a thin line.

"How's the Frenchman?" I ask.

Ryn met some rich French businessman in his late thirties while the company was in Paris, and they seem to be getting serious pretty quickly.

"He's coming to Saratoga," she says. "He told me he can't wait to see my Hippolyta."

"That's great, Ryn. You really like him then?"

"I love him."

"Whoa."

"We're in love."

"Like, you say it?"

"Yeah, we say it."

"In French or in English?"

"Both."

"Wow."

Our waitress comes over and we both order salads, though what I really want is a grilled cheese and a nice, cold Sprite. I seriously consider feigning an errand once we've paid the bill and coming back in once Ryn is gone, making sure I get a different waiter, and then feasting. But that's crazy. I order a Perrier.

"Remember that *Vogue* shoot?" I ask Ryn. "When all the Perrier was flat?"

Ryn laughs half-heartedly. "May as well have just given us tap, but we were trying to be fancy."

That was a fun photo shoot—Ryn talked me into doing it. Mostly it was us leaping around and posing with our arms draped over each other, cheeks pressed together, laughing. One of the staff members told us that we were like sisters. Today, though, Ryn seems off, a little cold.

Our drinks arrive and I sip at my sparkling water, trying to imagine the taste of added sugars.

"I was going to check out Adam and Milena's party tonight." She says this tentatively, like she's about to ask me for money. "You want to come?"

Adam and Milena are a married couple, and their parties are usually a lot of fun—they have rooftop access. Jasper will probably be there. "I shouldn't," I say. "I've got that all-day shoot tomorrow. I shouldn't even be eating, frankly."

I laugh but Ryn doesn't laugh back. She nods like she was expecting my answer.

"I'm not really looking forward to it," I go on. Our conversation feels difficult for some reason, like I'm running through water. "The shoot, I mean. I can't get used to all this"—I search for a word that doesn't sound pompous or like a humblebrag—"hubbub. I don't, I don't know, deserve it."

Ryn wrinkles her brow. "Of course you do," she says. "I've been with you this whole time—you've worked really hard. None of this just fell into your lap."

"Everyone works really hard. I'm not a superhero or anything."

"You are to a lot of people. You're a historic first. Don't downplay it."

"Fine. Then when you get promoted, do I have permission to go crazy? I'm thinking fireworks, maybe a safari."

"I'm not going to get promoted."

"Don't say that, Ryn."

She shrugs. "It's okay. Soloist is as far as I go and I'm happy with it. All I ever wanted to do was dance, and I've danced."

Our salads arrive. Ryn blots some of the dressing off of hers while I shove a forkful of leaves into my mouth.

"You talk like your career is already over," I say once I'm finished chewing.

"Oh, I've probably got another good ten or twelve years. Though if I marry the Frenchman I won't really have to work."

"*Marry?* You just met the guy." I don't know why, but I feel like a lost child all of a sudden. I could cry.

"I told you—we're in love." She gives me a little half smile. "When you know, you know."

I barely recognize my friend, my sister. She's holding her face in some new way.

"It's a little more complicated than that, isn't it? I mean, falling in love is easy—all you really need is a person with satisfactory parts and a nice attitude. But what about when the shine wears off? What about when you have to still choose that person even though they've gained a few pounds and they hate spending the holidays with your family and they've got kale stuck in their teeth?"

"Oh, Cece." Ryn sighs. "It's not that complicated at all."

She takes a moment to clean her teeth with the nail of her pinkie finger, using her butter knife as a mirror.

"Just don't put all your eggs in one basket, that's all I'm saying."

"Isn't that what dancers do?"

I suppose it is. It has never really occurred to me to plan for a future without ballet. I figure there's another fifteen or so years left to my career, twenty if I'm very, *very* lucky. And injury could end it sooner. I try to picture what my life will be like then, and my imagination is blank. I finish my salad before Ryn is even halfway through with hers, so I order tea. Again, there is this awkwardness between us, like we've had a huge fight we're not talking about, but the wave has already broken on the shore and receded, and now the sand is still hissing and bubbling. I remember Paul taking me to Coney Island when I was little, and he got me to stand far enough out that the waves died against our calves, and the sand seemed to rush after them, pulling us forward. He convinced me that it was whales underneath the sand, trying to drag us into the ocean. He was always so happy at the beach.

Ryn pays for us both, despite my protests. Outside, she lights a cigarette, takes a drag, and carefully blows the smoke away from me, using her hand as a shield. I have always found this gesture incredibly touching.

I slip an arm across her shoulders. I feel huge and bloated next to her. "What now?"

"Manicure?" she says.

I release her and we begin to walk to the salon we usually go to on Sixth Avenue. The place is actually a hair salon—they do nails in the back. It's one of those Dominican places where, for fifteen dollars, I can get someone to snatch my hair straight with a brush and a very hot blow-dryer. It comes out looking as straight and glossy as Ryn's hair until I sweat it out. I like to get it done before performances when I'm in between perms. I'd love to be part of the go-natural movement, but it isn't really an option for me. I already have the wrong skin for ballet; I can't afford to have the wrong hair. Maybe once I've been a principal for a few more years.

Ryn has gone quiet again.

"So Kaz has been hounding me to go over to his place for drinks," I say.

Ryn looks slightly alarmed. "Just you?"

I shrug.

"Will Cecilia be there?"

"I assume so."

Ryn does a half-snort, half-chuckle thing. "Yeah. Cecilia would never let you and Kaz be alone together."

"Gross."

"Are you going to go over to Jasper's tonight after he stood you up?"

I bristle a little at the judgment in Ryn's tone. "Probably not. I'm going to stay in, take a nice, long, Epsom salt bath, and catch up on shitty television. I might have a glass of red wine— photographers seem to like it when I look all vascular."

For some reason, this makes me feel alone and pathetic. Like a beached whale.

Ryn laughs. It's small, but it's genuine, I think. "I'll be out of your way," she says. "I've got to go find Josh before hitting the party."

Ryn's coke dealer is a smarmy Columbia grad student.

Her phone dings, and when she looks at the screen, she smiles.

"The Frenchman?" I ask.

She only giggles in a way that, again, makes her seem foreign to me. Distracted now, she slows her pace, leaving me to walk slightly ahead of her, exposed. I can be on my phone too. I text Irine something friendly and meaningless.

Usually, it's dehydration that kills a beached whale. Or they collapse under their own weight, suddenly magnified out of the water. Given enough time, they'll explode.

I haven't seen my mother since before I got promoted. I called to tell her, of course. I even called my father, but his phone just rang and rang, and I'm not even sure it's still his number. Aside from holiday and birthday calls, neither of us makes much effort to stay in each other's lives. My mother seemed happy, but not as happy as she could've seemed. The moment didn't have the *you see?* feel to it I'd always thought it would. I read a magazine as I take the A train to Brooklyn. I've picked one that doesn't have any mention of me in it—not an easy feat. My face is everywhere. I can't escape myself; it's like being in class all the time.

Yesterday's shoot was *NOTOFU.* I've been in that magazine before—a few years ago, Jasper and I did a spread for them where both of us were topless, our bodies pressed together in every shot, black skin against white. Or dark gray against light gray—the photos were in black and white. My mother had a fit. I couldn't get her to understand—my work is about the body, and so, to me, the body isn't really provocative as its own thing. She'll be happier with this spread; I am clothed the entire time, albeit in a flesh-colored leotard.

I get off a stop early because I feel like walking. Maybe I'm procrastinating. Whenever I visit my mother, I go with an internal flinch, like I've done something wrong and I'm waiting to be scolded. It is so hot outside that I can smell the heat itself, and I begin to sweat. Normally, this would distress me—I might try walking slower, or I might duck into stores for their air-conditioning—but I'm not wearing makeup and I have another tank top I can change into in my old bedroom. I don't know how people walk around in this heat looking pristine and dry. There must be some magic trick I was never taught.

"Hey sis," says a man sitting outside a bodega.

I ignore him.

He tries again. "Hey queen."

Part of me feels bad for ignoring him—he hasn't said anything overtly offensive. Maybe he just wants the time. Maybe he recognizes me. But I saw him leering at me from down the block. Now, my not speaking to him is a confrontation he has forced me into, a challenge to which I cannot predict his response. He waves at me as I get closer and I stare fixedly at the ground ahead of me. I stiffen as I pass him, try not to let it show in my gait.

"Fuck you, then," he says to my back.

I don't feel bad anymore, though, strangely, my eyes moisten like I might cry. How full of little violences this world is.

I have a key to my mother's house, of course, but I always still ring the buzzer and wait for her to let me in. My mother is wearing this bright orange romper and I'm taken aback. It's not really her style, and my mother is a fifty-two-year-old woman—she's always been vocal in her disapproval of women who don't dress their age, whatever that means. I don't comment on the romper, though. I just kiss her cheek and follow her into the kitchen, where she sits me down at the table and immediately sets a plate of peach cobbler in front of me. Normally, this would annoy me, but the cobbler smells incredible, and my stomach growls loudly. *Animal*, I think.

"You're all over the TV," my mother says, sitting in the chair next to mine. "You know that? Everyone keeps saying, 'Terra, isn't that your daughter I saw on the news?' They bring me magazines with you in them. I got a whole pile of them in the living room."

She says all this in a vaguely chastising tone, so that I'm tempted to apologize for the inconvenience.

"How's school going?" I ask.

"It's going good," she says. "Since I'm doing the summer classes, I'll have enough credits to graduate next spring."

She taps her fingers on the tabletop and I notice that her nails are painted bright red. Manicures have never been her thing. And her bare arms are toned. My mother has always been slim, but without any effort. Slender, but also soft. Not athletic. Not toned.

"Ma, have you been working out?"

She laughs a little, self-consciously, like she's a teenager. "Nothing wrong with getting in shape," she says. "I'm not getting any younger."

I narrow my eyes at her. "What's going on? You have a boyfriend or something? Is it Dad?"

Every decade or so, my parents revisit each other. It never ends well. I am the product of one of these rekindlings. It's why my brother and I are so far apart in age.

She sucks her teeth. "No, it is not your father."

I stare at her, eyes still narrowed, until she continues.

"It's this man from my cultural psychology class. King. He's very nice."

"Why are you being so secretive about it?"

"I'm not. I just haven't told you."

"Why?"

"Well, he's . . . younger."

I cross my arms. "How much younger?"

"A bit."

"How old is he, Ma?"

"He'll be forty in August."

I've eaten about half the cobbler, and it's sitting awkwardly in my stomach, an unsteady boat in an ocean of bile. I don't know why this bothers me. Jasper is older than me. But by six years. Not twelve. "That's a lot, Ma. Jesus. He's like Paul's age."

She rolls her eyes. "He's older than your brother, Celine."

"Not by a lot. Eight years. How is that not gross to you?"

"If it was the other way around, and he was the older one, you wouldn't have anything to say about it."

"Well, a man twelve years your senior would be in his mid-sixties, so yes, I think I would have something to say about that."

"This isn't really any of your business, anyway. He makes me happy. He calls me his queen."

I push the rest of the cobbler away. "Oh my God, Ma—is he a hotep? Are you dating a hotep?"

She frowns. "What the hell is a hotep?"

I lean forward. "Does he, like, *actually* believe he's long-lost African royalty? Does he make you watch lots of documentaries about the Black Panthers and Muhammad Ali? Does he make you cook for him and try to convince you to get pregnant and stop perming your hair? Does he say things like, 'Why be eye candy when you could be soul food?'"

She seems to think about this for a moment. "He's a very intellectual brother with some traditional values," she says slowly.

I laugh, slap her arm. "He *is* a hotep. Ma, you can't date a hotep."

She is amused, I can tell, but she raises an eyebrow. "And why not?"

"Because they're homophobic, misogynistic, and the absolute worst. I just got cat-called by one, and when I didn't respond, he cussed me out."

"King isn't like that."

"Maybe not now. But give him a few months and he'll be trying to convince you that Black men are supposed to have mistresses of every race, but the Black woman is his true queen."

She rolls her eyes again. "Why don't you focus on your own dating life, little girl, instead of worrying so much about mine?"

"I have no dating life."

I've never told her the truth about Jasper and me. It's not like it's a secret—everyone in the company knows, and I've even met Jasper's parents and younger brothers, one of whom is currently at SAB, and the other of whom just graduated with a doctorate in physical therapy. But we have cultivated the habit of not disclosing the full truth of our relationship to the public. The public's speculation, the company's PR director has said, is always more exciting, more tantalizing than the real thing. A hint of romantic tension is part of what makes a great ballet partnership—look at Margot Fonteyn and Rudolf Nureyev, or Suzanne Farrell and Balanchine. In ballet, the audience must know only enough to interpret, to project, to fantasize.

And though she shouldn't, though I resent that she does, my mother feels like the public. I don't tell her everything. I give her, in fact, very little. And this is a way for me to protect us both from her expectations. It's not like she pays attention, anyway. She might not even be aware that Jasper and I are celebrated for how well we partner.

We migrate into the living room and I see the stack of magazines and newspapers, all given to her. We sit together on the couch, which has been our couch for my entire life. Everything in this apartment is so old; when Ryn and I started furnishing our place, I came to the realization that I didn't actually know how to buy furniture. The financing, delivery, assembly—all this was a mystery to me.

My mother turns on the television, a gift from Paul, and, coincidentally, the only thing in the living room that is less than a decade old. He brought it here eight years ago. It didn't come in a box. He and my mother got into an argument about where he got it, but she never made him take it back. She turns to a reality show featuring a bunch of blond, Botoxed women with the emotional maturity of toddlers. There is this awkward silence between us that I hate. I wish my mother were a different kind of mother sometimes—the same woman but maybe a little cuddlier, more talkative, a little more maternal.

"How's Kathryn?" she asks.

"Good, I guess. She got herself some rich Parisian boyfriend, and now she's an expert in love and she doesn't even seem to care about dance anymore."

My mother smiles a little and shrugs a shoulder. "That's how it goes."

"What, so it's girl meets guy and then realizes that her career aspirations were just silliness and all she wants to do is stay at home and bake Bundt cakes?"

"No, but love is distracting. When you're young."

"Well, *he's* certainly not young. He's, like, almost your hotep's age. She just met the guy and she's already talking about marriage."

My mother raises an eyebrow. "You don't sound very happy for her."

"I . . ." I struggle to find the words for how I feel. Ryn is the sister I never had, and I don't appreciate the implication that I'm a bad friend because I don't feel what I'm supposed to feel. "I'm worried about her. Ryn could be a principal if she wanted. She has this crazy balance, and her technique is flawless. She just needs to *connect* to the steps. Emotionally."

"Mmm."

Now that I am talking dance, my mother's attention is waning.

"She gets it sometimes," I continue, "but it's not consistent. When she hits it, she's stunning. But I don't think she cares about getting promoted anymore. She'll quit and live off the Frenchman."

"Oh, good *Lord,* these children," my mother says. But she is not talking about me or Ryn or the Frenchman. She is responding to the reality-TV blondes, two of whom are screeching at each other at a charity event.

I snatch up the remote. "I don't want to watch this awful show," I say, and I turn to a documentary about Picasso.

"I only ever watch that stuff when you're here."

"Crap like that will rot your brain out."

The awkward silence returns. The documentary keeps featuring slow pans of that famous picture of Picasso—that one where he's in a striped shirt, and he looks like he's about to shake a fist at the camera. I'm not really listening to the narration. In the corner of my eye I can see the pristine stack of newspapers and magazines, and behind that, in the bookshelf, stands this year's Mother's Day card. It's a funny one. I never get the flowery, sentimental ones. It would embarrass us both.

There is a little photo album too. I used to like looking at it when I was a kid. It's mostly empty. It contains a picture of Paul as a baby, grinning a wide, mostly toothless grin, skinny little arms stretched over his head. There is a rare picture of my mom and dad together, fresh out of their wedding at city hall, my father with a 'fro and mustache, looking skinny and young in a polo and black jeans. My mother's hair is '80s big, and there's just the barest hint of pregnant curve showing underneath her pink dress. They are both laughing, arms slung around each other's waists. I always wished I'd known those people.

"Paul can't stand Picasso," I say, growing bored of the documentary and the silence.

"No?"

"No. He would always say Picasso is overrated. The only stuff worth looking at is his early work."

"Hmm."

"He's right, I think. I went to the Picasso museum in Barcelona when the company was there a few years ago. I liked all his old sketches and the pre-1901 stuff."

She doesn't answer and it irritates me. I am trying to goad her into talking about Paul. Or art, or *anything*. She is a rock. But she is my mother, and so I love her. But what do I love? Is she still, somewhere, that laughing woman in the photo, the one I'd like to know? Or if I got close enough to her, would I find only a collection of meaningless strokes, like Monet's water lilies? We sit in the stale stink of our quiet and learn about Picasso's last years and neo-Expressionism, and I think that we all die as stars die, an explosion of light and sound in a universe that is indifferent to both.

People often speculate that the extravagance of Kaz's apartment is Cecilia's doing. But I don't think so. I think that, despite his vaguely Sovietesque complaints about the capitalist West, Kaz has secret, poignant traces of nostalgia for a Russia that died suddenly and violently. Even though Kaz was born in the late 1940s, his grandparents remembered tsarist Russia, and it's in him too. It's in the shelf of Fabergé eggs, the mirrors with their gilded frames, the large volume on the Romanov dynasty. Ballet survived. It survived the Bolsheviks and the Soviets, it being both political ambassador and subtle dissenter. Kaz also survived, and he has similar dualities in him. His apartment is an ode to that, I think.

Cecilia is in the living room, encased in white—white jeans

and white blouse against the white couch. I think of snow blind-
ness. Kaz offers me brandy.

"Not just any brandy," he says. "Good, Armenian brandy."

I take the proffered snifter. The brandy's smell is too strong, and
I don't want to be buzzed, so I resolve to only pretend to sip at it.
Kaz gestures at me, indicating that I should sit on the same white
couch Cecilia is occupying. I do, with a hesitation that I hope doesn't
show. I have been here before, but for some reason, I am nervous
now. Part of me wonders if Kaz is going to un-promote me. Maybe
he has just realized I am a terrible dancer and he's going to fire me.
Though if he were going to fire me, he'd have called me into his
office. He does not typically handle business out of his home—his
apartment is usually reserved for dinner parties.

He is staring at me in his way and I try not to squirm. I try to
sit lightly on the couch, because I hate the idea of getting up and
having Cecilia glare at the imprint of my ass on her white sofa. I
am pulling my pelvic floor up, energetically lifting my muscles like
I do when I'm about to jump or be lifted.

"Go play the music, Ceci," he says, and for one horrible split
second before I discern the subtle phonetic differences between
my nickname and Cecilia's, I almost rise to obey, but I stop myself
in time, and no one seems to have noticed as Cecilia stands and
struts over to the piano. Disdain drips from her like pearls. I don't
hate Cecilia nearly as much as she hates me.

She sits down, arranges sheet music, and begins to play. Beautifully, I might add. I envy her talent—I wish I had taken piano
lessons. But the music itself is beautiful. It is not something I've
heard before. It is hypnotic. Mournful and sexy. I try to guess its
composer. Minkus? Adolphe Adam? Ponchielli? I close my eyes. It
starts slowly, but it's getting faster, gaining energy. My body is responding; I want to move.

"Stop there for now," Kaz tells Cecilia. "There are four movements," he tells me. "About two hours overall. Remarkable work from a little-known African American composer."

I open my eyes and meet his.

"You like it," he says, and he is not asking.

"It's beautiful." I stiffen a little, unsure what to make of this yet. How much of my promotion had to do with my dancing, and how much of it was optics?

Kaz stands, begins to pace on his Persian rug. "I am making a ballet on you," he says. "Full length. It is something I've wanted to do for a long time. Since I first saw you dance."

I can't help but smile. Our resident choreographer has created several ballets on me, but for Kaz to do it is something rare these days, an honor. A *claiming.*

"But it will be special," he says. "Something different. A story ballet that is both romantic and neoclassical."

I wonder how it can be both—neoclassical works so often push against the mystical female narrative central to romantic ballets. But I trust Kaz. Balanchine said that there are no new steps, only new combinations, but what Kaz can do with those combinations is miraculous.

"Are you familiar with the story of May and the Hag?"

I shake my head, though it does sound familiar. Like a story from one of the books of Black folktales my mother used to buy for me and Paul. Or one of the old Gullah stories my father sometimes used to tell.

"American folktale. Beautiful girl is cursed with the Hag, a vampire more or less, who snatches her and rides her around every night so she can't get any sleep. She can't scream or ask for help because the spirit shuts her mouth. The girl's mother catches on eventually and traps the demon. But once the mother dies, the Hag comes back and haunts the girl for the rest of her life. The end."

"Depressing," I say. I'm sure I do know this story—a piece of Gullah folklore. Something my father told me once. Or Paul.

Cecilia scoffs from the piano bench. "All folktales are depressing. You're familiar with *Swan Lake*, aren't you?"

Kaz continues as though he hasn't heard either of us. "I am interested in bringing the African American oral tradition to the stage, canonizing it as the old stories of Russian peasants have been canonized. If anyone's going to help me define a new American classical ballet, it's going to be you, darling."

For a moment, this resonates sourly. Every time I begin to feel at home in this company, Kaz's company, I am reminded of my own otherness. It figures that the first ballet Kaz makes on me after my promotion is, in effect, about my Blackness. Maybe the promotion was about my Blackness, too. But I am overreacting. Or I am reacting to the wrong thing. Kaz has chosen me.

He holds out his hand, and I take it, allow him to pull me to my feet.

"Of course," he says, "we have to change the story a bit. Make it more balletic. *The Nutcracker and the Mouse King* to just *The Nutcracker*, you know."

He nods at Cecilia and she begins to play again, from the beginning. Kaz leads me by my hand, using me to sketch steps.

"Beautiful May is adored by everyone," he says, just loud enough to hear over the piano. "All the boys love her, and—I don't know, we'll call her June for now—is jealous and spiteful. So she curses you to be haunted by the Hag."

He walks me in a square around the big white couch.

"Every night the Hag comes to you. Steals your breath. Makes you fly about the room. I'm dreaming of a spectacular pas de deux here. I'm thinking of Fran as the Hag. Or maybe Anya."

"What about Ryn?" I say.

Kaz shakes his head. "No, no. She's too small. She has to be able to lift you."

Cecilia has paused in her playing and now she snorts. "What girl can lift her?" she sneers.

Kaz ignores his wife's hostility. "That's the whole point," he says. "A pas de deux between two women done like a pas de deux between a woman and a man."

Kaz is known for this kind of thing. He likes to challenge the very traditional, very antiquated roles of men and women in dance, particularly partnered dance. For last year's fall gala, he made a piece on Rohan and Adam where they stalked around like jungle cats and danced an intensely physical, yet unexpectedly gentle pas de deux with each other.

He grabs my waist and begins sketching again, though Cecilia does not resume playing. "I want you to struggle. I want a fight. First she hovers over your bed, takes your breath. I want this very geometrical, very angular. A little erotic, a little Sapphic, but subtle. And then she takes you flying around the room. Here, we can be more classical. You're still struggling, but she lifts you, and lifts you, and lifts you. She *makes* you fly. Your salvation comes with the dawn. The Hag shrinks away from the rising sun. I want her to melt off the stage."

I demonstrate a little sickly, gliding step for him and he nods excitedly.

"That's it," he says. "Cecilia, what are you doing? Start the second movement."

She clenches her jaw but begins playing again without a word.

"During the day," Kaz continues, "you are exhausted. Weak and listless. You can't even speak because the Hag has stolen your voice—you can't tell anyone what's happening to you. I want you to dance like a wilting flower."

I kick off my sandals and begin a pretty little limp around the room.

"Not quite like that," Kaz says. "More up, like this. And your arms—here."

We all learn the language of ballet—the French words, the names of the steps. But after a while, it falls into disuse because dance is wordless. Yes, I know what an Italian fouetté is, but when Kaz says "more up" my body knows what to do.

"Now, a handsome stranger comes to town and falls in love with you, even though you never utter a word to him. But our June wants him for herself, and she flirts with him shamelessly. In trying to talk him out of his love for you, she ends up bragging about the curse. He resolves to save you."

"Ugh," I say. "Do you have to do that? You said it's the girl's mother who saves her. Why make it about some man? It's so tired and sexist."

Kaz holds up his hands. "I know, I know. It's for the audience. This is a new classic—classics are romantic. And this way I can cast that boy. The two of you sell tickets."

I put my hands on my hips. "Don't I sell enough tickets on my own?"

Cecilia has stopped playing again. "You're better with Jasper," she says.

Kaz frowns at her. "I don't know about *that*," he says, "but if I'm going to partner you with a man, then people are going to expect it to be him. Besides, there's a great pas de trois to be had here. The demon begins her mischief on you, but she is interrupted by the boy. Gorgeous battle: I'm seeing you flying between the Hag and the boy—we'll call him William or something—sort of like a game of catch. Lots of beautiful shapes. The arms, the legs—classical and modern clashing against each other. Finally, the boy throws a handful of pins into a jar, and the Hag, unable to resist counting them, jumps into the jar too. You both close it up tight and put it in the window until the sun comes and kills her. I still need to think about how we'll stage that."

"And then we get married?" I say.

"Yes. And then you get married." He gives me one of his unsettling stares. I know he is half in his head, choreographing, moving bodies across an imaginary stage. But I can feel Cecilia watching us. I try to look calm and relaxed. I'm not doing anything wrong, but once someone is suspicious of you, they can make guilt out of nothing. I should tell Cecilia that I'm not screwing her husband. That in fact, he only *thinks* he wants to screw me. It's the idea of me he's in love with. I'm a doll, a toy soldier. He hasn't considered that I fart and have morning breath and would probably get on his nerves. I want to say this to her, but she would never believe me. She's attached to an idea of me too. And Kaz— I'd rather have his gaze than have him not see me at all.

"African dance," Kaz says suddenly. "At the wedding. You know, in the great party scenes of the classics, there's those international dances? Russian, Spanish, Arabian, Dutch. We can turn all that on its head. An African dance, a Native American dance."

I cross my arms. "What, are we going to put people in blackface?"

He waves a hand at me. "Of course not. We're not the Bolshoi. Dance has no race."

I am suddenly dizzy, and I don't have the energy to unpack my objections. I sit on the arm of the white couch, holding most of my weight off of it so that my quadriceps begin to burn.

Cecilia rises, catlike, from the piano bench and glides over to me to peer into my face. "You don't look good," she says. There is something in her face—it's not quite concern, but something sharper.

I look down at my hands—looking up at her only makes my head spin more.

"Have you eaten today? When's the last time you ate?" she asks, not exactly friendly.

I have eaten today. A buttery croissant stuffed with bacon and cheese. It was delicious. I'm starving. It makes me sick.

"What are you saying?" Kaz says, coming to stand next to his wife and looking down at me too. His voice is chastising, disapproving—what Cecilia's trying to imply is taboo in the ballet world. "Of course she's eaten. Celine is strong—she eats. Isn't that right, Cece?"

I nod. "I ate. I'm just a little tired, I think. And I can feel a sinus headache coming on. That's all."

Kaz gestures at his wife. "Get her a glass of water. Cece, you need rest. We'll start setting the ballet in Saratoga, yes? I'll have it ironed out by then." He pats my thigh.

Cecilia brings me water in an exquisite crystal glass, and I wonder if she's done it to put me in my place. Or rather, to make me feel out of place. I'm afraid to handle it—my grip is weak. And why has Kaz asked me to his apartment to discuss this new ballet? Why not have me meet him at the studio? What are these people trying to do to me? I take a sip of the water and realize that I am very, very thirsty. Both Cecilia and Kaz are watching me. I'm not sure what they want me to do.

"I'm excited about this," I say, and Kaz grins, pleased.

Cecilia's face does not change.

Rohan throws a party the night before our Saratoga season begins. Jasper has convinced me to go with him. I haven't seen Ryn since we had lunch—apparently, the Frenchman surprised her by flying in early. She hasn't even been home. I tried texting her, but she hasn't responded. This irritates me—I need her, and she's hardly ever around lately. No one is ever there when I need them most. This thought summons a tightness at the base of my throat, Paul's ghost at the back of my mind, which irritates me even more. I gripe about Ryn to Jasper as we walk to Rohan's apartment.

"She can be so passive-aggressive," I say. "She always is. I never know what I did to piss her off."

Jasper is holding my hand loosely, and he gives it a squeeze. "It'll blow over in a couple of days," he says. "And then you, her, and Irine can get the old gang back together."

"That's the thing, though. Eventually, she'll just act like nothing was ever wrong, and I hate that. I'd rather have at it, you know? Just have the argument."

"Sometimes talking is overrated."

"She's all caught up in the Frenchman," I say, bitter. "Did you know Ryn is a relationship expert now? Oh, and she's the only person in the world who's ever been in love."

"Ah, young love," Jasper says, and he picks me up and spins me around.

I kick him gently in the shin once he sets me down. The fairy lights of the city are still spinning around me.

"Maybe she'll be at the party," Jasper says, "and you two can have it out there. I'll watch. You know, just to make sure it's a clean fight."

I roll my eyes. Straight ballet guys can be such cavemen. It's like they're overcompensating because they know everyone still assumes they're gay.

I'm surprised by how many people are crammed into Rohan's apartment. At least half the company is here, as well as a handful of people I don't know. I lose Jasper pretty quickly and I feel alone and claustrophobic. I drift from group to group of dancers, looking for someone to stick to, someone to anchor me. I feel strangely exposed, a lone antelope or zebra or something, caught in a nature photographer's lens. *Here we find a young female, separated from her pack. She must find another to join if she is to have any hope of survival. But will the new pack accept her?* Those nature shows are always so smug. And we all know the poor antelope is going to get eaten by a lion in the end. And you will cry ugly tears because you've loved that antelope for the past forty minutes. And we're all the antelope. Except for the sociopaths who think they're the lion.

I pass through the living room, where a few people are doing lines off the coffee table, and another group is passing around a bong. Someone offers me Percocet and I decline. I make my way over to a card table that is crowded with bottles of alcohol. I stare at the myriad of choices—rum and gin and vodka and tequila and whiskey and room-temperature beer and even some shitty wine. There are mixers too. I don't really want a drink but I feel like I should have one. Anya comes up to the table—she looks like a ballerina Bettie Page in a red crop top. I smile at her and she looks startled.

"You look pretty," I say, hoping she'll invite me to hang out with her, since Jasper has abandoned me.

"I love your shoes," she says without looking down. She smiles—a stage smile—and heads off without getting herself a drink.

I mix vodka and tepid orange juice in a red plastic cup. I make it stronger than I normally would, hoping the alcohol will make me feel less out of place. I take a sip and try not to pull a face. The orange juice is cheap—pulpy and watery—and the vodka tastes like rubbing alcohol. I look around, searching for Jasper, but I don't see him. By the time I'm nearly a quarter of the way through my screwdriver, I'm already feeling buzzed. I'm a lightweight, but even for me, it usually takes more than a few sips. From the corner of my eye, I think I see people's faces turning toward me. When I turn my head to meet their gazes I can see that it's just my imagination. I decide that this will be my only drink, and I will drink it slowly.

"Hey."

I look up and see Ryn, who looks like an angel in a white dress, her enviable blond hair flowing around her face.

"Hey," I respond.

An awkward pause. Ryn touches her collarbone, flicks a lock of hair over her shoulder. The room seems to blur in and out, in and out, like someone's adjusting the focus.

"Is the Frenchman here?" I ask.

She looks at me like I've just said the dumbest thing in the world. "No." She makes the "no" last for two beats. "This isn't really his scene."

"Dancers aren't his scene? Isn't that a little problematic?"

I'm trying to be funny, but Ryn frowns at me. "I mean parties like this. He'd be uncomfortable. His English isn't that good, you know."

"Well, either he'd better spruce up his English or you'd better spruce up your French—communication is key, as they say."

"We manage," Ryn says. She's looking at me hard, like we're playing charades or something and she's trying to give me a hint with her eyes. My vision is a little blurry, like I have a slight astigmatism. I'm getting something wrong, but I don't know what it is, and it's irritating me.

"It's weird," I say, "that I've never met him. You ashamed of me or something? I need to look him over, see if I approve."

Ryn's pale face turns ice cold. "I'm probably going to head out," she says. "We have plans."

She's walking away from me now, her beautifully muscled back shifting like a mirage as she goes. I stand stunned. I have no idea what I've done. I take a big gulp of my terrible drink.

The sense of wrongness is immediate. Luckily, I've been to Rohan's apartment before, so I know where the bathroom is. I push past the line of people waiting to use it and burst in, startling the girl in there. She's only washing her hands. I don't have time to apologize before I throw myself over the toilet bowl and vomit up my screwdriver. I am peripherally aware of the girl rushing out of the bathroom. I've never been someone who throws up from drinking, and I haven't even had a whole drink, so I think there must have been something wrong with the orange juice. I try to remember whether it's salmonella or listeria you can get from juice. Listeria would make more sense.

I flush twice and go to the sink to clean up. I wonder how many people just saw me throw up. I try not to look. There is a bottle of mouthwash in the medicine cabinet and I pour some directly into my mouth without letting my lips touch the rim of the bottle. As I gargle someone pushes the hair off my neck. I look in the mirror and see Jasper standing behind me.

"Whoa, babe," he says. "Anya told me she saw you book it in here and puke. We've only been here for like an hour—what the hell did you drink?"

So then Anya saw me. Between her, the girl I startled, and the people in line, that makes at least five. I cringe inwardly.

I turn around so I can glare at Jasper directly. "Where the hell did you go? You completely ditched me."

He steps back a little, instantly defensive. "I was socializing. It's a party."

"I thought we came to this party *together*."

"Didn't realize that meant I had to babysit you all night."

I start to push past him but he grabs my arm.

"Jesus, can you fucking relax?"

I glare at him, mouth squeezed shut against a retort. I don't want to escalate this; I don't want to fight with him too.

"How much did you have to drink?"

Now his tone is softer. I simper, half hating it but doing it anyway, wanting him to take care of me. Ryn's coldness is a persistent sting, like a paper cut.

"Just one," I say. "I didn't even finish it."

"You sick?"

"I feel fine now. Maybe the juice was off or something. Does vodka go bad?"

He laughs. "I think after a while it just turns to ether."

I'm relieved he's joking with me. This feels good—I want it to be like it was in Europe again. "Maybe someone tried to roofie me."

"Guilty."

I follow him out of the bathroom and we join a group. I take some gentle ribbing for being such a lightweight. And this isn't so bad. I don't know why I was so worried about my witnesses. We've all thrown up before. Jasper offers me a gin and tonic but the thought of more alcohol makes the bile rise up in warning, so I get a cup of room-temperature ginger ale, which I sip on for the remainder of the night. When we leave, Jasper is drunk and I am starving. We stumble, laughing, into one of those grimy pizza places that always have the best pizza, and we eat out of greasy, folded paper plates in the wet night as cabs glide by like anglerfish. I try to kiss him after we're done eating, but he pulls away.

"You threw up."

"I washed my mouth out," I say. "You *saw* me wash my mouth out."

"All right, all right."

He kisses me, but tepidly, his mouth firmly puckered, firmly closed. He's like a kid being forced to eat his broccoli. I am tired now that my stomach is full, and I don't feel like walking the ten blocks to Jasper's apartment.

"Can we take a cab?" I ask.

"What? No—we have to walk this pizza off."

So we walk. I sense eyes peering out of every cab that passes. I wonder, randomly, if a pair of those eyes might belong to Paul, if he's still in this city somewhere. Now is not the time to think about Paul. Already, I can feel the wave of panic-like emotion. This is all Ryn's fault. She's been so bitchy lately and it hurts and she *knows* that when I'm feeling vulnerable the memory of Paul glues itself in my mind and I won't be able to concentrate or sleep. Now I'm furious with her. The only thing that relieves the feeling is dance. That's why I don't dwell on my brother unless I'm at the barre, in class. That's when it's safe. Otherwise, the questions, the hurt, the anger—all of it—would roll together and rise in a tsunami of panic, blacking the sun, burying me, blocking out all the beautiful music.

Ryn knows this. So her cold shoulder feels extra malicious. I focus on being angry at her. I let it heat me until I feel like screaming, like breaking something against the dirty sidewalk. I repeat our earlier conversation obsessively in my head. She was so condescending. So passive-aggressive. My fingers itch to send her an angry text, but I resist. I don't want to give her ammunition to play the victim. Instead, I grab Jasper's hand and try to keep up with his long strides. He glances down at me, a quick smile. He squeezes my hand, a little too hard. We're already on Ninety-Eighth. Two more blocks to go. It's been three since I've thought of Paul.

Intermezzo

When I got my contract with the company, my mother and I got into a fight because the first thing she said wasn't *Congratulations* or *I'm so happy for you* but "What about college?"

"What about it?" I said.

"It's just a couple of years away. I don't want you getting sidetracked."

"Sidetracked? Mom, I just got hired by one of the best ballet companies in the world."

"I told you from the beginning you were not sacrificing your education for this."

"You don't understand. You're not even *trying* to understand. This is my *dream*."

"I understand a whole hell of a lot more than you, little girl. Dreams end—you wake up. What's your backup plan? What if you get injured and can't dance anymore?"

"I can always go to college later, if I want to."

My mother shook her head. "By then, you're going to want kids. You think it's easy studying with a crying baby?"

"I'm never having kids."

"You don't know that. You don't know what you want—you're just a kid yourself."

I was so tired of her telling me that I didn't know anything, of her acting like she knew more about me than I ever could, that she held some secret of the universe which I couldn't yet handle. I yelled, "I know exactly what I want."

"Don't you raise your voice at me in *my* house."

"I'll move out. Kathryn's getting her own place—I'll move in with her."

My mother laughed. "Go ahead, then," she said. "You've been thinking you're grown since you were ten—go on ahead and see how grown you really are."

"I will."

"Good."

"Fine."

"Good luck finding a landlord that'll rent to a minor without a cosigner."

"I'll get Paul. *He* was happy for me. He'll help me."

"Please. Your brother can't even help himself—you think he's going to help you?"

"God, you don't even care, do you? What kind of mother are you?"

"The worst kind, I guess."

I called my brother and an automated voice told me his number was out of service. I went to his apartment and knocked and knocked until an irritated neighbor told me the apartment was empty. Paul had sold his things and left—the neighbor had bought his toaster for two dollars. Out of desperation, I did something Paul had forbidden me to do; I went to the restaurant where he worked. They weren't open for dinner yet. I tapped on the glass doors until someone opened them a crack to tell me they were closed.

"I'm looking for my brother," I said in a rush. "Paul Cordell? He's a chef here?"

I saw the recognition in the man's face. I also saw the hesitation. "Oh, yeah—you must be Cece, right? Paul didn't tell you? He don't work here no more."

"What? What do you mean?"

The man—a waiter, I guessed from his black uniform—looked uncomfortable. "You should really let Paul tell you about it." He began to step back.

I grabbed the door, realizing that I looked like a nut. "*Please,*" I said. "Tell me."

The waiter looked over his shoulder nervously, licked his lips, and then leaned in. "Look," he half whispered, "he got fired. A week ago."

"What happened?" I whispered back.

He licked his lips again. "I don't feel right telling you this. But me and Paul were buddies, and I'm worried for him. He came into his shift, well, you know—"

"Stoned?"

"Outta his mind. We're used to that, to tell you the truth, but this time, he was, like, on some other shit. Acting crazy. I didn't see the whole thing, but the owner tried talking to him, and Paul ended up hitting him. Punched him right in the face. So he had to fire him. Had to. And he liked Paul—everybody liked Paul."

"So no one's seen him? No one knows where he is?"

He shook his head.

I tried Paul's cellphone countless times in the vain, irrational hope that I'd reach him if I kept trying. I remembered what he said to me when I called to tell him I'd been hired: *You're going to be great, Cece. So much better than me.* Why hadn't I recognized that as a goodbye when I'd heard it? I went to my mother, but she insisted that Paul was fine, that I shouldn't be so dramatic. *He'll turn up once he gets himself together,* she said. Frantic, I called and appealed tearfully to my father, who said more or less the same thing.

I felt like I had slipped into an alternate universe where a loved one's disappearance was no big deal. I needed to speak to someone who would make sense. I told Ryn. Told her everything. When I was done talking, she sat quietly for a long time.

"Maybe," she said carefully, "you have to let him have his journey."

I felt like screaming. "What are you talking about?"

"My friend back home has an older sister who was addicted to, like, Oxy or something. And then she got into heroin. She would disappear all the time—that's what drug addicts do, you know. But she always came back. Every time they tried to help her, she just got worse. Then their pastor or something told them that she needed to take her journey on her own, and that God had a plan. So they stopped trying to force her to get better. And, yeah, it was hard, but it worked. I think she's been clean for, like, five years."

"But it doesn't always end that way, does it? What if he never comes back?"

"He will. From what you've told me, he obviously loves you. My dad always says, 'You have to allow people to be unhappy.' I think it means you have to, like, let people make their mistakes so they'll learn."

I thought of all the times I got on Paul's nerves, all the times he'd gone above and beyond to take care of me. Maybe he was tired. Maybe it was my fault he'd snapped. Maybe he just needed a break, a rest, and then he'd reappear and be better. I didn't think he'd do anything drastic, like kill himself. And deep down, I didn't think he'd just leave me forever. Maybe I needed to let him have his space. That saccharine adage came into my mind: *If you love something let it go . . .*

So I let him go. I turned all my missing him, all my wonder, all my anger, all my worry, all my love into dance. In the end, I graduated from high school early and my mother couldn't force me to go to college. She had nothing to threaten me with. Everything I had, I had gotten without her help, and therefore, it was out of her power to take it away. This was when I became a dancer.

III

BALLABILE

The Saratoga season is short, but from day one, I am exhausted. We begin setting the new ballet right away, and the role Kaz has created for me is extremely challenging. I have rehearsal for *A Midsummer Night's Dream* and *Theme and Variations* as well. And then there are phone interviews, emails back and forth with bloggers, fan mail, shoe signings. Dancing is my ecstatic meditation.

Ryn is second cast for *Theme and Variations,* and so we rehearse together. We haven't spoken to each other at all. Rehearsal is the only time I see her since she's not staying in the renovated farmhouse the company has rented. The Frenchman probably bought them a sweet little house near town. During our first rehearsal together I notice the giant diamond on her left ring finger, and I nearly cry. She didn't tell me she got engaged. When did this happen? After the party? She'd said she and the Frenchman had plans. No one is reacting to the ring—no one is squealing or offering congratulations. My heart breaks as I realize what that means: Everyone knows but me. Ryn is marrying a stranger, and she has cast me aside, a dead pointe shoe. I dance badly during rehearsal; my shoulders are stiff and my left calf cramps painfully. Ryn does not so much as look at me. Not even once.

Jasper and I go together to a quaint, market-like grocery store to grab something to eat even though I feel sticky and salty from sweat, and I'm not sure I'm fit to be seen in public. Just water and some cheese and fruit—we're performing later.

"Did you know Ryn got engaged?" I ask him.

He shakes his head. "Just found out this morning. I guess she did a big reveal at Rohan's party. Totally missed that."

"At *Rohan's party*? I spoke to her—she didn't even tell me." This is making me unbearably—perhaps unreasonably—sad. I am heavy with it. I think I am keeping myself under control, but Jasper is able to see how upset I am.

"Oh, hey, calm down," he says. "Maybe she wants to tell you when it's just the two of you."

I shake my head. "She could've told me. She didn't want to. She's supposed to be my best friend."

I won't allow myself to cry, but I feel as though I've been stabbed. Jasper puts an arm around my shoulders.

"I don't even know why she's pissed at me. She's being so . . . so *mean*."

Jasper hugs me into his chest and kisses the top of my head, digs his blunt fingertips into my trapezius. "You two need to talk."

"Didn't you see her at rehearsal? She's not talking to me. It's like we're in middle school."

"It'll blow over." He's rubbing my back now, digging his knuckle into a knot in my rhomboid. I breathe into the pain, smelling his sweat, his deodorant, his musk, until the knot releases.

"I mean, we're roommates. Is she going to move this guy into our apartment, and they'll both give me the cold shoulder? I don't want to live like that. Or maybe she's planning on moving out. Then I'll have to pay the rent myself or find another roommate. God, what a pain in the ass."

"Just move in with me."

I go completely still, my heart beating a little quicker. We've never really broached this subject. I haven't wanted to scare him. "Really?"

I feel him shrug. "Sure. I mean, it makes sense, right?"

I nod slowly against his chest. "Yeah, it does make sense." I say it slowly, half afraid he'll realize what he's saying and take it back. I know Jasper loves me, but love is nothing, a feeling. It's not binding at all. He could walk away from me at any time.

"There," he says, sounding a little smug. "You feel better now, don't you?"

I don't want to admit that I do, that he has pacified me as easily as one pacifies a baby, so I say, sarcastically, "Four years later."

He shrugs again. "You were just a kid when we first got together."

"And what does that make you?"

"A creep. You knew what you were getting into."

He tickles me and I laugh, squirming away from him. I am embarrassed by how happy I feel now. I was near tears a moment ago, but now I am as giddy as I am right after a performance. We kiss fully, deeply. He's been letting his beard grow in a little, and I hate it, but I don't tell him this. He's kissing me like he's hungry, starving, and I'm the only one who will satisfy that hunger. Ryn no longer makes sense to me. But Jasper—he makes sense. There's a small part of me that doesn't trust it, that argues that the world is unstable, that the ground beneath me is just an illusion, and as soon as I begin to trust it, it will disappear. I can't wait to get onstage. There, the light is bright and the music is loud, and the dance is everything and I won't be able to hear myself anymore.

Jasper wakes me up early to drag me to the gym with him. I am so tired it sickens me; it takes forever for my eyes to grow accustomed to being open, and my vision is still a little blurry by the time I'm dressed in my workout clothes. The smell of Jasper's coffee makes me queasy. Because it is so early, the gym is nearly empty, but it reeks of metal and body odor. I don't know what they've done to make the smell so bad and so powerful—gyms have a particular odor in general, but I've never been in one that stinks this badly. I try to breathe through my mouth, but then I swear I can taste what I'm smelling, and it makes me want to gag. Jasper doesn't seem to notice as he dictates that today will be arms-and-shoulders day. We work out together frequently, but he's been bossy in the gym lately, and I can't help but wonder if he thinks I'm getting fat.

Weight training is not my favorite thing. The guys have to do it so they can perform lifts, but I only go because Jasper seems to like working out with me. But today, I am weak. My normal weights feel heavy and I shake, even during our warm-ups. It must be exhaustion, but after last night's performance, I pretty much went directly to bed, so I don't know why I'm so tired. My body is not playing the obedient instrument today. By the time we're done, I'm ravenous and overheated. I lie on my back on one of the stretching mats while Jasper takes mirror selfies.

"Come here and let me bench-press you for Instagram."

I roll my eyes. Jasper is a social-media junkie, whereas I have very little use for it. He and Ryn basically run my Instagram account, and every now and then Ryn renews her thus far unsuccessful campaign to get me on Snapchat. There is a sharp little twinge of hurt as I think about Ryn. Jasper MacGyvers a stand for his iPhone using a bench and some weights and films as he raises and lowers me over his chest, me as flat and stiff as a board. Then he makes me pose with him for a picture, Hermia and Lysander in sneakers and sweaty gym clothes. After we leave the gym we take a shower together, and I don't tell him how overrated I think shower sex is because I am being a good girlfriend today. And then he goes to do some radio interview and I'm left with a couple of hours to myself before class.

I consider going back to bed, getting another hour or so of sleep, but I am so, so hungry. And I have the most bewildering and unthinkable craving for an Egg McMuffin and hash browns. Just the craving is making me feel fat. In the farmhouse kitchen, which is, mercifully, still empty, I try to quell the craving as best I can with scrambled eggs and half a slice of toast, but when I'm done, I want the other half of toast, this time with butter, *and* an Egg McMuffin and hash browns. I am mildly panicking, like when I snuck into my mother's room and tried on her old wedding band and then couldn't get it off my finger. I remind myself to take deep breaths. Class is only an hour and a half away now. Then I'll be distracted and I'll go back to normal. There's nothing wrong with me. Just because I'm craving fast food after eight years of not touching it *doesn't* mean I'm going to lose control, gain fifty pounds, and destroy my career.

I am constantly off-balance lately, like I'm lurching through my days, constantly on the brink of falling over. Simple things seem to take more muscle, such as getting dressed and packing my dance bag. Like after years of discipline dedicated toward building physical control, my body is now resisting me. And shit. The cravings. I'm an idiot, because what's dawning on me now should have been obvious. But no. No. Right? No.

I try to stay present as I get dressed: the leotard with the tights on top to make going to the bathroom easier, the shorts on top of that, the long-sleeved shrug that'll probably come off after ten minutes of barre, the leg warmers for my tight hamstrings and calves. I pack my ballet slippers and my pointe shoes, the REI booties that keep my feet warm and flexible. A pair of sweatpants, a couple of tank tops, some socks, more leg warmers. Junk clothes. And then extra tights, lamb's wool, hairspray, a sewing kit for my shoes, hair pins, deodorant, cocoa butter, two spare leotards, a towel for sweat, Band-Aids, Neosporin, roll-on perfume, some fruit and protein bars, my makeup bag. I name each item in my head as I stuff it into my bag. Stay present. Stay present.

Of course, I think, I *could* be pregnant. The thought is glib at first, almost a kind of joke. Of course I'm not pregnant. But then it begins to mutate and I'm suddenly certain that I am. I can almost feel the parasitic bean at my core. The disease that has been taking my body away from me. Jasper and I have never been particularly consistent about protection; my period has never been particularly consistent about showing up. But Europe—I think back to Jasper and me having sex on dark, pebbly beaches, in alleyways, him holding me up against rough walls, in my tiny sublet apartment, the balcony doors open to the distant sounds of guitar players and drunken tourists. There was never any protection, but Jasper always pulls out. I didn't even think about it. I groan, letting myself fall forward until my forehead rests against my bag, which is cool.

But I *can't* be pregnant. After four years, now? This must be something else. Maybe I'm having a psychotic break. I hurry to the bathroom, pull up my shirt in front of the mirror. My torso is a sculpted work of ribs and abs. I squint at my reflection. Look down and compare what my naked eyes are telling me to what the mirror is telling me. My stomach is flat, but it's little consolation; I'm not sure, but I don't think I'd show this early on. I wrap my hands around my waist, pressing my thumbs against my spine and squeezing slightly until my fingertips meet at my belly button. I imagine something rippling across my stomach from the inside, pushing the skin out, like in a horror movie. If there's something wrong with me, it's nothing I can see. At least not yet.

I place a hand lightly on the vanity for balance, and then lift my left leg up into a développé à la seconde, just to prove that my body is mine to command; it does nothing without my consent. I hold my leg up for as long as I can, breathing stubbornly through my nose, not backing off even after my leg begins to shake. By the time I let my leg back down, my panic seems silly. I cannot be pregnant. I will go to class, get my mind back together, and then I'll take a pregnancy test, which will put me at ease. And then I'll be able to focus again.

The first pregnancy test I take after class is positive. So are the next three. I sink to the floor in the single-stall restroom of the café I've snuck off to. My thoughts are wild. I can't do this right now—I'd lose at least a year, probably more like two, and I'd never get that time back. Everyone would forget me. And I've never wanted kids.

I have to get rid of it.

I almost don't even want to tell Jasper because telling him— telling anybody—would make this a real thing, and I don't want this to be a real thing.

"Shit," I whisper.

I don't know the first thing about abortion. I don't even know who I'd ask. I peel myself off the floor and stuff the tests into the trash, piling paper towels on top of them before hurrying out of the bathroom and out of the café. No one to talk to and nowhere to go. I nearly run, my head ducked, until I find a cemetery, the only place where I can find some seclusion. I need somebody, and all the people who should be there when I need them—my mother, Ryn, Jasper . . . my brother—are woefully deficient in their own ways. I glance around, and, with shaking hands, take out my cell.

The phone rings and rings and Irine doesn't answer. Her voicemail kicks in and I hang up, crushed, humiliated. I'm pathetic. She probably doesn't have time for me. I don't think I've ever felt more alone, not even when Paul abandoned me. But then my phone buzzes and it's Irine's name on the screen.

"Cece!" she exclaims. "How are you? How is Saratoga?"

"Irine," I say breathlessly, "I . . . I want to tell you something. You can't tell anyone."

On Irine's side of the line, something rustles, a door closes. When Irine speaks again she sounds closer, like she's leaning in. "Are you okay?"

"I'm pregnant."

Irine is quiet for so long that I can't help but to fill in the space.

"I'm sorry. I know this is weird. I don't know why I'm telling you this. I mean, you're probably really busy and—"

"Cece," Irine interrupts, "I am your friend."

I take a breath.

"You . . . don't want the baby?" Irine asks this slowly, carefully.

"I don't want to be pregnant."

I hear faint typing. "I just looked it up—there is a Planned Parenthood there," Irine says. "But do you think you should come back to the city?"

"I'm—not sure," I stutter.

Irine pauses. "*Do* you want the baby?"

I am dizzy. I think I hear a leaf crunch, so I look around again, see no one. I whisper, "It's Jasper's."

Jasper, who just asked me to move in with him. Jasper, who I'm terrified of losing, who is such a large part of my proxy family—the company. I lean against a headstone to steady myself, and then, guilty, switch to a nearby tree.

"You know," Irine says, "Matan and I had an . . . incident, before we were married."

"You did?"

"It's more common than you think. Really."

I cup my hand around my phone and talk softly, urgently. "I feel like I'm going crazy."

What I can't tell Irine, what I can't tell anyone, is that I so often feel as though I'm passing—not for a white woman but for a dancer. And now this will be the thing that gives me away. It will be the thing that gets me expelled from the family I've fought to belong to.

"I don't want to lose the time," I say. I'm overheated. Clashing emotions hurtle into each other. I was so sure, only moments ago, that there was no way I'd carry this pregnancy to term, but I am suddenly aware of my inability to say aloud that I don't want this baby. I don't, exactly, but—

"Irine," I say, my voice still hushed, "do . . . do you think it'd be like, I don't know, throwing myself off a cliff? What I mean is, do you think I'd disappear?"

Irine knows exactly what I'm talking about, though I'm sure I'm not being coherent now. "Having kids is not a career-killer for ballerinas anymore, Cece. You're young—your body will bounce back."

I imagine coming to company class, my leotard stretching farther and farther away from me. I've seen those women—modifying to accommodate their new center of gravity, pausing every now and then to stretch their hip flexors.

"Look," Irine says, "you don't have to decide now. Have you told Jasper?"

"I don't know how he'll be." Could he possibly be happy? Would it repel him?

"How about Ryn?"

"We're in this stupid fight."

Irine tsks. "You and Ryn don't fight. Go make up. It'll help."

"I should go," I say. "Rehearsal. I'm sorry I unloaded all this on you."

"Celine, don't be stupid. I'll check in with you later, okay?"

After we hang up, I hurry out of the cemetery. I find Broadway and take it back into the main part of town, scrutinizing the faces of every mother I pass. Inside, I am pure chaos. I wonder whether motherhood is madness, if it's already started to infect me. Because even as I feel my body has betrayed me, I can also picture me and Jasper searching for the perfect two-bedroom in Harlem or Brooklyn, or maybe even a house, a fixer-upper out in Westchester. I can see us picking a neutral color for the nursery, fighting over names. This is what normal women want, isn't it? And maybe I wouldn't mind being normal, just a little bit. Normal does not have to mean average.

Tonight, we have a dinner with some of our wealthiest donors, which we have all been "strongly encouraged" to attend. I am exhausted, but I throw on a loose-fitting dress and some lipstick, and carpool with Jasper, Gwen, and Rohan. Everyone else is full of energy while I am exhausted. I never like going to these things—it feels like prostitution. I'm also queasy and full of heaviness tonight. I'd love nothing more than to stay in bed and watch Netflix. I keep imagining I can feel the fetus inside me, like a mote floating around.

The dinner is at a donor's house—a ridiculous mansion just outside of Saratoga Springs. When we walk inside, I am a bit overwhelmed by the opulence. There is catering, a live jazz band, and multiple fountains. As soon as we enter, donors swarm us. I do my best to mingle, smiling as they tell me about the shows that stuck with them, thanking those who congratulate me. I wonder what I look like to them.

To my right, I see Jasper surrounded by women. Not out of the ordinary—he is charismatic and handsome. And usually, I pride myself on not being the jealous type. But one of the female donors near him is on the young side—not that much older than him—and she's pretty. Blond-haired and slender. She is leaning in close to him, laughing, and he has his hand on her arm. I frown. I see him look up and around, and his eyes graze over me, but he acts as though he doesn't see me. The queasiness reaches my throat. I refocus on the donor who is speaking to me, a kind man who I think looks a little like Jerome Robbins.

Our host calls everyone into the garden for the sit-down dinner. I don't see Jasper until he grabs my elbow, and leans down to speak to me in a low tone.

"I'm going to sit by one of the donors tonight. You're good, right?"

"The one you've been flirting with all night?" I ask. Immediately, I regret saying anything. I am *not* this kind of girlfriend. But that fleck is floating around inside me, making itself known, and I can't help but wish that Jasper would act like he's mine, or I'm his.

"What are you, jealous?" Jasper laughs. "Doesn't hurt for them to think they have a chance. The fantasy, right?"

"What about me?" I am so tempted in this moment to throw in that I happen to be carrying his spawn.

"Come on," he says. "You're a big girl. This is work. This is what we do."

I glare up at him.

"Cece. Can you not be difficult tonight? You look after your career, right? Let me look after mine."

Before I can ask him what that's supposed to mean, he is saun-

tering out into the garden, charm back on. I end up spending the
evening next to the Robbins look-alike, a fate that isn't so terrible
except that my stomach won't stop lurching, and I want to bury
my face in Jasper's shoulder, but that woman's hand is there instead. But he isn't wrong. We put our careers first, both of us. All
of us. We have to.

I leave at the end of the evening without Jasper, letting him
look after his career. He crawls into bed with me later that night
and snuggles into my side. He is still in his cocktail attire.

"You should've stayed," he eventually says. "One of the donors
got wasted and jumped into a fountain."

I smile unconvincingly into the dark.

"Adam took that woman home," he tells me.

"The donor you were eye-fucking? How'd you let that happen?"

Jasper chuckles, slips his hand beneath the waistband of my
shorts.

We're rehearsing *Theme* onstage, which is a little disconcerting because there are no mirrors, and the stage is open to the outside.
People can and do watch us. Jasper and I only have to dance
Theme and Variations twice this Saratoga season, which is good
because—and I don't think I'd ever say this out loud—it's not my
favorite Balanchine ballet. It is, in fact, my least favorite. It feels
like sacrilege to even think this. But there's something very bland
about it. The first cast has been getting all the praise for *Theme*,
and I wish they had to do the last performance and not me. Our
summer gala is coming up in two days and after that, for the rest
of the two-week season, it's all twenty-first century choreogra-
phers and Robbins and Balanchine shorts and tributes to the
French.

Ryn, who is dancing one of the demi-soloist roles in *Theme*, glances over at me and frowns as though I've done something wrong. I still don't know why she is angry with me, but at this point, my own resentment is overshadowing my curiosity. She hasn't spoken a word to me, not even to say "good morning" or "excuse me" or to wish me merde before a performance. And every time I see her, unless she's about to perform, she's got that giant diamond choking her knuckle. This pisses me off even more.

I pretend not to notice her and lean into Jasper's damp chest, hoping he'll wrap an arm around me. He does. I consider telling a few people that we're moving in together and letting the news spread like floodwater. Letting it reach Ryn in her delusional bubble. Now, I frown at myself: I can't be this petty if I'm going to have a baby. *If.*

I throw it all away as we begin our final run-through. I like to be a little careless during rehearsals. Or, it's more like I'm being playful. I experiment, toss things out there. I can get away with this because I've been with the company for six years now—people know me, my creative process. I set myself free in rehearsal—especially if I already know the ballet—and then once I go onstage to perform, I get this balance of technique and organic feeling. That's what they call stage presence. And that feeling—there's nothing like it.

Despite *Theme* not being my favorite, there *is* something poignant about it. A Balanchine tribute to Imperial Russia, a world that died violently. A lot of dancers who've danced the principal role go for the regal, ice palace thing. But that's not what's in my body for this piece. I tap into the poignancy. I want the audience to feel like they're looking at one of those rare films from 1910 or something—it's startling and fascinating and beautiful and, ultimately, haunting.

This ballet goes by quickly—it's only about twenty minutes long and the steps are so fast. Jasper and I are whirling through the last pas de deux. In the end, he throws me up onto his shoulder and I perch there, crystallized and august. There is a smattering of applause, both from company members and from my cygnets. I wave subtly at them and watch them squeal to each other. I have a blissful hour and a half of free time before I have a phone interview and then I'll be back here, getting ready to perform. *Theme and Variations* is up first in tonight's program, and then it's some jazzy modern piece and a short from our resident choreographer.

I take off my shoes, and, barefoot, make my way offstage to grab my things. I'm just about to slip out of my practice tutu and put on my sweatpants when someone bumps into my side, knocking me off-balance a little. I look up and see Ryn, who is trying to take a selfie in front of a plastic bag stuffed with pointe shoes. I imagine she'll upload it to Instagram with some almost witty caption like *Where pointe shoes go to die. #SPAC #nofilter.*

I glare at her wordlessly until I hear her phone's camera go off. "Excuse you," I say.

She glances at me, rolls her eyes, begins to walk away.

But I am tired of this. I grab her wrist. "Ryn, what the hell is your problem?"

For a moment, her expression goes ice-cold. Even her lips turn white before angry color lights up her face. Then she flips my grip on her wrist so that now she is clutching me. She drags me into the first room she can find, an empty dressing room, and throws the door closed behind us. Kaz was wrong not to consider her for the role of the Hag—Ryn is stronger than she looks. Her fingers clamp down on me like iron cuffs. I am glad when she lets me go. There is a moment of silence as we stare venomously at each other. Blushing sunlight drifts in through the venetian blinds.

"What is *my* problem?" Ryn says, breathless with fury. "You. Have been being. Such. A bitch."

I have the urge to slap her.

"Are you crazy? I haven't done anything to you—you don't even tell me you're engaged? What the hell is that?"

"I tried to tell you. At Rohan's party. You were so caught up in yourself you didn't notice me trying to show you the ring. You never even said congratulations."

"Flashing that thing at me does not count as telling me, Ryn. I didn't even see it until we got to Saratoga."

"Bullshit. You just don't approve of my fiancé. Even though you're my friend and you should be happy for me."

"It's hard to be happy for someone who dates a guy for a month and is suddenly the fucking oracle of love."

"Oh, fuck you, Celine."

"Fuck you, *Kathryn*."

"You know what makes it even worse? For years, I've been listening to you bitch and whine about Jasper, and I never judged you, never made you feel like you didn't deserve for things to work out. But as soon as *I* find someone, you start acting like I'm beneath you. Like, what, because I haven't stuck by the same asshole for years my relationship isn't valid? I thought we were friends, but now I see: If it's not about you, you're not interested."

"You're just trying to find a way to justify the fact that you dropped me like a sack of trash as soon as you got with this guy."

"That's not true. I tried. You always had something negative to say."

"I think you're moving way too fast." I shrug. "Sue me. I thought we were close enough to tell each other the truth."

"Well, Jasper's a dick. He's *been* a dick. You're smarter than this, and every time I listen to you complain, knowing you're just going to run back to him, I lose respect for you."

"I've lost respect for you ever since you abandoned your best friend over some dude you don't even know. You should be smarter than to let some stranger lock you in way too soon, and then isolate you from your work and your friends. But, apparently, you're just another basic bitch ready to choose a man over everything else."

Ryn slaps me. Not very hard. But enough to sting. Rage comes bursting out of its pen. Although it's more than rage. Somewhere, a voice inside of me is pleading, *Not again*. Ryn is disappearing on me just like my brother did. I am powerless, furious. I bring an arm around and my hand connects with the side of Ryn's head. I am holding back a little, because, deep down, I don't really want to hurt her. But still, she looks stunned before she lunges forward and grabs me by the shoulders, pushing me back.

It occurs to me now that I need to protect myself, that, more than ever, I can't let myself get hurt. My legs are stronger than my arms, so I allow her to push me back until I can hop onto the dressing table for leverage. I lift my feet, intending to kick her in the stomach, knock her away from me, but because of her position—hunched over me, hands reaching for my face—I find not hard knots of muscle there but softness. And it's so rare to find softness on a ballerina's body, and it feels so unexpectedly good underneath my bare toes, that I dig them in and she gasps in pain.

I am aware of what we must look like, tussling as we are. What if my brother saw me now? We're both still in our practice tutus, and so I imagine we resemble ducks bobbing for small fish, tufted asses turned up in the air. The whole thing is rather cute, actually. I chuckle at the image. A laugh like a spasm—I don't even feel it coming, it just escapes. This seems to give Ryn more pause than my feet in her gut. And then, with one of those horrible snorts that are as involuntary as a sneeze, she laughs too. Now we are both laughing, infected by it. My hilarity feeds hers and hers feeds mine and we can't stop.

She gestures down at my feet, which are still at her stomach. "What are you even doing?" she says as she laughs.

"I don't know," I say, wiping my eyes. "You hit me."

"I know. I don't know what came over me. I've been so mad at you."

I tap my feet lightly against her abdomen. "You fight like a girl."

"And you fight like—I don't even know what. A kangaroo?"

She grabs my feet and shakes them before stepping back, shimmying out of her tutu, and hopping up next to me on the dressing table. We both lean back against the mirror.

"We should probably talk this out," she says. "Like adults."

"Okay. Why were you so angry at me?"

Ryn shrugs. "I didn't think you cared about me anymore. Every time I spoke about my relationship, you just seemed annoyed. It hurt my feelings."

"Of course I care about you. I was worried, that's all. I want you to be happy. But I also don't want to lose you. You're like my sister."

"You're not losing me, stupid. I admit I've been a bit distracted, but I didn't mean to abandon you. You're like my sister, too. Frankly, I like you a lot more than my actual sisters." She grabs my shoulder. "I'm not Paul, Cece."

I nod, fighting down a lump in my throat. Ryn knows me all too well.

"I'm sorry I didn't congratulate you," I say. "I just saw you wearing the ring and then the fact that you didn't tell me hurt my feelings, and then I got angry. Like, *really* angry."

"I should've just told you instead of playing peekaboo at Rohan's party. That was kind of a setup."

I lean over and rest my head on her shoulder. "Should we hug and say sorry like we're in kindergarten?"

Ryn laughs, but we do just that.

"Are we done with this fight now?" I ask.

"Yes, please."

"Good. Because I've really needed my sister lately. You have no idea."

She sits up straight. "I'm ready. Tell me."

"So, Jasper asked me to move in with him."

Ryn squeals and claps her hands. I'm a bit envious of her ability to be this excited for me even though she thinks Jasper is a dick. "Finally. Did you say yes?"

"I did. I feel like something's changed. Ever since Europe. Like, maybe he's finally growing up."

"Good. This does show that he's willing to commit for once and for all." She holds up her hand, the one with the giant ring on it. "Maybe you're next."

A murky wave of anonymous feeling rises at that. "We'll see," I say. "But there's something he doesn't know yet. I'm not keeping it from him. I just haven't had the chance to tell him yet, and I . . . well. I think—I need to tell you."

Ryn's eyes widen.

"Irine knows," I add a bit guiltily.

Ryn leans farther into me.

"I'm pregnant."

She gasps. "Oh. My God. Are you sure? Did you take a test?"

I nod. "Like, four."

"And you're going to . . ." She gestures with her hands, reluctant to ask the question.

"I don't know, that's the thing. And I feel like I'm going crazy, because I always thought that if this ever happened, it'd be a no-brainer. But, like I said, things have been different lately. I'm a principal now—maybe I could, you know, just bounce back. And I think I could make it to the new ballet without showing."

Ryn seems to be momentarily at a loss for words. Her stare is switching between my face and my stomach, her green cat eyes wide, hands spread apart like she wants to grab me but is afraid to. I am flinching internally. I don't know what I'm going to do, how it's going to feel, if Ryn tells me that I'm a colossal moron, a monster for even considering this.

"Oh my God," she says, "and I *hit* you. Are you okay? I didn't hurt you, did I? You should've hit me over the head with a chair."

I laugh, relieved. "That's why I was kicking you. I'm fine. Really. Like I said, you fight like a girl."

"This is—wow. I didn't think you ever wanted kids."

"Well, I'm not sure yet. I'm just, you know, *thinking* about it."

I wonder if this is some kind of prenatal madness. I wonder if this pregnancy is somehow delusional, hysterical. I wonder if Jasper really does think I'd be better off in Irine's company, if this pregnancy would only confirm that. Or if it would make me even more firmly his. I wonder what a child of mine would be like. Would it be a dancer like me? Would it be pragmatic and stubborn like my mother? Would it be temperamental and irreverent like my father? Would it disappear like Paul?

I wake to Jasper settling his body over mine, early-morning sun reaching for the bed. I sigh into his mouth, forgiveness coming quickly. He cups my face with a hand, uses the other to pull my knee up. My hip cracks loudly and we laugh, our foreheads pressed together. I hook my arm around his neck, use it as leverage until I fall back, turning my face and burying it in the pillow to muffle myself. I enjoy the aftershocks with Jasper's body still pressed on top of mine, his weight a ballast, our sweat mingling, and—and this mass, a clotted snarl of cells between us, beating against my abdomen, his abdomen. I shudder and Jasper kisses me nearly hard enough to bruise.

I shower first, and when I emerge Jasper, still naked, is sprawled across the bed on his stomach, looking at his phone. He waves it at me as I approach. I sit down next to him and he plays me a YouTube video—a line of black-clad dancers on a stage undulate in a wave to a haunting score of polyphonic overtone singing. It's strange and beautiful, the dancers sinewy and fluid. I note that one of the Black women has a large 'fro.

"I googled your friend's company," Jasper says.

One of the male dancers breaks the line, stepping forward and doing a kind of grand fouetté sauté. The line of dancers behind him spin around in quick succession, turning their backs to the audience. The polyphonic singing is unsettling, it's nauseating me. I lean down to rub my face in Jasper's hair.

"We'll be late," I say.

Jasper takes his shower and we dress and carpool to the studios with Rohan and Fran. I keep unconsciously putting my hand to my stomach, like worrying at a wound; my knuckles press into my belly during the drive. I can feel my own fraught heartbeat.

Kaz is giving class today, which is good because he gives complicated combinations. Maybe it'll help me not think. My teeth hurt as we begin and I worry that they're going to fall out. I read somewhere that women in the old days used to lose their teeth when they got pregnant. Something about insufficient nutrition. Don't I need folic acid? Where does one get folic acid outside of prenatal vitamins? I don't even take a regular multivitamin.

Front front side side back back. *And . . .*

I imagine the fetus as a bloody clump of flesh at my core, both revolting and somehow not, like a vital organ. I heat up quickly at the barre. I take off my cardigan, exposing my glistening, bony décolletage to the air. The gradual removal of junk clothes in class is a performance in and of itself. Every discarded garment means something—signal of another movement, cuing of the next act.

Tendrils of hair stick like wet tentacles to my temples. I will have to use the flat iron later.

And fondu and relevé and second plié passé passé retiré and stay stay *stay* . . .

I check my silhouette in the mirror, half expecting to see some kind of bulge, some kind of tell. But I look the same, I think.

Développé and open relevé extend hold hold to the back arabesque and balance . . .

My right side is always the weaker when it comes to balance, and today, it is especially pronounced. When we switch to the right side, I wobble in the arabesque, and as I fight for control, my lifted leg drops a little. Kaz comes to the rescue, supporting the faltering leg with one hand and spreading the other across my stomach. Something in me wants to curl away from his touch. Either a burgeoning protective instinct or self-preservation.

Mi Yeong is in front of me at the barre, moving slowly and throwing me off—she is still recovering from her injury. But she's so beautiful—she's spare, just bone and muscle. Thinking of my conversation with Irine, I try to catch Ryn's eyes in the mirror. But I catch Anya's eyes instead. Kaz has decided on her for the Hag in the new ballet, my character's antagonist. I smile at her, admiring her long, clean lines. She smiles back quickly, averts her gaze.

We take a break before center, Kaz giving us the length of a song. Jasper is across the room, taking a sip of water before dropping onto his back to stretch his hamstrings, pulling one leg at a time into his face, pointing and flexing the foot. He's taken to wearing these neon shirts to class. They're '80s vintage, and totally not his style, but I can't deny that they look good on him. He's always been handsome, but it's like lately, he's been commercializing his handsomeness more. Participating in mainstream millennial flashiness. The girls are putting on their pointe shoes.

Once mine are laced up I open my legs wide in a quick split before standing and doing a few relevés to keep my feet warm. Ryn and I catch each other's eyes. I notice her gaze flit reflexively to my stomach. She turns pink and it makes me laugh. She has no guile, Ryn. Now she laughs too.

I'm not quite on my leg today, but I mask my wobbliness by trying to play up my strengths: I use my famously flexible back to make my movements extra sumptuous, I make my turns extra sharp, my extensions even longer. This last earns me a "Good girl" from Kaz, which pleases me more than I want it to. Normally, a bad-balance day would irritate me, and I'd approach the rest of the day with a grim perfectionism to make up for it. But I actually feel proud of myself—even pregnant, I'm still a good girl.

After one particularly challenging combination Kaz calls me forward.

"Arabesque for us, darling," he says.

I rise en pointe and lift my right leg up and back, reaching it behind me. I am determined to hold the balance now—I fight for it. I know that Kaz is going to make me hold it.

"Put the tension in the right place," he tells everyone. He grabs my right ankle. "Remember that a spring does not just hold on to energy." He moves his hand up to my thigh, scooping my waist with his other hand. "It releases it, directs it outward. *That* is what moves you."

Kaz lifts my right leg up higher and higher, forcing me forward into a penché. I have to keep fighting for balance as Kaz pushes my right leg up far higher than I would take it on my own; my left hamstrings complain. He is overextending me—a quick glance in the mirror tells me that he has taken my leg a little beyond a hundred and eighty degrees; his fingertips dig into my hip bones, his other hand squeezes into the muscle of my right thigh. Just when I think I will have to roll my left foot down to flat, he releases me, and I manage to land in fifth position rather than falling over like a felled tree.

As I return to a corner of the studio, I notice for the first time a group of girls—baby bunheads from SAB—peeking in at us through the door. The SAB students have been around because there are some kids' dances in *A Midsummer Night's Dream*. When they see me noticing them, they giggle, their eyes wide and astonished, and disappear. I wonder what I look like to them, what they would think of me if I came to company class with a stomach distended by pregnancy. Would they find it abhorrent, cautionary, or would it give them hope that they could have more than one thing? These days, I am ever aware of the wake I leave. Two of those little dancers were Black.

After class I walk up to Jasper. We have about an hour before we're scheduled to work on the new ballet, and then it's rehearsal until seven. Our closeness from this morning is still perfuming the day, and it's making me think it might be okay to tell him now. Maybe he'll help me sort out what I feel. Maybe he'll be a pillar. Part of me regrets telling Irine first, or at all—I wasn't thinking clearly. Why tell the one person who still thinks I'm not quite a fit for City Ballet? This is my family—*Jasper* is my family.

"Hey," I say, stepping close, "you wanna go for a walk?"

"Can't," he says. "I'm going to get a quick adjustment. Gotta have time to miss each other, right?"

He gives me a playful slap on the ass as he steps around me to go.

As complicated and exhausting as it often is, it is difficult not to love Kaz's choreography. He is not a fan of eating up music with things like running and pantomiming, and so we are constantly dancing. He, quite literally, keeps you on your toes. I am falling more and more in love with this new ballet, though I am sore and drenched in sweat.

The part where I'm being attacked by the Hag is brilliant. Anya lifts me, throws me, spins me. We fly, a series of sissonnes, her supporting me at the waist—it's exhilarating. Of course, since women don't usually partner other women, Anya is inexpert at lifting me, and there is a sore spot on my shin that will become a bruise later.

"Like this," Kaz says. "Bourrée, bourrée, Italian fouetté, bour-rée, bourrée, Italian fouetté. Like before you were cursed, only now you're exhausted. Watch your head. And Jasper, maybe you can be more masculine, hmm? Again."

Jasper and I start our pas de deux over again, Anya watching us, seated on the floor near the piano. She is a pale shape in my peripheral vision as I keep my eyes on my reflection in the mir-rors. I droop through a pirouette, nearly fall and let Jasper catch me. He drags me into a lift, and this is the hard part—I have to look limp, but really I'm working to hold the shape. And then Jasper puts me down and I bourrée away from him. Bourrée, bourrée, Italian fouetté, bourrée, bourrée, Italian fouetté.

"Stop," Kaz says. "I don't like it."

We all titter, unsure.

"Cece, I'm sorry, but you don't look like you're being tor-mented every night. You don't *look* exhausted. Beautiful as always, yes. But not exhausted, darling."

The thing is, I *am* exhausted. I'm not even halfway through my day yet, and I'm ready for a nap. But I'm so used to masking how I truly feel while I'm dancing that I can't figure out how to dance like I'm depleted and lethargic. And at this point, I know I'm thinking too hard.

Anya stands up slowly. "Could I make a suggestion?"

I am impressed by her bravery. Kaz can be mercurial, especially when he's creating. But he only makes an irritated gesture, indicating that she should go on. She steps forward with a shy, red-lipped smile and takes her position—my position—to Jasper's left. She sketches the pirouette, Jasper catches her, they do the lift, and he sets her down.

"I think the problem," she says, "is that it's so hard to look weak while doing an Italian fouetté. But what if you—" She does a little ghost of the turn, dampening the extension and slowing it down, and after the last one she sort of swoons. "And then Jasper can catch you."

Kaz is nodding, a finger on his chin. "Let's see you do it, Cece."

I can't deny that Anya's suggestion is a good one, but I also can't help resenting it, and the fact that her perfect ivory skin is dry and clean, her blush leotard unmarred by sweat, not a strand of her black hair out of place. So when I copy what she's just done, I make it mine with the arms, the head, the eyes.

"Dial it back even more, darling," Kaz says. He puts a hand on my waist and walks me through the turn slowly, placing a hand on my thigh as I begin to lift my leg up in the développé. "Don't even go all the way up. Only about three-quarters. There. And maybe keep this bent, just a little. Yes. Now fall."

I let myself fall out of the balance and Kaz catches me. He smells like cigarettes and laundry detergent. The smell is strong and I don't want to breathe it in.

"Jasper, what about a cambré press here? And, Cece, like you're fainting. Let me see."

He claps his hands and the piano starts, and we begin again. After the last turn I fall into Jasper's arms, and he lifts me, hands on my waist. I fall back, arching over his head, and I decide to add my own port de bras, reaching feebly with one arm to the ceiling, letting the other dangle behind Jasper's back. I let one knee bend, pointing the toes back.

"Gorgeous, darling," Kaz says. "Jasper, move your hand there, so she can—good. Now take her for a little walk. Cece, pivot."

Jasper walks around in a circle, holding me aloft, and I shift so that my head is over his head, my legs hanging down the left side of his body. He is holding me up with one hand now, so this is difficult. I let the upstretched arm fall back over my head to act as a counterbalance. He is digging his fingers into my ribs a little, so I know he's beginning to strain. He wasn't straining with Anya. Could I already be gaining weight? I grow hotter and irrationally annoyed at Anya.

"Now," Kaz says. "Let's see something. Turn her to face you as you bring her down—yes, like that—and catch her around her knees. Cece, you stay straight and steady. Make sure you've got her, now. Get down to your knees, and darling, you sink your hips, like you're sitting in a chair, but lean away from him. Lovely. Dainty with the arms. Good. Now let her go because I have to think what comes next."

We all titter again and Jasper sets me down, using the bottom of his shirt to wipe the sweat off his chin. Some of that sweat may be mine. I take a sip from his water bottle. As I go to screw the cap back on I notice a small smear of ruby red lipstick along the rim. I frown over at Anya, and she catches my eye, smiles sheepishly. That's fine, I tell myself. We have these little intimacies, dancers. No big deal. We're a goddamn family.

"All right, all right," Kaz says.

He lowers himself to one knee and holds his arms out to me. I step into them, let him wrap his arms around my legs and lift me so he can show us what he wants.

"Straighten," he says. "Bring it down. Arabesque, through to attitude devant, and fall back. He'll catch you."

We sketch this out together, and, not for the first time, I wonder what it would have been like to dance with Kaz when he was at his prime. Even now, he is still graceful, agile, the only sign of wear on his body his caution with his knees, arthritic after years of coming down from flying. Still unmistakably a dancer.

"Now you two," he says, waving a hand at Jasper. "From the beginning, if you please."

I spare a glance at Anya as Jasper and I get into position to begin once more. She is sitting on the floor again, long legs stretched out in front of her, pointing and flexing her perfect feet. The music starts and I rise onto my toes, lift my arms in a deliberately flimsy port de bras. Jasper leaps to me. But Kaz calls a halt to the piano, stomps his foot.

"*No*—you are early, Jasper. Can you not stay on the music? Let her breathe."

He gestures for us to start over. I make eye contact with neither Jasper nor Kaz. The polite thing to do after one of Kaz's little fits of pique is to pretend nothing happened. But I can see Jasper's irritation. If anything, he's probably frustrated at himself, though, honestly, if he was early it was by a split second. Kaz's flare of temper was an overreaction. We begin again and this time Jasper is exactly on the music. I wilt through my Italian fouettés, doing my best to make them mine even though they kind of feel like Anya's now. I swoon out of the last one, let Jasper catch me and lift me up over his head.

I get ready for him to switch to just one hand and pivot me. Lifts like this often look easy on the girl. They are not. Always, she is using resistance to create stability, engaging her entire core to become solid and steady, using muscle control to balance and counterbalance, add weight and become lighter, stay in shape, stay en pointe, solidify the supporting leg. Keep the hips in position. It can be difficult, being easy to lift. Jasper and I partner so well together because we trust each other completely. We are adept at reading each other's bodies. And we communicate. We have full conversations onstage without the audience being any the wiser.

But Jasper has gone quiet on me today. I can see that he is in his own head and I don't want Kaz to notice; it'd give him an excuse to yell at Jasper again. So as Jasper begins to pivot me, I add a flashy movement of my legs. But Jasper is not prepared for this. It throws him off-balance and he loses his grip on me. He catches me, of course—Jasper has never dropped me. I get approximately one second of air and then Jasper is holding me, princess style. He is furious, though. His cheeks flame bright red and he all but tosses me out of his arms.

"What the *fuck*, Cece?" he hisses.

I flinch. This venom stings.

He leans down toward me, hands on his hips. "If you're going to go heavy on me, maybe you *should* let Irine poach you."

I stand stunned. I cannot believe he's just said this to me—he knows how it felt to have Irine tell me I don't belong in this company. And I can't believe he's said this right in front of our boss. He's towering over me, eyes full of fury. I think I see disgust there, too. And then, to my utter dismay, I burst into tears. I have *never* cried during a rehearsal. It is unprofessional, it makes me look weak. I am mortified, but the tears have an agency of their own. They come despite my horror—blood seeping out of a fresh wound. Careful not to see myself in any of the mirrors, I walk out of the room. And I'm careful to walk, too. Somehow it seems worse to me if later they can say I *ran* out of rehearsal sobbing. By some grace of the universe, I don't encounter anyone as I make my way to a changing room. I sit on a bench and will the tears to stop. This will not go on longer than two minutes, I decide. I assure myself that there are no cameras in here, nobody hiding in a dark corner. I am not being watched. I am safe. I take deep breaths, slap at my cheeks, try not to dwell on that moment in the air, unsupported, when Jasper threw me out of his arms.

And it's *his* fault he almost dropped me. He wasn't paying attention; he wasn't paying attention to the music's accent correctly; he should know how to read my body better than that. I was trying to make him look better. I want a new partner. I want a new boyfriend. He will *never* talk to me like that again. The tears fade away now that I'm good and angry. My little crying jag was humiliating, but I lift my chin and set my shoulders as I burst back into the room. Kaz tries to coo over me but I wave him away. Anya gives me a small, pitying smile, which pisses me off even more.

"Sweetheart," Kaz says. "Perhaps we should step away for now. Go get a massage."

"I'm fine," I say, my tone cool and clipped.

Jasper steps forward, arms spread low in the ballet mime for "why." Or maybe it's the normal-person mime for "forgive me." It all gets mixed up, sometimes. "Cece, I—"

"I said I'm fine," I snap. "From the beginning."

In a bit of irony, we now dance perfectly. We are back in tune with each other, our internal music in sync. When he lifts me this time, the lift feels easy, the pivot natural. Everything graceful. I breathe in the steps and let this lingering heaviness I feel feed my acting. When we're done I nod at Kaz and Anya, and then stride out, not so much as a glance or a word for Jasper. My cellphone buzzes and I check the screen, see it's my mother. I hate that I'm a little disappointed it's not Jasper. I ignore the call and keep walking.

A full day has not cooled me down. Despite his attempts to talk to me, I have not uttered a word to Jasper unless necessary. He still doesn't know I'm pregnant. The truth of that sits somewhere at the bottom of my throat, sticky and shy. I will tell him, of course. But we need to be in a better place first. I must've been asleep when he came home last night, and he was gone by the time I woke up this morning. I didn't see him until class. And now we are performing together, business as usual. Sort of.

I have just finished running off into the forest to elope with Lysander, and instead of exchanging notes and encouragement backstage with Jasper like normal, I scarf down half a banana and glare as he practices his pas de deux with a bewildered Helena on Gwen's understudy. They are laughing together and I know she must be flattered by the attention he's giving her. Like he wants to partner with her from now on. Because I don't even belong here. I glance over my shoulder at the sound of giggles and see the five baby bunheads I'd noticed before watching me during company class.

They are in their warm-ups and stage makeup. They are part of the quick-footed flock of fireflies that flit across the stage at the beginning and end of this ballet. They unnerve me, their frank admiration is disarming. Again, I wonder what they're seeing as they look at me; it can't be accurate—a distorted reflection. I smile at them, especially at the two Black girls, and they look at each other in astonishment.

"Looks like you have a fan club," Jasper whispers.

I don't know when he stopped flirting with Gwen's understudy and snuck up next to me. I glance at him balefully and make no reply.

Before long, Jasper is back onstage being drugged by Puck and falling in love with the wrong woman. I don't have much time before I have to go out there and cry over the betrayal. I put my banana down—I'll eat the other half at the end of this act, when

I'll need to refuel for the big wedding—and take a swig of water. I kind of wish Hermia would stop moping around and just go beat the shit out of both Helena and Lysander.

I am scrubbing my makeup off after the show. I am wrung out, with barely enough energy left to hold myself upright. I place my fingertips against my abdomen, wondering at the strength of that clot of matter, my baby, to hold on to me as I throw my body into dance. I wonder what it would look like. Would it be long-limbed like Jasper? Would it want me for a mother?

I startle when I hear someone behind me say, "Excuse me?"

I turn and find the baby bunheads, a little group of cygnets, shifting nervously on their feet, looking at me shyly through their lashes. One of them, a little blond sprite, steps forward, blushing furiously and proffering a bouquet of grocery-store flowers.

"We wanted to give you these," she says, not looking at me.

"Thank you," I say, genuinely touched. "They're beautiful."

One of the Black girls, emboldened by her friend, says, "We admire you a lot."

I smile, my body warming from the belly out. "What are your names?"

Danny is the little blond one who handed me the flowers; Sunny—real name Soo-Hee—is tiny and doe-eyed; Priya speaks barely above a whisper. The two Black girls are Michelle and Denisha. They're all very cute, with their neat little buns and chicken legs.

"I hate my name," Denisha says almost as soon as she's offered it.

"Why?" I ask.

"I . . . it doesn't sound like a ballerina's name."

I feel a surge of protectiveness toward these little dancers of color. Already, she has absorbed the message that the ballet world doesn't want her, that she must assimilate to even be tolerated.

"I think Denisha is a beautiful name for a ballerina," I say.

The girls titter. I remember being this age—they must be about twelve. Every compliment feels like a mortifying lie.

"Hey," I say. "Maybe you guys could come sit in while I rehearse *Theme and Variations*?"

Their faces light up.

"Really?" Sunny says, her voice breathless. "We could do that?"

"I'd really like that," I say, and it's true.

They run off, chattering excitedly, and I wonder if I could ever possibly live up to their awe. I want to, I really do. Through the work, the sweat, the doubt, the pain, the constant pushing, I try to remind myself that I am now a Black ballerina, that there are people who need me more than I need myself. I am trying to be good at this. Or at least to be acceptable. Because they'll call me an inspiration, an icon, no matter what I think of myself. More and more, I'm starting to see that. It's terrifying. But it's also touching. Again, I place my fingertips on my stomach.

I've always assumed I never wanted kids, that I'm not maternal. I come by it honestly—my own mother isn't exactly what I would call maternal. But these little dancers—that's what Paul always used to call me: his little dancer, like Degas—have touched something I didn't know I had in me, something close to that knot of cells at my core that is somehow a part of me, and yet apart from me.

It is our day off, and so after the gym, Jasper and I find a diner where we wolf down pancakes, eggs, sausage, and bowls of yogurt and underripe fruit. I want to tell him—he has been so sweet lately—but it doesn't feel like the right time. This morning, before we got out the door to head to the gym, he grabbed me roughly, pulled down my leggings, and pushed me to the floor. I was taken aback—Jasper usually initiates sex with some slightly tentative, lingering touch, like knocking on a door he's unsure will open. Now he is making playful faces at me because, next to us, there is a family with two frazzled-looking parents and three young children who are all either cranky or maniacally excited, and therefore all screeching. I think of a nest full of baby birds, calling for their mother's spit-up.

I have been thinking a lot lately of this singular love you supposedly feel toward your child. So often, it's described the same way one might describe a bear attack—you don't see it coming, it changes you forever, there's nothing like it. Almost as though it has some magical quality, which makes it seem improbable and even a little frightening, like death. Should it have already happened to me or does it come just after birth? Will I be okay when it happens to me? Will I still exist? Did it ever happen to my father, who I saw infrequently growing up even though he lived a subway stop away? If it didn't happen to him, could I have inherited his immunity? Did it happen to my mother?

I have considered asking her, but I'm not sure she'd know how to answer. And I'm not ready to tell her I'm pregnant. I'm not ready for her questions, her disapproval. Her righteous glee. I watch Jasper wash down a huge mouthful of food with his coffee, and instead of telling him I'm carrying his child, I complain about the LA filmmakers who have been getting increasingly insistent about meeting with me. The whole thing is a little embarrassing and very overwhelming. Who would want to watch a film about me? It is my present that is interesting, not my past.

I have to talk fairly loudly so I can be heard over the children, and the mother glances at us and takes out her phone.

"Are you going to do it?" Jasper asks.

"I don't know," I say. "I've already got interview requests and photo shoots up to here. And I have the endorsement contracts— four different brands. They're going to pounce on me as soon as we get home. I'm already stretched thin."

The mother appears to be looking something up on her phone.

"Is it, like, a documentary?"

I shake my head. "From what I gather, it's this weird hybrid of a documentary and a 'narrative film.'" I put air quotes around *narrative film* because it is not my term but one I only just learned from the latest email.

"Sounds cool," says Jasper.

Now the woman is leaning in close to her husband, whispering. They both glance at us, trying to appear as though the glance is casual, meaningless, like the glance you might brush over someone as you step into an elevator with them.

"I just don't think my life is that interesting," I say. "They want a ghetto Cinderella, and that's not really what it was. I don't want to pretend."

"You *are* from Brooklyn."

I snort. My mother's neighborhood is full of families, cooking smells, cats that everyone takes care of, hardworking Caribbean immigrants. "There are enough people who don't remember Brooklyn before it was gentrified that being from there isn't even that badass anymore."

Jasper reaches over to brush a thumb across my lips. "You don't see yourself the way other people see you," he says. "Think about it, babe."

The husband and wife are watching something on the phone. They have the volume down low, and the kids are still making a bunch of noise, but I think I can hear the familiar, dramatic percussion that accompanies Odile's entrance. The black swan is always so much more fascinating to people than the white swan. She should have her own ballet.

"I'll think about it," I say. "Maybe they'll get Misty Copeland to play me," I joke.

"That would be so cool."

I purse my lips.

As we get ready to leave, the wife approaches us with sweetly timid little shuffling steps.

"I'm sorry," she says. "I don't want to bother you. You're Celine Cordell, right? And you're Jasper Campbell? We—my husband and I—we loved you two in *Swan Lake*."

She gestures back at her husband. The kids are all quiet now, watching their mother with interest. "Would you mind taking a picture with us?"

She holds up her phone, like she's ready to demonstrate exactly how the picture will be taken, should either of us ask. Why do they always do this?

"Of course," Jasper says, smiling his stage smile.

I'm thankful we stopped to take a shower after the gym instead

of coming straight to breakfast. I'm even wearing a little mascara.
I do wish I'd done my eyebrows, though—they tend to disappear
in photos. We pose around the table with the husband and wife
and their sticky kids, and we grin while the waitress snaps several
pictures with first the wife's phone and then the husband's. The
waitress is taking this job very seriously, moving around to capture
us at various angles, taking several shots in portrait and landscape
modes.

The other patrons are not lining up for their turn to take a
picture with Jasper and me. Some look over with studied disinterest or mild irritation. But many take out their own phones and
record the scene. They mostly try to do this covertly, but I see
them, and I wonder what they're going to do with these videos.
Maybe they will whip them out at parties, say, *Look, Dawn. This is
a video I took of somebody else getting their picture taken with Celine
Cordell and Jasper Campbell. You know, the dancers? You ever see* Nutcracker?

The wife takes a picture of just me holding her youngest, a
little girl who can't be older than three. She is wearing a sparkly
pink tutu that had previously been hidden by the table. The tod-
dler wraps her arms and legs around me as I hold her, and it melts
my heart, how trusting she is. I try to imagine a child like this
being mine, the soft little arms and legs something I created with
my own body. I can't. The girl has a pleasantly sour smell, and
when she smiles I can see her teeth, small and a bit sharp, with
spaces in between each one. I imagine the fetus as a tiny, angel-
faced piranha. Eventually, the girl grows impatient with all the
picture-taking and squirms, reaching her arms out to her mother.
I am relieved.

"You seriously need a manager, you know," Jasper says once
we're outside. "People love you. The offers aren't going to stop
coming."

"Then you be my manager."

Jasper actually has a manager of his own. Frank. He's led Jasper into two major endorsement contracts and facilitated a partnership between him and this charity that distributes fresh water in underdeveloped countries and in Flint, Michigan.

"I'll share Frank with you," Jasper says, "though you might be better off with a Black woman."

"Or a Black man," I say, and Jasper playfully spanks me.

"Let's get drunk tonight," he suggests. "We're all going out for dinner, and afterward, let's find a bar with live music and just get wasted."

I would love to get drunk tonight. But, of course, I can't. I don't say that to Jasper, though. "Sounds good to me," I say, not quite lying. We'll go out and I'll come up with an excuse for not drinking.

Jasper pulls me into a shadowed alley and shoves his hand into my underwear.

"What has gotten into you?" I ask.

He grins impishly at me.

"It's broad daylight," I protest, but it's half-hearted. I'm excited by this new aggression and he knows it.

He doesn't last long, which is somewhat of a relief—I'm still sore from this morning, and I'm half afraid someone is going to catch us. I can't help but think of the fetus as he presses my back into the rough brick wall of the building. I don't orgasm, but I pretend I didn't need to. As we're walking back out into the street, after adjusting our clothes, he kisses me softly on the temple.

"Just like Europe," he whispers. "I love you, kiddo."

And I almost tell him then, I really do, but before the words form themselves enough to be spoken properly we are across the street and there is a great white dog barking and tourists walking by with their white legs and the exhaust fumes of a passing bus and the wide-open street with its cars and the hot, bleached sky.

Deprivation is a phase dancers go through when they're young. Especially the girls. The ballet body is an intimidating mystique, and the ritual of denial is seductive to those whose entire lives is discipline. But then we get older, we join companies, we become professionals who dance upward of twelve hours a day—deprivation is no longer sustainable. I look around at this table of feasting artists—muscled danseurs in their V-necks and tank tops, ballerinas who are so used to stage makeup that their going-out makeup is either minimal or over the top. I look at beautiful, underweight Ryn, remembering the days we used to split a granola bar for breakfast. Now both of our plates are piled high with pasta.

Because I am the only one not drinking tonight, I am feeling tender toward everyone. I watch one of the soloists flirt with Gwen, feeding her a neat forkful of his eggplant Parmesan. I watch Rohan guffaw around a mouthful of bread in response to something Fran has whispered in his ear. I keep my eyes on them for a little while, looking for signs that their secret is about me. I force myself to look away. Mi Yeong is sitting on the other side of Ryn, and Ryn is letting her try on the giant ring. It dangles, too big for her tiny finger.

Beyond them is Anya, who finishes her glass of wine in one

gulp and then reaches for the bottle. She's the only one not gorging herself—she picks at a small garden salad—and I sincerely hope she's not sick. I am proud of myself for having such a charitable thought toward her because when she first got to the restaurant, all the seats were taken except for the one next to me and Jasper, and rather than sit there, she pulled up a chair all the way at the other end of the table, and I can't help wondering what I ever did to her.

Jasper throws his arm around me and gives me a little squeeze, nuzzles my hair with his nose. He indicates my untouched glass of cabernet sauvignon. "I thought we were getting wasted tonight," he says, and I can tell he's already halfway there.

I smile at him, savoring this warm secret between us. Even if he doesn't know it's there yet, it still belongs to both of us. "You know me," I say. "Best not to get started too early, or else I'll be out by midnight."

On my other side, Ryn tickles my thigh under the table. I glance over at her and she gives me a wide, knowing smile. I gently slap her knee for being so obvious.

After dinner we find a dark, roomy bar featuring a Southern rock band. The music is terrible. The percussion is way too loud and the lead singer sounds like he has bronchitis. But everyone—except for me—is too drunk to care. I discreetly order a ginger ale, which I pretend has rum in it. Pretending to be drunk may be even more fun than actually being drunk. I dance with Rohan. I dance with Mi Yeong and Fran. Ryn and I sandwich Jasper between us, all of us laughing.

This is the kind of night I imagine is par for the course for other twentysomethings. I can see us all as though we're in a movie, some comedy montage of a Typical Night Out, all swinging hair and beer bottles and straight white teeth and lights in bleary blues, greens, and purples. And then the next day, the adorably painful hangover, which will coincide comically with a job interview or the sudden appearance of a baby or something.

It's nice, being in this movie, just for tonight. The bar is getting pretty crowded, and before long, I lose track of Jasper. But Ryn is still with me. It feels good to have her back. I loop my arm through hers and we sway together to the slow song that's closing out the band's set. When the song ends, Ryn tugs at my wrist.

"Come to the bathroom with me," she says.

The bathrooms are in the back, and we have to swim through a river of beer-sour bodies to get there. I check my makeup in the mirror while Ryn slips into a stall. I like how I look tonight; my skin is clear, my hair is behaving, and—perhaps thanks to the ever-flattering filter of a good mood—I'm seeing my lips as beautifully plump instead of grotesquely bulbous. I steal Ryn's red lipstick from her clutch and smooth it on, pouting at myself in the mirror.

I hear a stall door open and I glance over my shoulder, expecting to see Ryn, but it's Anya. She looks surprised to see me—even takes a startled half step back into the stall. But then she seems to get ahold of herself and begins walking toward the sinks. I smile at her, but she doesn't see because she is looking down. I wonder exactly what her problem is, but then, remembering my charitable concern earlier and how proud of myself I was for it, I reframe the thought: I wonder if she's feeling okay. When she gets closer, I can tell that she's been crying.

"Anya," I say, my concern genuine now, "is everything all right?"

She smiles weakly down at the sink and nods. "I'm fine," she says.

Ryn comes out of her stall and takes the sink on the other side of Anya, so that now she's caught between us.

"Have you been crying?" Ryn asks. "What happened? Are you okay?"

"It's fine. Really. I'm just drunk."

Ryn shakes her hands dry—the paper-towel dispenser is empty—and places one on Anya's back. The water still on her fingers stains Anya's T-shirt a wet gray.

"You can tell us," Ryn assures her. "You're protected by the sacred covenant of girls being in the bathroom together."

This makes Anya laugh a little, but she shakes her head. "I can't," she says.

She is getting more and more splotchy, desultory blossoms of angry red and pink on her cheeks, her neck, across her collarbone. I am reminded, randomly, of headcheese, and a deep nausea begins building in me. Ryn is rubbing small circles on Anya's back.

"Tell us," I say.

She begins to cry again, teardrops dyed a murky gray by her mascara. They land on the lip of the sink. I go to a stall to get a wad of toilet paper and come back, hand it to her. She takes it, but she seems reluctant, like I may have dipped it in poison or something.

"Ignore me," she says. "Seriously. I'm not even really upset or anything. I don't know why I'm crying. I'm just drunk."

"Bullshit," says Ryn.

Waves of bile break against the walls of my stomach. I am seasick. I place a hand on Anya's arm, half to comfort her and half to steady myself. Her arm is fully ineffective at the latter—it's twiggy; there's not enough to hold on to. Anya looks up into the mirror and meets my eyes. Or rather, she meets the eyes of my reflection.

"Please," she says. "Don't be nice to me."

The room seems dimmer than it was moments before. I know what's wrong with Anya. Know it with the same instinctual surety with which I knew I was pregnant.

"I feel woozy," I say, and I begin to shimmy up onto the sink so I can sit.

Ryn rushes over to help me. "You didn't even have anything to drink," she exclaims.

That was a slip. Ryn is terrible at keeping a story straight. I should find some subtle way to chide her for it, but I can hear my own breathing; whisper of breath rushing in, rubber-band creak of contracting intercostals, bellows whistle of lungs expanding, music of bronchioles like leaves in the wind, tiny, wet pops of alveoli, and then the rushing out, mostly carbon dioxide, which, if you listen very closely, has a much thinner sound. Ryn has a maternal hand on my forehead.

"You feel warm," she says. "Are you okay? Should I get Jasper?"

I rest the back of my head against the mirror. It is cool, even through my hair. Anya is standing with her hands on either side of the sink, gaze no higher than her own navel in the mirror. She looks frozen that way. Someone has removed her batteries. Breathe in, a chorus of wind, breathe out, an epilogue. Forever and ever until I die. We are steampunk machines; these bodies are haphazard and arbitrary. Bricolage.

"*Celine.*" Ryn's voice is a little shrill.

"I refuse to be mean to you." My own voice sounds strange to me, slow and ghostly.

Ryn looks baffled, but Anya lifts her head, meets my real eyes this time.

"Tell me," I say.

Ryn glances, wide-eyed, between me and Anya. The room has become almost black but for the white of Anya's shirt, her skin, silver glint of the mirror, wet red of her lips.

She is shaking her head so slightly it could almost be a muscle spasm. "We were both super drunk. Wasted. I know that's no excuse."

Ryn makes a noise that is half gasp, half squeal, but she is on the periphery of my attention. All I see is Anya, her wet, teary face.

"It was before Paris. I just thought," Anya continues, "I mean, you aren't, like, *out* about it, I thought maybe you two weren't—"

"No you didn't," Ryn interrupts sharply. "Everyone fucking knows, Anya."

I place a hand on Ryn's shoulder to quiet her, restrain her.

Anya flinches like Ryn has slapped her, but she agrees. "No. You're right. I'm so sorry. We were just drunk, and I swear it was only the one time, and he made it very clear that it was a mistake and we were to act like it never happened."

This does not satisfy me. I want to know more; I want her to kill me with the details. I want her to give me everything so I can choke on it. I want her to choke. I want her to give me everything so I can find the one thread to pull that'll make this whole thing fall apart, collapse into nothing. Cease to exist. I want her to give me everything until it is nothing. I know this is impossible. I know that I can't be satisfied because she's just kicked a black hole into me. I don't want to hear any more.

Breathe in, breathe out.

Everything starts to make sense. Jasper's attentiveness. Anya's behavior. Not sick, not just quiet. Ashamed, shrunken. Like a kicked dog. I know all too well how cruel Jasper can be when he wants to.

I narrow my eyes at her. "What did he say to you?"

She bites her lip and her red lipstick smears on her teeth. "He just told me to stay away from you. He told me"—she hesitates—"he told me not to fuck this up for him. I was just something he needed to get out of his system."

"That piece of shit," Ryn growls.

I slide down off the counter and once I'm on my feet black

spots appear at the top of my vision. I ignore them. I don't have a plan. I just grab Anya's wrist, march out of the bathroom with her in tow. Ryn follows us, grabs my other hand so we don't lose each other in the crowd. Breathe in. Breathe out. I don't know where Jasper is. I pull all three of us through the press of bodies without direction, without discrimination. I am Giselle, maddened. Anya and Ryn submit to my tugging. They follow.

We don't find him. It is unbearably hot, so I pull them out of the bar. Only once we're outside do I let them go. I run a hand over my face, swiping at the sweat. I've forgotten that I put on Ryn's lipstick earlier—now my hand is marred by an audacious streak of red, I can feel it smeared on my face. I either look like a lioness fresh from a kill or a battered woman. Either way, bloodied, and Jasper is nowhere to be found.

The tears come suddenly, and Ryn gathers me into a tight hug, shoves my face into her bony chest. The ground is uncertain, there's nothing holding me in place. Anya apologizes over and over. I grab her wrist again, in part to shut her up, but also to keep her from leaving. She will witness my pain if Jasper will not. I am branding her with my sorrow.

Like any good perfectionist, I have been gruesomely critical of myself. I have believed that I don't have the mental fortitude a dancer should have; I have believed that I'm not strong enough, skinny enough, fit enough, creative enough. When I finish a performance, what I feel is more often than not an inchoate disappointment, both in my climax being over and in having squandered it. What I have now is relative fame, and it has fractured me—there is that person and there is also this person. This, who is hiding behind That. That, who is at the apogee of her career, who some call one of the best dancers in the world, who is well-spoken, intelligent, an artist. But then there is the woman behind the curtain. This woman who is sure of being unmasked as mediocre; who makes stupid mistakes; who, if she is so good, should've taken less than six years to become a principal; who fell in love with a careless narcissist; who is not your Black ballerina; who can never do enough. What holds me together—what has always held me together—is dance. That I am a dancer. I cannot be anything else. I cannot let him strip me of myself. He has never been an anchor—only the illusion of one. An illusion I trusted even as I sank. And it's like I've been walking around with a sinus infection and, suddenly, it's cleared. That sense of things being right again, of relief, of clarity. I can breathe again. I don't want to have a baby. With the same urgency of not wanting to die.

Ryn helps me move my things into the spare bedroom of the furnished apartment she is renting with her fiancé. I finally meet the Frenchman. The circumstances probably couldn't be any worse, but he is nice, if a little shy. I have not confronted Jasper, have not spoken to him, but he knows. In less than twenty-four hours I have racked up thirty-four missed calls from him, ten voicemails, and sixty-three unread text messages. Ryn took my phone away from me when one of the text messages—it said only "please"— sent me into a fit of sobbing so violent I gagged. Kaz is making one of my solos in the new ballet, and both Anya and Jasper are smart enough not to show up for it. Though Ryn reports that his calls have not stopped, Jasper knows better than to bring drama to work. It is agonizing to walk away from him, but he isn't safe. He never was. It's like being tied to the back of a truck.

Tomorrow is the only day for the entire Saratoga season when I'm not performing, so Ryn and I plan accordingly. She texts Irine on my behalf and reports that Irine sends her love and support. Today, Ryn comes with me to the clinic, where they tell me I'm five weeks along, where they ask me if I'm being forced, where I don't look at the grainy black-and-white image, where they give me a bunch of advice about my physical activity that I will probably have to discard. Where they give me a pill that, after twenty minutes, it is clear I will not throw up, and it's like nothing, like I've done nothing at all. They send me home with four pills that I am to take in twenty-four hours, and I'm told that's when the process truly begins, but really, the process has been well underway for weeks now. This seed-sized bundle of cells, this nascent life, was never mine.

. . .

Performing in and attending the summer gala hours after taking mifepristone was a gamble, but I came out feeling fine. I swallowed a combination of ibuprofen and Tylenol beforehand just to be safe, but I felt nothing. I avoided Jasper everywhere but onstage, and Ryn stayed glued protectively to my side during the reception. The next morning, my day off, I skipped class, called Kaz and told him I needed to nurse a sprain, and took the four misoprostol tablets in Ryn's kitchen with her standing over me and the Frenchman tucked respectfully away in their bedroom.

Aside from the expiatory foul taste of the pills as they dissolved between my cheek and gums, there was mostly just fear. I'd stayed up late reading horror stories of women hemorrhaging, going into shock, enduring excruciating, labor-like contractions. Women who'd been destroyed by the experience, a permanent emotional disfigurement. None of this happened to me. I cramped, though not severely; I bled, though only moderately. I took two naps and both times I dreamed of my brother, his face so vivid I didn't think it could be a dream, though I knew it couldn't be real either. By dinnertime, the cramping subsided and I knew I wasn't pregnant anymore. And it was no great trauma. It was like coming out of delirium.

At the clinic, they advised me strongly against returning to work the day after taking the misoprostol due to the physical demands of my job, but I kept insisting that wasn't a possibility for me until, eventually, a pink-faced nurse placed her warm hand over mine and said, "You're the expert on yourself. The most important thing is that you listen to your body."

When I woke up the next morning I stayed perfectly still in bed for a while. I was on my back, which I considered the best position for self-assessment. I did a mental check of every important muscle, head to foot. For a few long, silent moments, I concentrated all my attention on my pelvis. There was a vague undercurrent of activity there, like the subtle shifting of tectonic plates. It felt no different than a regular period. I could tell by the germinal quality of the sunlight that it was very early—no later than six in the morning. I know I dreamed of my brother again, but the details evaporated in the soft morning light. Somewhere in the apartment, there was a faint buzzing.

I get up as quietly as I can and tiptoe into the kitchen, and then out into the living room. The buzzing is coming from an antique secretary desk. I go over and slowly open the drawer. My phone is inside, and, predictably, the display tells me it's Jasper who's calling. I wonder if his calls were keeping Ryn and the Frenchman up, and that's why she moved my phone here, where I could easily find it. Either that, or she figured she could trust me by now. I slide my finger across the screen to answer, hold the phone up to my ear without saying anything.

"Hello?" Jasper's voice is gravelly; he's just woken up. "Cece? Are you there?"

I keep my silence as I creep back into my bedroom, close the door.

"I know you're there, Cece. I can hear you breathing."

I hold my breath.

Jasper sighs. "Fine. At least hear me out, then. You don't have to talk."

I don't hang up.

"Look, this thing with Anya—it's not what you think. I mean, there *is* no thing with Anya. I don't know what she told you."

He pauses, perhaps waiting for me to respond. I don't.

"I made a mistake. I know that. I'm sorry, Cece. It meant nothing, it really did."

A thousand angry responses crackle just behind my teeth, but I don't let them out. I'm not ready to give him my voice.

"You weren't in class or rehearsal yesterday."

No shit, I want to say. I'm furious at him for not guessing the reason, for never noticing a change in me at all.

"You can't go on like this. You'll have to talk to me eventually, at least at work."

Another pause. Why is he so convinced he needs me to speak? Has he deluded himself that this call is about me, instead of about him?

"*Please,* babe. I'm an idiot. I never meant to hurt you."

I warm up my feet. Point and flex. Point. And flex.

"I know what you're thinking."

I almost laugh.

"You're thinking if you let this go, I'll think it's okay and do it again. But you're just scared, Cece. We can't throw away four years because of this. The sooner we get over it, the better."

I wish he were here so I could throw something at him. I'm shaking a bit, a little involuntary rock as I sit on the bed. I'm that mad.

"Cece?" he says. "You really won't talk to me? Just tell me what I have to do and I'll do it."

"Leave. Me. Alone." I hate that my voice is a raspy half whisper, hate that it trembles slightly.

A long pause, and then Jasper sighs again. "Okay," he says. "I'll give you space. Nothing but work stuff until the end of the season here, I promise. Just say we'll start over once we get to Wyoming, all right?"

I hang up. I curse myself for answering in the first place. I was looking for something I knew I wouldn't find. I lie back and close my eyes, try to reconstruct the dream I had about Paul. It had been as warm as bathwater, soft. Here is his face: light brown eyes, skin a shade darker than mine, rash of acne scars at his sideburns. Maybe those are gone now. Maybe his face would be unrecognizable to me now. Transformed by the erosion of five years. How have I let five years go by? Ballet has been my everything. Again and again, I have chosen it above everything.

I need to move. My body is lamenting my full day of inactivity. I make the bed and change into yoga pants and a long-sleeved shirt. I consider making Ryn and the Frenchman an elaborate breakfast as a thank-you, but I doubt any of the stores are open yet. What I really want to do is hit the gym and swim a few laps, but, given my increased risk of infection at the moment, swimming is strictly forbidden.

So I head out the door, settling for a long walk. The apartment is close to Broadway, the hub of Saratoga Springs, and that is where I go, marveling at how different streets look when they're empty. Or mostly empty. There is an elderly couple walking hand in hand across the street. A gaunt man in a grimy American flag bandanna and a holey shirt leans against the side of a building, smoking a cigarette. He holds the cigarette like a flute, squints his eyes as he inhales the smoke. I notice the black lines of dirt under his fingernails.

He notices me looking at him and I quickly look away, keep my eyes averted until I pass him. But then I stop, turn back, meet his eye.

"Good morning," I say.

He smiles, his teeth shockingly white and perfect, except for the bottom one that's missing. "Morning."

I resume my walk. I am light, new. As shiny and clean as a second chance. I've done something life altering, and so now, I am going to pick the ways in which I am altered. It is a satisfyingly tedious task, like decorating a new apartment. I've decided that I am now bolder, less avoidant. From now on, I'm not going to look away anymore.

· · ·

Cecilia is giving class this morning. Before, I might've thought to myself that this is the last thing I need, but I've decided that another alteration is that I'm now unflappable. Not in a cool, aloof way, but in an innocent, nothing-bothers-me-because-I'm-just-so-sweet kind of way. So when Cecilia tells me I need to actually open my hips if I'm going to dance ballet, I smile at her, cute and wide-eyed, and execute a perfect grand plié, blinking up at her for approval. She grunts and gives the next combination.

I ignore Jasper, though I feel his eyes on me. I tell myself that this does not count as being avoidant—I told him to leave me alone, and I think meaning what you say is an important part of boldness. Ryn, in a slight breach of etiquette, has taken a spot near the front of class, where she can watch me—I swear she is watching me in the mirror more than she is watching herself. She is looking for signs of fatigue, signs that I really shouldn't be dancing right now. But I feel reasonably fine so far. I feel like I'm on my period, and that's all.

It isn't until we get to jumps that I notice anything out of the ordinary. I'm heavy, I can't get the height I'm used to, and I have this strange awareness of my pelvis whenever I land. It doesn't hurt or anything, I just . . . *feel* it. As a result, I'm being cautious, holding back a little. I can tell Cecilia notices because she looks at me with an eyebrow raised, but she doesn't say anything, which is out of character for her.

She pulls me aside after I finish a jeté combination with two other dancers. Her espresso breath warms my cheek as she leans in close and says, in a low voice, "You are bleeding through your leotard."

My immediate reaction is to smile and nod because I was sure she was about to criticize me. As what she said registers, I remind myself that I am to be unflappable and I keep the smile. It's not at all unusual for company members to leave class early. If you're nursing a knee injury, for example, you might duck out during jumps. So I collect my things as unhurriedly as possible. It's the most normal thing in the world. I even wave at Cecilia and the pianist as I slip out the door. Before the studio door closes, I see Cecilia staring at me with an unreadable expression on her face. I most decidedly do not run to the bathroom.

There is a good chance that no one but Cecilia saw me bleed through my leotard this morning. I had been wearing a sheer black skirt. I decide that no one saw. The rigorous demands of class, setting the new ballet, and rehearsals do not seem to have *harmed* me, but my bleeding has increased at least threefold. This is heavier than any period I've ever had by far, but according to some thorough internet research and an apologetic (on my part) bathroom stall examination from Ryn, it's nothing to be alarmed about.

Luckily, my costume for tonight's performance is a solid black unitard, but just to be safe, I've lined my seamless performance briefs with two heavy-duty pads. Tonight I am dancing a sleek piece with no story. There's this technically difficult contrast of energetic movements and stillness. And everything is so smooth, sumptuous—I feel like I'm underwater dancing it—with these gently curved lines and ripple-like movements that you'd be hard-pressed to find anywhere else in the company's repertoire.

Thus far, Jasper has stayed true to his word and has been keeping his distance except when we're partnering together. Earlier, during rehearsal, I was so sure he'd touch me and know everything. It terrified me even as I wanted it, wanted him to wrap his hands around my waist and squeeze and sense my womb's trauma. Of course, he didn't sense anything, went on knowing nothing, and it's strange, letting him touch me so intimately while I'm in the middle of grieving him.

We do a slow walk onto the stage together, our legs long, until we reach the center. I lift my right leg in a développé, him supporting me at the waist, and then I hold it, balancing, my whole body tight as he lets me go, pliés under my leg, does a tour in front of me and lands on my left side, grabbing my hand. It's about six seconds of unsupported balance that feels more like six minutes, and it earns us applause from the audience.

"Here we go," he says under his breath.

What follows is an explosive eight bars of jumps that ends with me kneeling at Jasper's feet, trying not to look like I'm gasping for breath. We are back to stillness for several counts. I slowly raise my arms and he draws me up. We undulate together like we're breath itself or some underwater plant being swayed by the current. I extend into an arabesque that then becomes something softer, more rounded. I stay there, center stage, gradually metamorphosing, while he stalks off to stage right. There's this pause in the music here, like a preparatory inhalation, before Jasper travels back to me in a chain of cabrioles, leaping, beating his legs together, and seeming to hang in the air for a split second before coming down.

He lands on one knee before me and I arabesque again, bringing my face down close to his in a penché.

"You got it," he whispers.

It is my turn. I start slow. Pirouettes à la seconde, which are actually much harder when trying to do them slowly. My right leg, extended out to the side, is not as steady as I'd like it to be, and by the last turn, it has slipped out of ninety degrees. I do a deep plié and hold it, thighs burning, and I am acutely aware of my bleeding. I pray nothing shows. There are several counts of silence as I raise back up and make a series of shapes until I land at stage left, and then I am exploding into a chain of spinning jumps, my knees bent, heels tucked up into my crotch, landing in a lunge, arabesqueing, and then doing the jump again.

This kind of virtuosic leaping is usually reserved for male dancers, but one of the things I love about this ballet is that it has these androgynous moments. For one of the last arabesques, I don't have the stability to roll up onto the box of my shoe, and after the last jump, Jasper intuits my unsteadiness and saves me by rushing up and grabbing my arm early. The audience doesn't notice. I get plenty of applause. We slow down again, make languid shapes together. I partner him, he partners me. A leg hooked over his arm, his foot on my bended knee, arms, hands, legs, feet. We pulsate, evolve. We are one organism.

More androgyny: Together, we barrel turn, jeté entrelacé. There are coordinated detournés, Russian fouettés, pirouette piqués. Classical steps with modern quirks. Serpentine twisting, creative interlocking of our bodies. I am not as tuned in to him as I normally am, and I'm cramping. My pelvis, my hips are tight. It restrains me. Again, this is not something the audience notices. They are cheering like they're at a baseball game. We have a lively crowd tonight, which I like. Sometimes, audiences don't know when to clap during the more modern pieces—the music is strange, full of gaps; they don't know when we're pausing and when we're stopping.

Jasper is compensating for me, covering up my imperfections. I hate him for it. This hate is distracting, distancing. The piece ends with him walking offstage hunched over, me on his back, spine to spine. As soon as we're out of sight, I roll off him. Kaz has been watching from the wings. He frowns at me. There's no time to react before our curtain calls begin. By the time the audience is done applauding, Kaz has disappeared. I leave Jasper in the wings, down two bottles of water, and rush to the bathroom, certain I have soaked through my pads and soiled this unitard. I haven't, but it's clear that doubling up on pads was a good decision.

In the dressing room I run into Cecilia. I suspect she has been waiting for me.

"What's the matter with you tonight?" she says.

I'm exhausted. All I want to do is wash off my sweat and makeup and go home. I'm in no mood for Cecilia's venom. But I remember to be unflappable. "I know," I say. "I wasn't at my best tonight."

She narrows her eyes, looks down her prominent nose at me. "And why is that?"

I scrub at my face with baby wipes, force my voice to be non-chalant. "Oh, I don't know. I bet I just need a good night's sleep. Plus, as you know, I'm on my period."

Admittedly, I added that last part to shock her a little.

Cecilia narrows her eyes even more. Now they are black slits in her face.

"That is some period," she says.

There is something in her tone that disquiets me. Cecilia is not dumb, and if there is one thing she does more than criticize me, it's watch me. What has she observed? And, more important, what conclusions will she draw? I don't know what expression I'm making, but it seems to satisfy her. Or it answers some belief, closes her curiosity. She leaves me. I curse myself for being not unflappable but nonplussed. Entirely flappable. I scrub at my eyelids with coconut oil to remove my eye makeup, and then I rip my false eyelashes off, enjoying the brief crackle of pain.

Kaz calls me into his office after company class and I know it is not going to be good. I sit down at the chair in front of his desk and remind myself to be bold. Whatever is coming, I will defend myself against it.

"Cece," he says, "you know I adore you, so I will be forthright: I think you need to have some time off."

"What? Why?"

He stares at me knowingly a moment before going on. "You are not . . . *yourself* lately, my beauty."

"Look, I know I had an off night last night, but, I mean, come on—that wasn't even the worst off night."

He holds up an elegant hand. "It isn't that. I don't mean to be indelicate, darling, but you never get emotional during rehearsal. I like to think I know you, Cece. Better than you think I do. I know what's going on with you. Do you think I haven't seen it before? I know what that *boy* has brought upon you."

"Whatever is or isn't going on between me and Jasper is personal."

"You know what is personal to me? This company. This seventy-year-old company that I have been entrusted with for almost *thirty* years. And you, Celine. You are personal to me too. From the day I first saw you at the summer intensive. I've watched you become a woman. I've watched you become a ballerina. Those are two separate things, you know. A woman's body can be many things, do many things in her lifetime. But a ballerina's body can belong to no man, nor even to herself—only to ballet, you understand?"

"I don't think I do," I say, jaw tight. "Plenty of girls here have gotten married, had babies. Principals do it. This is not the fifties."

Kaz nods. "Yes. But make no mistake: There is always a cost."

"You're being dramatic."

He laughs. I can see his top and bottom teeth, the dark glint of his fillings.

I sigh. *Make no apologies,* I tell myself. "It's really none of your business," I say, "but I had an abortion, okay? I'm fine, my body still belongs to ballet or whatever. I don't need any time off."

It's a relief, saying this to Kaz. More than I expected it to be. It's also safer than saying it to Jasper, and I'm a little ashamed of myself for that.

Kaz looks neither surprised nor shocked. "Have you told the boy?"

I look down at my hands, two dead birds in my lap.

"I thought not. I am not judging you, darling. And I am not punishing you. But I insist that you take the rest of the summer off. Finish out the season here, there are only four days left. And then don't go to Wyoming—go home. We will tell everyone that you are out. I will keep the board at bay. When the fall season begins, you will be refreshed, we will premiere the new ballet, and it will be marvelous."

I shake my head. "I told you I'm fine. I can dance. I feel fine."

He leans forward, resting his elbows on the desk. His eyes crinkle at the corners. They are full of some deep emotion I don't care to dwell on. "And I told *you* I've seen this before. You feel fine, so you jump right back into full days of dancing, even though the doctors tell you not to. The company's touring, so you skip your follow-up appointment. You dance well, because dancers at this level always dance well, even on strains and tears and hairline fractures. But your stamina isn't the same. Maybe you faint after class. Maybe you faint onstage. Maybe you hemorrhage, you get an infection, you perforate, you get septic. Maybe you're fine. But you, my Cece, are much too precious for the risk. Please. Take the break."

"But," I scramble for a compelling objection, "we're still making the new ballet. If I'm out, we'll have to rush to finish it in time."

He waves a hand in the air, dismissing my argument. "The new ballet is almost done," he says. "And you have always been more than able to pick up new choreography in a hurry."

I begin to object again, but Kaz interrupts.

"Look," he says. "It's just Wyoming. A couple of master classes, some open rehearsals, two performances. Nothing. Better to take care of yourself."

He stands, glides over to me, and kneels next to my chair. He takes my face in his hands, and I am surprised not so much by the intimacy of the move as I am by how soft his hands are, how old he looks up close. "This is better," he says, the words low but forceful. "For everyone."

I see Cecilia as soon as I leave Kaz's office. She is standing right outside the door. I know it was she who reported her suspicions to Kaz. I know she probably pushed him to force me into a break. I know she thinks it was Kaz, and not Jasper, who got me into this situation. I am too weary to feel betrayed. Instead, I am defeated. She wins. She and Jasper win. And maybe I deserve it. I've always known of her suspicions of me and Kaz's relationship, and I've never done anything to assuage them. I've always known Kaz's love for me is not quite grandfatherly, and though I've certainly never encouraged him, I've never dissuaded him either. I've enjoyed being the chosen one. Cecilia's hatred was as flattering as Kaz's adulation. I couldn't blame her for reveling in my disgrace.

But she does not look triumphant. She looks sympathetic, consoling. She even smiles at me. It is the kind of smile you might give a child after disinfecting a cut. Yes, it burns, but it's over now, it's going to get better. It's unnerving, this smile, this beatific sympathy. I keep my face blank and hurry away.

IV

VARIATIONS

[A]

I am home, but "home" is not quite the right word. Nothing feels right. All of a sudden, my everyday movements—picking sleep from the corners of my eyes, walking from my bedroom to the kitchen, chewing, putting deodorant on—seem performative, artificial, like I'm doing them for the benefit of an unseen panel of critics. Which, given that no such panel exists, means there's no real reason to do any of it at all. I stop wearing deodorant, stop making my bed, stop exfoliating. I don't leave the house except to get the fruit and eggs I subsist on.

The only time I feel like myself and not like someone playing me—badly—is when I give myself class. I could just go to Steps on Broadway, but everyone thinks I'm out with an injury, and I don't want to be answering questions. And I don't want to be watched. I use one of the dining-room chairs; that they are exactly the right height to substitute for a barre is one of the reasons Ryn and I bought them. I pick music that features piano—Chopin, Rachmaninoff, Liszt, Satie—and I play it on my phone, the volume turned up all the way.

Front front, side side, back back back. The music makes me cry. I don't stop. *And* down, two three four, and up, two three four, and sous-sus and balance. The clear morning light, as crisp as celery, crystallizes tiny specks of dust. You can smell its woody heat. Here I am; here I am in now. Ballet, as the master once said, must always be in the present tense.

Paul picked me up and spun me around. He was my first partnering class. We were dancing to Tchaikovsky, and I was five years old. At that age, there wasn't much of a difference to me between Paul and my father. In fact, in my early-childhood memories, Paul often obscures my father, who is little more than a shadowy half presence. But this was Paul, my brother. He wasn't sick yet, or at least not that I knew.

Earlier that day, Paul had taken me into Manhattan—I don't remember why. It wasn't important to me at the time. My child's joy lay in the fact of my brother, his attention. The city was a great wave of sensation, so different from, so much larger than Brooklyn, our earthy street in Bed-Stuy. We passed through Lincoln Center, and there, I was arrested by a huge black-and-white poster featuring three women in a misty garden. They had flowers in their hair and were wearing beautiful dresses, with flowers around their arms and long, floating skirts.

I asked my brother about them. *Ballerinas,* he said. The word to me was beautiful.

When we got home, Paul put on his Tchaikovsky record, and I pranced around on my tiptoes. He showed me how to wave my arms in the air like they were the wings of a swan. He showed me how to balance on one foot. He laughed as I twirled in haphazard circles. He picked me up and spun me around.

"You're not half bad for a little monkey," he said. "What if we talked Ma into classes? Would you like that?"

"Yeah," I bellowed, exhilarated.

Paul laughed. "Who knows? Maybe one day you'll be a famous ballerina."

I was already dancing again.

I haven't seen the Espositos since before my promotion. They were there the last night I danced Aurora—I got a huge bouquet of flowers from them and a note in Luca's hand that read, *Stunning. We are proud.* I got a text from Galina once the news of my promotion came out. It read, simply, *It is good.* Galina's typical Eastern European Spartanism. Coming from her, this was basically a declaration of undying love. Other text gems from her have included:

I see you in Agon. *Hips don't turn out anymore?*

Why feet so straight en pointe? You need to push metatarsal.

You make very pretty Odette. Odile, I don't like.

It would be easy to read her as unkind, but, really, she's just an Old World perfectionist. She only bothers to criticize those she loves the most.

I don't think I can handle being recognized today, so I call an Uber and let a bearded hipster—whose car smells, unexpectedly, like watermelon Jolly Ranchers—drive me to the Upper East Side. This is my first major excursion since coming home from Saratoga Springs, and I'm dressed in cotton armor: yoga pants, oversized Black Lives Matter T-shirt. I have my dance bag with me—I know better by now than to come to Luca and Galina unprepared. It is hot outside, and there is no relief upon walking into the familiar building, which is old, and its air-conditioning has never been a match for the city heat.

I step into the studio as a rush of little girls bound out. I can't help but note that only one of them is brown. Luca and Galina seem happy but unsurprised to see me. I wonder how they could possibly have expected me—it's not like I called beforehand. My decision to venture this far out of my house today was an impulsive one. Galina performs her ritual of making tea and serving her Ukrainian cookies, and we sit together in the office. Luca and Galina sit so close their shoulders touch. They hardly seem aware of it. Every now and then, randomly, it feels as though I've been hit in the gut. It happens now. I take a sip of tea, though it's still too hot.

"That Rose Adagio," Luca says. "My goodness." He puts a hand over his heart. "Even Galina cried."

"Only a little," Galina says.

Luca winks at me.

I could swear that show happened years ago.

"But what is the matter?" Galina asks. "Paper says you are out." She looks me up and down. "You don't look injured."

I should have anticipated this. Not much gets past Galina. I try to think of something to say, something that is not a lie but not the truth either. But Galina is quicker than me.

"Ah," she says. "I see. Injury is not on outside, eh?"

There is no use denying it. I shake my head.

Luca puts a hand on my shoulder. "But what could've happened? You've achieved everything you've ever wanted. You are one of the most important ballerinas in history. You are not happy?"

"I am happy. It's not that. It's just . . . it's complicated." As much as part of me wants to, I can't tell them everything. I'm embarrassed, I realize. Not because I got an abortion, and not because I got pregnant in the first place. But because I'd gotten my heart broken. Because I'd been immature and delusional. Because my own weakness is the reason I'm here instead of in Wyoming.

Galina has told me before that Luca was her first love. *It was accident,* she said. *I made mistake to let him walk me home and then poof—love. I tell him, "Now, we get married. I don't want this to happen again." So we get married.* Galina had protected herself from the distraction of heartache by committing herself forever to the man she'd unintentionally fallen in love with. And then she'd gotten on with her career, never pausing for kids or divorce or disillusionment. I wish I had that knife-sharp, Eastern Bloc fortitude.

I have to tell them something, so I tell them about Irine. I tell them about her company, her insistence that I'd be more at home there than at City Ballet. I even show them a bit of the dance Jasper played for me on his phone. All the while, part of me hisses that I am committing a cowardly betrayal—I'm not representing Irine fairly. I haven't said anything untrue, and she's also been nothing but kind and supportive ever since I called and told her I was pregnant. She checks in on me with daily texts, never pushing, never prying.

Galina makes a small, disapproving noise. "Tell friend you will take her class."

I look at Galina in surprise, hurt already welling up behind my breastbone.

"What?" she says. "You do not think you learn nothing from *modern* company class?"

"But," I sputter, "she only wants me there because she doesn't think I belong at City Ballet."

"I don't understand, Celine," Luca says. "You've just been promoted. How can you have any question?"

"You go take class," Galina orders. "This have nothing to do with if you *belong* at City Ballet or no."

I lower my eyes. Hesitantly, I tell them, "I didn't want to take time off. Kaz made me."

"Why?" Luca asks.

I can't bring myself to answer. Nor can I bring myself to lie. My throat clogs as I try to come up with something to say.

"It is good for woman to have secrets," Galina says, giving

Luca a meaningful look. Sooner or later, she will probably guess. She will probably get pretty damn close to the truth, too. If she hasn't already. "How long is break?"

"Just until the end of the summer."

"Good. Time is best thing for injury on the inside."

I rub at my forehead with my palm, which is warm from my mug of tea. "I wish I were stronger," I say.

Galina throws her hands up as though to slap away my words. "Don't be dumb. Point of being strong is not to be without pain. Point is to go on."

She stands to get more hot water from the kettle on the hot plate.

"Luca," I say, "I wonder if you could do something for me. It's a little strange."

Luca raises an eyebrow but gestures that I should go ahead.

Out of my dance bag, I pull the Italian picture book Paul gave me when I was a kid. The book with the illustrated dancer whom I believed was the epitome of balletic perfection. The book onto which I projected all my hopes as a little girl. I hand it to him, and he digs reading glasses out of his shirt pocket, squinting at the book's cover.

"This is Italian," he says, sounding delighted.

"Could you tell me what it says?" I ask sheepishly.

Luca opens the book and begins to translate.

The story is about a young girl who prayed so fervently for grace that she attracted a demon, who, under the guise of an angel, promised to grant her wish under the condition that she never take her pointe shoes off. The trick is that the pointe shoes force her to dance at inopportune moments, causing her to be ostracized. In the end, the shoes never allow her to rest. It is nothing at all like what I always thought. On the last page, the watercolor ballerina I'd aspired to—she must be in agony.

[A1]

And tendu front front, side side side, back back, side side side, plié, relevé, passé, and balance. I am listening to nothing. No music to distract me. I hear the soft whisper of my foot against the hardwood floor, subtle creak of my joints. Lichine's *La Création* and Gat's *Silent Ballet* are both scoreless ballets that I have never danced. Robbins's *Moves* is also a ballet without music; I have not danced it since I was in the corps. Generally, Anya occupies the role of the girl at the head of the opening line of dancers, the female half of the first, violent pas de deux.

Without music, I have no choice but to get lost in movement and movement alone. There is an automatic, obsessive part of my brain that can't help counting. I do my best to ignore it. My movements are aggressively adagio, in contrast to the famous quickness my company is known for. I exaggerate my développé, pushing my shin in toward my ear, push my arabesques until I can see my entire calf sticking up behind me in the full-length mirror in front of me. Wherever there is pain—a twinge in my hamstring as I extend, a pinch in my low back—I linger.

My phone dings with a text message. *Look what I found,* Irine writes. She has texted both me and Ryn an old picture: the three of us as teenagers in matching leotards, our arms slung around one another, our smiles practiced, insecure, our front legs bent at the knee and turned out, front feet en pointe. I look closely at my teenage self, my gaze falling forward into my wide young eyes, back into time. Wherever there is pain, I linger.

They teach you, in ballet, to leave it all at the door. They drill this into your head as soon as you become a serious student. That whatever has angered you outside the studio doors, whatever hurt you, frightened you, betrayed you, could not come into the studio with you. In there, it was to be dance, and dance alone. And yet here I am, dancing and feeling at the same time in the imperfect silence of my adagio.

The ocean was a shining strip of blue that sped by my open window. Paul pointed it out to me with wonder in his voice, but I found it unremarkable. I was more fascinated by the lightning speed of the train we were riding. Or it was a bus. Or a plane. Though if it was a plane, my window could not have been open, and I remember distinctly the whip of the strange-smelling air across my face.

I was wearing a new dress, stiff and, I believed, hideous. My parents' voices seemed to fade behind Paul's.

"Look, Cece," he said. "Look."

Against the bright square of window he was pointing out of, his long finger was pitch-black. I squirmed. There were the sharp points of his knees against the backs of my thighs—I was in his lap. I wanted to get up, to stand on the unsteady floor, but a seatbelt clamped me in tight. Or it was Paul's arms.

My parents were arguing. They were not screaming—it scared me when they screamed—but their voices were sharp and red. I knew that Paul was trying to distract me. The ocean looked endless, blue, and not unlike the sky, except that it moved like it had a mind of its own. I didn't like it.

"There are fish in there," Paul said. "They don't even know how many. And if you go swimming in it, sometimes the fish tickle your feet. It's a whole 'nother world. Isn't that cool?"

In the background, my father's voice disappeared. Our mother came to sit with us. A bump in the road sent me flying. Or I was transferred from Paul's lap to hers.

"We won't be back for a while," my mother said. "That was the last of them worth visiting."

I looked forward to watching the ocean end outside my window. Would it narrow to a sharp tip, like a knife? Or would it grow thinner and thinner, until it disappeared? But, in the end, it was just that a sudden cluster of buildings blocked it from my view. Or it was clouds.

I have been ignoring my mother's calls for far too long, and so I agree to a visit. Kaz emailed me this morning to tell me that Wyoming isn't the same without me, but, really, this little break is for the best, and he has some ideas for the wedding pas de deux in the new ballet that he'd like to go over so when would be a good time to FaceTime, and, by the way, how am I feeling? I haven't responded yet. Among my other unanswered emails is a draft of a contract with one of the big brands, several interview and guest-appearance requests, and an email from the director in LA asking me for a Zoom meeting.

I think about these emails on my ride over to Brooklyn and feel not guilt, not stress, but a kind of apathy. They seem so far away, and the person they're trying to reach isn't exactly me. I make a note to start looking into a manager. I can pay someone else to care. When I walk into my mother's apartment, it is filled with the smell of food. She is in the kitchen, furiously cooking my childhood favorites—chicken gumbo (tomato-based, as it ought to be), buttery cornbread, doughnut holes fried in her ancient cast-iron skillet.

"Sit down," she says.

But she is not in the kitchen alone. There is a man at the table, lanky, deep brown, dreadlocked. He stands.

"Well, hello there, sister. You must be little Celine. I'm King."

He holds out a hand, but I just stare at it.

"Ma didn't tell me you'd be here," I say, glaring at my mother's back as she attends to something on the stove.

So it was a trap, her asking me over. Not about me at all.

King laughs. "I've heard all about you," he says, and he pulls out a chair. "Sit down?"

I am filled with an unexpected and violent flood of resentment. Who does this hotep think he is? Instead of sitting, I stride over to the kitchen counter, snatch up a doughnut hole, still hot from the oil, and shove it into my mouth.

"*Celine,*" my mother hisses.

King laughs again. "It's all right, Queen," he says. "She just didn't expect to see me, that's all."

My mother glares at me as I lift the lid of the pot to get a sniff of the gumbo.

I can't take my mother's glare anymore, and so I settle down at the kitchen table with King, though not in the chair he pulled out for me. "It's nice to meet you," I say. "So, my mother tells me you met at school?"

"Yes," King says. "Your mother is going to work for the NAACP one day. And you're the first Black ballerina? What a family."

My face heats, either with embarrassment or irritation. It's hard to tell. "I'm not the first Black ballerina," I say.

"Your mother showed me some YouTubes of you dancing. I don't know much about ballet, but you sure are something, aren't you?"

"Yes," my mother says, her voice crackling like electricity, "she *is* something. I've been calling you. Your phone broken or what? I had to find out from the paper that you're injured."

She appraises me and I squirm under her gaze. "I'm fine. I'll be back in a little over a month. It's nothing—a vacation, really."

She looks me up and down. "Humph. You're full of beans. Look at you. I can see every bone in your body. And your eyes don't look right."

I roll my eyes and my gaze lands briefly on King. He raises a stern eyebrow. Infuriating.

"Eat some cornbread," my mother says. She butters a square of it and sets it before me. "I swear, you dancers all look like you could use a good meal. The men too. But just try that anorexia nonsense— don't think I won't still cart your grown ass to the hospital."

"I'm not anorexic, Ma, Jesus. See?" I take a huge bite of the cornbread. It's delicious.

"Good. A Black woman doesn't have any business being an-orexic. That's for white girls."

"Just like following your dreams, right?" I turn to King. "She used to tell me and my brother that Black people can't be artists."

She looks at me wide-eyed with shock. "I did *not*. What are you talking about, little girl?"

"You told us that following your dreams is for white people."

"I tried to get you and your brother to be practical about your future," she says in a measured tone. "I don't know what you're mad at me for—it's not like either of you listened to me anyhow."

"But what kind of thing is that to say to a child? Don't you know you're supposed to encourage your kid's dreams?"

She crosses her arms. "You're doing all right, aren't you?"

"Because I had Paul. *Paul* encouraged me." I bounce my leg up and down, my knee bumping against the underside of the table. If I keep it up, eventually I'll bruise.

"Right, I had nothing to do with it. Thank God your brother kept me from holding you back."

"That's not what I'm saying. It's just that, as a kid, it was really hard to have this thing I loved and have my mother tell me it was pointless. Sometimes, I wished you were at the recitals and the auditions like the other girls' moms were."

I don't know why I'm going down this road. But it's like I'm speeding downhill without brakes.

"I was *working*, Celine. I didn't have a husband bringing home a paycheck for me. I was on my own."

I consider, unkindly, bringing up the fact that she and my father never actually divorced—I wonder if King knows that—but I don't do it.

"I just wanted you to have a backup plan," my mother says, as close to conciliatory as she gets. "So you didn't get stuck here. Like me. And your father. Like Paul."

"Wait," King says, sounding confused. "I thought Paul *is* an artist."

I snap my head to him, glaring. He is not allowed to say Paul's name like he knows him. "Has she told you about my brother?"

"Your mother talks about the two of you all the time. She brags about you in particular, Celine. No one can hear her talk about you and not realize how proud she is."

I want to snap at him for presuming to know more about my mother than I do, for stepping into the middle of a dance that has nothing to do with him, but I'm more curious to know how much he's heard about my brother. I look at my mom. "You talk to him about Paul?" I say, my tone skeptical.

She gives me a little self-conscious shrug.

I turn back to King. "So you know he's been missing for five years."

"He's not *missing*, Celine," my mother says. "He's just . . . not in the city anymore. And that's for the best, I think. Lord knows being here wasn't doing him any good."

I narrow my eyes at her. "You're talking like you know where he is."

She shrugs again. "I know he's all right. I'd know if he wasn't. Where he is—that's his business."

"Your brother," says King, "descends from royalty. A king's got to follow his calling out into the world. He'll come back when he finds what he's looking for."

I stand abruptly, and the feet of the chair scrape against the linoleum. If I hear one more word of this man's nonsense, I'm going to either scream or vomit. I flee the kitchen, close myself into my childhood bedroom. The room I used to share with Paul—the two heavy bookcases dividing the room in half gave us the illusion of having our own spaces.

My side of the room is filled with detritus of a childhood fully lived—a few deteriorated stuffed animals, a Ballerina Barbie, face inexpertly colored in with brown marker, stacks of *Girls' Life*, *Pointe*, and *Dance*, a neat row of nail polish on the dresser, a few orphaned stilettos in the closet, a lacy bra hanging from a bedpost, an old dance bag stuffed with ballet slippers I've outgrown and dead pointe shoes.

The bookcase that faces my side of the room is full of assorted dancers' autobiographies—Allegra Kent, Jacques d'Amboise, Gelsey Kirkland, Suzanne Farrell, Carlos Acosta. There are the picture books Paul used to read to me when I was little, a few high-school textbooks, titles straight off of summer reading lists, a decent collection of psychological thrillers.

Paul's bookcase used to be full of art books: books on photography, on street art, on the history of hip-hop, on philosophy.

There were stacks of records and CDs, sketchbooks, some filled and others never opened. It's all gone now. He took everything with him when he moved out, and now, who knows where it went?

I cross over into Paul's side of the room, something I never did as a kid—even when he wasn't living with us—unless explicitly invited. It truly is like entering a separate space; here, it is barren. It even feels a little colder. The bed is bare, the wardrobe empty except for a pair of old black sneakers. The lamp has no lightbulb. But it is not a shrine. My mother clearly cleans in here regularly— it's as spotless as the rest of the apartment. She's got a stack of her sociology textbooks sitting in his bookshelf, and it looks like she's germinating seeds in the egg carton on the desk.

Because no one has come after me, I'm feeling alone and unwanted, pushed out of my own childhood home, though, at the same time, part of me recognizes this as melodrama. I sit on what used to be Paul's bed and lean back. I imagine finding him in any number of heroic and dramatic ways. I imagine catching a glimpse of him on a crowded subway, of chasing him through the cars until he gives up running and collapses, sobbing, into my arms. I imagine following clues to an upstate meth lab, breaking into the underground cell where he is being kept prisoner. I imagine finding him strung out under a bridge somewhere, forcing him to come home with me, enduring his cries and rages and feeding him thin soups as he detoxes in my room.

I've grown so accustomed to avoiding this kind of meditation, to keeping these thoughts tucked neatly in a box that I only opened when I could safely look at them from the shark cage of class, the rhythm, the ritual, the counting of my protective metal bars. Now I experiment with feeling his absence. The grief, the anger, the overwhelming guilt. I imagine finding him and slapping him. I imagine embracing him. I imagine him screaming at me, telling me it was *I* who'd abandoned *him*.

My mother enters the room without knocking, as she has always done. She is carrying a bowl of gumbo with a slice of cornbread sticking out of it.

"I made you a plate," she says, setting the bowl down on the
desk. "Eat. I don't like how skinny you are."

"It's my job to be skinny," I grumble, but I do what she says.

What is it about food that can be so profoundly comforting?
The gumbo is delicious; it is satisfying more than one type of hunger. My mother watches me eat in silence for a while.

"Tell me, now—what did that boy do to you?"

I look up at her sharply. "What boy?"

She rolls her eyes. "Don't take me for stupid. I know that white
boy was more than just your dance partner."

"How?"

"Same way I know he's hurt you bad—because I'm your
mother. Now, tell me what he did."

I look down at my bowl, my appetite waning. "You know. The
usual. He's just . . . a jerk."

My mother purses her lips.

I don't say anything more.

After a while, my mother gets up, rubs two tentative circles into
my back, and leaves me alone.

[A2]

Last night, I dreamed that Jasper showed up at my apartment, and I let him pull down my pajama pants right there in the open door. The dream sex was terrible, and I awoke with the nauseating sense of having let myself down. When I checked my email, there was a new one from him. I deleted it without opening it. I e-signed some endorsement contracts, set up a couple of meetings, and arranged a time for a Zoom meeting with the director in LA. I emailed the company's publicist to ask for help procuring a manager.

When I text Irine, I can nearly hear her screaming in excitement through the phone. I'm not sure what to wear to her company's class, but when I arrive, I find that my junk clothes and socks fit in just fine. Irine herself is giving the class and, mercifully, she doesn't draw any particular attention to me before she gets started, though people definitely notice. Two people excitedly introduce themselves, their curiosity plain. And I can feel the excitement in the room—I can see the dancers pushing themselves more than they normally would, performing. It embarrasses me that this is on my behalf.

The entire class is accompanied by drums, sharp and primal. There is no barre. We begin in the center of the room in one large group—the opening exercises seem to mimic a seedling's struggle out of the earth toward the sun. Down, and slowly rise, relevé, and open the chest. The pace is much slower than what I'm used to, and this feels like an indulgence. Irine directs us into a kind of plié where we are bent at the hips, arms in first, and then, as we lift our torso, we open the arms like great birds. She comes over and offers me a wordless correction, urging me to open my chest more by pulling my torso into her chest. I think I can feel her heart beating against my shoulder blades.

Much of the class is variations on pliés, relevés, birdlike crouches and catlike lunges. Tendus, lots of breath, half-collapsed arabesques, strange asymmetrical balances, turns on flat feet or on the heels. Galina was right—I am learning. By the middle of class, the drums have gotten into my body. I can tell who has been classically trained and who has not. At the end of class, Irine hugs me tightly despite my sweaty body, kisses both my cheeks.

"How do you feel?" she asks.

"It's amazing how quickly I get out of shape."

"Oh, stop it. What did you think? You'll come back, right? You're welcome any time."

There is a light in Irine's eyes, a hunger. It unnerves me so I hug her again. She hugs me back tightly.

Irine's class has left my creativity inflamed, my body ravenous for ballet. I don't just want to exercise—I want to *dance.*

I buy yards and yards of rope from Home Depot. While I'm in the area, I go to Eataly and buy powdery nests of tagliatelle. I eat small pinches of the raw pasta on the train ride home. I stare at the coils of rope in the giant plastic bag. The choice is this: I can either hang myself or dance.

In the living room, I move furniture and secure the ropes to the exposed beams on the ceiling, letting them hang down to the floor. I grab a rope and test my weight on it, and then I begin to swing because I once heard that objects are heavier when in motion.

The rope supports me, and the beam does not so much as groan. I begin to dance.

I can't exactly replicate the support of a partner, but I can approximate it with the ropes. I can do supported jumps and pirouettes, I can do promenades, I can lift myself. I can even approximate a shoulder sit. My abs and arms burn deliciously. I descend an imaginary flight of stairs, run half-heartedly, arabesque. Use a rope to lift myself, back arching—cambré press, or something like it. And again, this time running toward stage left, arabesque, lift. Two more times. I pirouette, feeling imaginary hands on my waist, supporting me. Attitude devant—I hold my leg up to the front, and then derrière.

I grab a rope and hold my position, spinning in a slow circle like I'm a diamond in a rotating display—promenade. And then promenade, arabesque, another pirouette. I pause to look on lovingly while my invisible partner leaps around. If I really am being watched, as I so often feel that I am, and my watcher can hear the music playing from my iPhone, then they might be able to guess that I'm dancing the famous balcony pas de deux from *Romeo and Juliet*. But maybe only if they're balletomanes. Without a set, and without a Romeo, maybe this is indistinguishable, to the untrained eye, from the dozens of other classical and neoclassical pas de deux between man and woman.

I do another series of lifts and arabesques, arms wide open, heart wide open. I watch my invisible Romeo leap around some more. It's been a long time since I've danced Juliet—the role really belongs to Gwen, because she's elfin and makes a good thirteen-year-old. The last time *Romeo and Juliet* was in our calendar, I was third cast. I pretend to jump into Romeo's arms, and then fish dive, which is basically impossible with the ropes, so I just penché. The supported grand jeté is much easier.

But I'm behind the music now, so I hurry through the attitude pirouettes, the chaînés, promenade arabesque, and repeat. And then a pause—I'm looking at an imaginary audience, seeking approval—and another fish dive turned penché. Now my favorite part: grand jetés, bourrées, attitude pirouettes, arabesques, all of it exuberant, exhilarating. I throw my arms around Romeo and dance away, sissonnes, supported grand jetés, my approximation of a cambré press lift. Expansive, I spread my arms wide. Another cambré imitation, arms and hearts fly open. Port de bras—just the arms, room for creativity here. A chance to catch your breath.

Romeo is kind of a dick if you really think about it. First of all, when the play starts, he's madly in love with Rosaline, another Capulet—clearly, he has a type. But she's not into him and has sworn to a life of chastity (which means he can't get up her skirts). Still, the whole reason he crashes the Capulet party is to see her. Then, once he spots Juliet, he totally throws poor Rosaline aside. Which makes you wonder if he would've gotten bored with Juliet had they given it a few weeks. Then he stalks a thirteen-year-old, claims his love for her is emasculating him, and kills her cousin. And, apparently, nobody knows how to check for a pulse. The whole thing is ridiculous.

The first time I danced Juliet was in 2002. I was six. It was some simplified version Señora Sandy had dreamed up, condensed into two ten-minute acts. I don't remember the choreography well now. I think mostly it involved me running back and forth onstage and putting my hands over my heart a lot. In the end, instead of dying, Romeo and I just fell asleep, and were then awoken and led off by our mothers, played by Señora Sandy and one of the resident dance moms.

I was so proud to have been chosen to play Juliet, especially since Señora Sandy had made it clear that the role usually went to an older girl, and the night of the big performance, my mom was in the audience, front and center. Paul was not living with us then—she'd kicked him out a week before. I begged my mother to let me go visit Paul at our father's house. She withstood my relentless whining for quite a while before agreeing to drop me off at my father's apartment one Saturday afternoon.

My father was living in a one-bedroom above a bodega. There was a musty, greenish-brown carpet throughout—even in the bathroom—all the windows had bars, and there were roaches in the rust-stained kitchen sink. Paul was different. He sat on the couch, which was also his bed, smoking cigarette after cigarette, and every now and then, he'd jerk up and peek out of the cloudy window. I asked him who he was looking for, but he just laughed a shaky laugh.

Our father, a big, dark shape in the doorway, said, "I keep telling him to join the army. Military'll get him together."

Paul sucked his teeth, returned to the couch. "I ain't signing up to die nowhere. You even know how old I am?"

"Go and get in that junior ROTC," our father said. "Army'll let you in with parental consent at seventeen. I'm your parent, you living with me, and I'll consent. You got to do something other than stink up my house with them cigarettes, boy."

Paul rolled his eyes. "Ignore him," he said to me.

I was uncomfortable. I wanted to call my mother and tell her to come get me, but I was afraid to ask my father if I could use his phone.

"Here," Paul said, handing me a watercolor he'd done on a sheet of notebook paper.

It was me as Juliet, hands clasped over my heart, colors swirling out from me like moving wings. I beamed up at my brother. "You were there?"

"I'm always there," said Paul. He mussed my hair with a dry, ashy hand. "You were really good, little ballerina."

Our father snorted. "Whoever heard of a Black ballerina?"

"Leave her alone," Paul said. "You've never even bothered to come to her recitals. She's a prodigy."

"Of course she's a prodigy. She's my kid, ain't she? But they don't want to give us anything—she could be the best dancer in history, and let some white girl clap her booty and *that's* who gets the Nobel Prize."

"Jesus, man, she's just a kid."

"So? Ain't no 'just a kid' with us. Your mother's raising y'all too easy."

"At least she's raising us."

"Look here, boy. I *am* your father."

Paul fell into sullen silence. He lit a new cigarette off his old one and blew smoke over his shoulder, away from me. My mother picked me up around dinnertime. She didn't come up to get me— she just called my father and told him to send me down. Paul walked me down the dark stairwell and sent me into the bodega so he could talk with our mother. I bought a Kit Kat bar and watched them through the glass doors.

Paul was animated. He gestured up, toward the apartment, toward me, to himself. Our mother stood with her arms crossed, shaking her head. Eventually, Paul, wiping his face on the sleeve of his sweatshirt, went back inside. On our way home, my mother held my hand so tightly it hurt.

Any Psych 101 student will tell you it's my father's fault I'm attracted to men like Jasper, men who will fail me. But I don't blame him. I've always known where he was. I've always known who he was.

It's Paul's fault. He's the one who left me. He's the one who loved me so well for the first part of my life, and then suddenly disappeared. So now, more than ever, I need to find him. The circumstances are right for me to be more successful than I was before: I'm on a hiatus, I'm older, I'm not so easily distracted. I don't know what I'll do or say when I see him again, but he took my power away from me when he left, and I need it back.

My father does not live in that apartment over the bodega anymore. He lives in a garden apartment on Hancock. I haven't been there in four years. He had a girlfriend last time, Taisha, who has since moved out, but everything else is the same. The dead vines woven into the chain-link gate out front, the dirty white lawn chair on its side in the backyard, the framed painting of Black Jesus above the television, the dog, Isis, a Rottweiler-Doberman mix.

And my father, handsome still and tall, sinewy, a basketball player's body. He does not so much sit in his armchair as fold himself into it, his long arms and legs not quite seeming to fit. I have his nose, I realize, and his jaw, but everything else in his face is Paul's. Isis rests on the floor between his legs, and every now and then he rubs at her haunches with a socked foot.

"Been a while since you came to see me," he says.

I'm not sure how to answer this. I want to point out that he's visited me exactly never, and he's never made it to even one of my performances, but instead, I answer him with silence.

"I read all the articles with you in 'em. Show 'em to everyone. 'That's my daughter,' I say. Some of 'em don't believe me til I take out the picture I got of me and you."

This irks me. Who is he to go around bragging about how great his kid turned out? He had nothing to do with it.

"I wanted to talk to you about Paul," I say.

He raises his eyebrows. "Your brother? What about him?"

"Do you know where he is?"

He glances at Isis. "Ask your mother," he says.

"She doesn't know."

He scoffs. "Your mother knows where that boy is."

"She says she doesn't."

Now he laughs, snorting, his shoulders shaking and his hands clasped over his stomach. "You think she don't know where her own son is? You think, if that was true, she wouldn't have every cop in the country out looking for him? You talking like you forgot who your mother is. She knows exactly where that boy is."

"But she says she doesn't," I repeat, but I'm less sure now. *Did* she say that? Had she ever actually said the words "I don't know where Paul is"?

"I remember one time," my father is saying, "down in Pinckney, South Carolina. We was visiting my grandma and my cousins. Paul was just a little boy—you weren't around yet. Grandma Ondine raised me, was as good as my mother. She died when you were only three or so. We took you to her funeral—you remember that?

"Anyway. We were having a family reunion, a barbecue, you know. And all of a sudden, we realize we don't see Paul anywhere. No one knew where he was. We were in this park, you know, and your mother, she never lost it. She wasn't running around crying or nothing. She managed to get three other families out there looking for Paul. Don't know how she did it. One of the families was Mexican or something. Didn't even speak no English."

He shakes his head, laughing to himself.

"Where was he?" I ask.

"Paul? Don't you know that crazy kid had walked to the beach? That boy loved the ocean. Lucky he didn't drown his fool self."

"What did Ma do then?"

"Sat with him. I told her to beat his ass and take him back to the barbecue, but she just stayed with him." He shakes his head again, this time, I think, out of incredulity. "Some kind of woman, your mother. You a lot like her."

I bristle. "No, I'm not."

He leans forward, resting his elbows on his bony knees. "What's wrong with being like your mother? That's a good woman. Me and her could never hold it together for long, but that doesn't mean she ain't good."

I don't want to think about my mother right now. I'm still trying to sort out whether or not she's been lying to me for the past five years. "How come you didn't come around to see us more often?" I ask. "It's not like you lived far away or anything."

He looks down at Isis again, scratches in between her ears. Momentarily, it seems like he's not going to answer me, and my muscles, unbidden, begin their preparations for retreat.

"You kids hated me," he says.

I'm taken aback. I would've been less surprised if he'd said he was a secret agent. "I never hated you."

"Your brother sure did. And you used to scamper away from me like a skittish kitten. Some men can stand that. Some men might say that's better than nothing. I guess I'm not that kind of man because to me, that's worse than nothing."

He settles back into his chair, crosses his ankle over his knee. Isis, disturbed by the movement, gets up, yawns, and saunters over to me, presses her butt into my thigh. I give her a few pats and she presses harder.

"You want a beer?" my father asks.

I shake my head.

He shrugs, and leaves to get one for himself.

[A3]

I'm sore, which is satisfying because it indicates that my DIY classes are actually enough to keep me in some kind of shape. I sink into a bath that is heavy on the Epsom salts. During performance season, I take baths like this every night. I love being in the water—there's no comfort like it.

Is this what Paul feels when he's in the ocean?

I have a blurry memory of learning to swim. I've never been more than a decent swimmer. Paul and my father, both of whom may as well be mermen, taught me. Feet clumsily splashing, arms cycling in a jerky port de bras—swimming above water was an awkward dance for me; my body did not seem to want it. But once I dipped below, swam underwater, it became effortless. Suddenly it was dance—the great breath before going underwater like the great breath before running out from the wings and onto the stage, and then the ease of it until you come up for air and you feel everything again.

Was that in South Carolina? My brother loved it there. I have a memory of resurfacing and seeing my mom and dad together, shoulders touching, watching me. I sink my head into the bathwater, not caring that I'm getting my hair wet, trying to submerge as much of my body as I can. Underwater silence is a silence unlike any other. All I can hear is myself. The water is a silent pressure against my inner ears, against my eyelids. I can feel the abrasion of the few remaining undissolved salt crystals against the backs of my thighs.

The truth is, sometimes I *wanted* him gone. He frightened me a little, my brother. As much as I loved him, I knew something was wrong with him. I knew he did drugs, but there was always something else. He could be moody, lethargic one moment and giddy the next. He could be buoyant, and sometimes his liveliness had an indescribable edge of rage to it, so that when he picked me up and spun me around, I wasn't entirely sure whether he was giving me flight or preparing to throw me.

But if I were a better sister, if I were a better *person,* I would've gone looking years ago. I wouldn't have let five years go by. I was busy, caught up in my career—this was true. But there was time. There had always been time. The truth is, I hated watching Paul destroy himself, once I was old enough to realize that's what he was doing. So when Paul abandoned me, I abandoned him too. Because holding on was beginning to hurt. And, I think, he must know it. He must know that I let go too. I am just as culpable as Paul. Just as fallible.

I open my eyes. The warm salty water stings. *Paul.* It almost chokes me to even think his name—bubbles rise to the surface of my bathwater. I remember him backlit by the sun, gulls swirling high above his head, the ocean roaring in front of us.

I can't hold my breath anymore, and I push my face up into air. It is very cold compared to the hot water.

My God—Paul is in South Carolina. He's there, and it's so clear now I can feel it inside, coaxing my heart into a frantic allegro. *Paul.* I can go get him. For so long, this has been a fantasy, but it can be real. I'm full of the urgency of it. I rush out of my bath and sit on my bedroom floor, a pool of bathwater spreading around me, phone in my hand. I am looking up plane tickets. I know where he is, and it's time. I need him. We need each other.

And it seems crazy, but why not? I have the money and the time, so why not?

And maybe, if he'll look at me now, we can forgive each other.

Intermezzo

"*Plié et grand plié et relevé, et garder le dos droit,*" Señora Sandy said, and we—me and four other seven-year-old girls—bent at the knees, hips open, and then straightened, rising into slippered demi-pointes, careful, as directed, to keep our backs perfectly straight.

"*Non, non,*" said Señora Sandy, rushing to my side. "*Ton genoux, Cece, ton genoux.* Your knees go over the second toe. When I studied with Alicia Alonso at the Escuela Ballet Nacional de Cuba, wobbly knees were never tolerated. Everyone, try it again. *Un, deux, trois, quatre.*"

Señora Sandy had a collection of ballet music CDs—*Coppélia, La Bayadère, Giselle, The Nutcracker, Don Quixote*—that she used, in rotation, for our accompaniment. The walls on three sides of the room were tiled with cheap acrylic mirrors so that my view of myself was always somewhat kaleidoscopic, and you had to be careful where you put your hand on the barre because it was so old and worn in places that you could get a splinter.

"Cece, *venez ici,*" Señora Sandy said, snapping at the floor in front of her. "Demonstrate a saut de chat for us, please."

By now, I had been taking ballet with Señora Sandy for two years, and there were two things I loved about ballet more than anything: leaping and spinning. Señora Sandy did not believe in simplifying anything just because we were little kids. She spoke to us in French, she taught us the skeletons of advanced steps, she did not mince words. I already knew the preparation steps— tombé, pas de bourrée, and glissade. I stepped forward with a flourish of legs and feet into a lunge, took three quick steps, and then a low, gliding leap, and then the bigger jump, the saut de chat, my working leg kicking up through a développé as though throwing up a long skirt with my foot, and my back leg following, reaching back behind me. I landed and promptly fell out of fifth position.

"*De nouveau,*" said Señora Sandy.

I did it again—tombé, pas de bourrée, glissade, saut de chat— and this time I landed in fifth position and stayed there until Señora Sandy tapped me once on the shoulder, her signal that I'd done well. I relaxed, as pleased as a cat.

"What is the difference between a grand jeté and saut de chat?"

"In grand jeté, you don't développé," I said quietly. I was a little shy of the other girls, who swore outrageously when there were no adults around, and who, though they were never outright mean to me, I sensed did not like me or how frequently Señora Sandy asked me to demonstrate something.

I got another tap from Señora Sandy and then a pat on the bottom, which meant I was done demonstrating and should return to my place with the other girls.

"All right, *mes petites haricots sautants,*" she said, "*sauté, sauté, sauté, échappé sauté, trois fois, tombé, saut de chat.* Try to remember, my little jumping beans. I did not make it as *una primera soloista con el* Ballet Nacional de Cuba by forgetting steps. *Allons-y.*"

After class, I watched the other girls leave, giggling with one another in their tiny velour sweat suits with glittery words like LOVE or PRINCESS or DIVA across the back. I waited for Paul to come get me—I was not allowed to walk home by myself. My mother had begun making noise about pulling me out of ballet a year ago. I was getting too caught up in it, she said. And it was too expensive. But when Paul started paying for me to go, he took it upon himself to walk me to and from class, even after our mother made good on her threat to kick him out of the house. He'd been living with our father for months. And our mother had just allowed him to move back in now that he had a "real" job. I thought that must mean he'd had a pretend job before, but no one would talk to me about where he got his money from. I rolled out my arches on a tennis ball while I waited for him to come—Paul had taught me to do that after my mother told me ballerinas couldn't have flat feet.

He was late, but I didn't mind. When my brother was late, Señora Sandy let me stay for a bit while her intermediate class arrived. The older girls—and one boy—came into the studio to warm up, and sometimes they liked to play ballet mistress with me, teaching me the things they were learning. Some of the girls let me try on their pointe shoes, and though Señora Sandy wouldn't let me stand in them yet, I lay on the floor with my feet pointed against the wall and pretended to bourrée.

I was surprised when it was my mother, and not my brother, who came to pick me up that day. Our walks were the only time we really spent together lately. Instantly, I was worried. Either my mother really was going to pull me out of ballet or something had happened to Paul.

I ran up to her. "Where's Paul?" I asked.

"He's fine," my mother said. "He's sick, that's all."

I knew that wasn't the truth, or at least not the whole truth, but before I could say anything, Señora Sandy interrupted us.

"Mrs. Cordell," she said. "I've been hoping to catch you. Do you have a minute? Cece, go into the studio for a little longer, Mami."

They were both staring at me, waiting for me to go, my mother with a look of irritation and impatience on her face. With reluctance, I slunk back into the studio with its mirror tiles and splintered barre. A few of the older girls were warming up. One was doing a split against the wall and another was pointing and flexing her bare feet, one at a time. I was trying my best not to be noticed, but it was impossible—the older girls smiled and waved at me.

"Hey, Cece," they said.

I waved back but didn't go over to them. I crept toward the doorway, pretending to be preoccupied by stretching. If I did a side stretch, leaning toward the doorway, I could hear a little without being seen. Maybe my mother wouldn't have to pull me out of ballet after all; maybe Señora Sandy was kicking me out. Their voices were low. I could only hear snatches of their conversation.

"Don't want her . . . expensive . . . to her head . . ." This was my mother. She was using her proper voice, the one she used with white people, especially if she thought they were dumb.

"Understand . . . I see . . . exceptionally . . . Ballet Nacional . . . I can . . ." Señora Sandy was using a different voice too, her accent less pronounced.

"Practical . . . better than me . . . her brother . . ."

I strained to hear more clearly, wondering why my mother was bringing up Paul. I wasn't supposed to talk about him too much to other people. He was what my mother called "our own business."

"Unusually talented . . . potential . . . bright future . . . gifted . . ."

I felt myself flush.

My mother lowered her voice even more and her response came to my ear as a chain of unintelligible syllables, but Señora Sandy raised her voice a little, though not angrily, her words a bit clearer.

"*The* Alicia Alonso," I heard her say. "So I know a dancer when I see one. Celine is a dancer."

My flush deepened. Señora Sandy was telling my mother, the toughest person I knew, that *I* was a dancer. It didn't matter that I couldn't picture it yet; I could feel the fact inside myself, germinating. It was an instinct, like how infants know to hold their breath underwater. My worry for Paul faded into a corner of my mind. He was probably fine, I told myself. I could see his face, as familiar and sure as a sun. He got sick sometimes, but he was always fine. But Señora Sandy thought I was a *dancer.*

V

LA DANSEUSE

Pinckney is a town with two cemeteries but no hospital. The nearest is in Georgetown, about a half hour north on Route 17. Although I'm no stranger to travel, this place disorients me. I'm an orphan, a floating point in a void. I haven't had this much unstructured time since I was a child. I've never been out before—injured yes, but never *out*. My time has seldom been mine alone. This little odyssey may not be exactly normal, but it *is* mine.

There is only one mirror in my hotel room—the one in the bathroom—and it is woefully untrustworthy. It distorts my image depending on which angle I'm looking from—I can see the distortion happen in a wave as I turn my body about—so that I can't be sure of what I really look like. I resort to contorting myself in an attempt to see my own body without a mirror, the way other people see me. For a moment, I worry that the room is equipped with cameras and somewhere, someone is watching and laughing at me. But this hotel doesn't even have elevators. It is disconcerting, not being surrounded by mirrors most of the time.

I do yoga on the beach named Cape Rush on Google Maps, but called the Sickle by locals. With my earbuds pumping Mozart, and then Kendrick Lamar, into my body, I stand where the sea eats at the sand, watching the waves, how they dwarf me, how hungry they are. I can't bring myself to go in. Before I know what

I am doing, I am doing ballet. I stretch, looking for the resistance in my muscles and tendons, stretching past it. My spine pops deliciously to the birdlike fury of the Night Queen's aria. I warm up my feet, ease into a split, the sand abrasive against my calves and inner thighs. I give myself class—just center—aware of a small audience of locals and tourists. And all the while, the ocean rises and falls in front of me.

Afterward, I find a restaurant that looks like a Hooverville lean-to. There isn't much that isn't fried on the menu, and so I give in: I devour all the fried clams, crab balls, grilled shrimp, oysters, and key lime pie I can eat. I feel so guilty after my meal that I make my way determinedly back to the beach, and, pushing past my fear of the sea, dive straight into the next big wave that comes. All around me, saltwater presses in, somehow both soft and full of might. I force myself to open my eyes, let the blurry blue underwater world burn my gaze.

I start by finding and going through all the local phone books and directories, which yields me nothing. I had expected as much. There are no Cordells listed, and my great-grandmother Ondine's last name was Brown. It would take me more time than I have to get through all the people listed under Brown. I have to be back at the company to start preparing for the fall season in a week. The next step in my strategy is to start asking around. I wrote the words "ask around" in my notebook as if I'd know what they meant when the time came, but I have no idea how to "ask around."

For dinner, I return to the seafood place, order a somewhat healthier meal of scallops and fried green tomatoes. My penchant for self-criticism is automatic, unstoppable; I make myself leave most of the green tomatoes on the plate. I stare at the basket of cornbread. *No no no.* My server—a whippet-thin woman with the kind of smooth, nearly black skin that defies you to guess her age—remembers me from the day before, and with a maternal smile, asks my name.

"Cece," I tell her. "And you?"

"Janine. Where you from?"

"New York."

"Thought so. I usually guess right. Now, what you down here in Pinckney for?"

I had guessed this question was coming, and so had time to formulate a suitably vague response. I tell her I have family here, and then quickly change the subject to the tourism industry in this part of South Carolina. But as I finish my second refill of sweet tea—the sweet tooth seems to be the slowest of my pregnancy symptoms to subside—my nagging inner voice begins to admonish me for holding back. Reserve is an old habit, ingrained in me by my mother, but I am here to get information, not withhold it.

Tucked in my purse is a picture of Paul. It's an old picture—taken not long before he was kicked out of the School of Visual Arts—but it is how I remember him, and even after all this time, I can't imagine looking at his face and not seeing this Paul I knew. When Janine comes to bring me my check—"You sure you don't want any pie this time?" she asks, grinning—I pull out the photo.

I take a breath. "This is my older brother, Paul. Cordell. I think he's here in Pinckney. Does he look at all familiar to you?"

Janine takes the picture from my hands and squints at it for a long time. Then, she lets out a slow breath. "No, honey. I'm sorry. I don't know him. But take this down to Pat at the marina—all the restaurants get their fish from him. He knows everybody."

I thank her and she hands my photo back.

.   .   .

Janine was right—Pat does know everyone. And everyone knows
him. Everyone I ask knows exactly who I'm talking about, speaks
of him familiarly. But he is not at the marina when I go looking
for him bright and early. He has sent his apprentice to handle his
business for the day, and the gawky teenager barely seems to know
his own name, let alone anyone else's. I spend my morning at the
marina, showing Paul's picture and asking people if they've seen
him. No one has.

By the afternoon I am discouraged, the heat has made my face
oily, and my hair is sticky and stiff from the salt air. I know I
shouldn't be surprised—the whole trip was a shot in the dark—
but part of me had been certain I'd find Paul here. And that it'd
be easy. I am weighed down by weariness. I trudge back to the
hotel for a nap.

I ache for ballet. I ache for the ritual of it. The shark cage. My
mind is untamable, unsteady. My mother kicked Paul out because
he was both selling and using drugs—the selling may have been
my fault, since he was paying for ballet. Maybe the using was my
fault too. Maybe he's the local drug dealer here, and that's why no
one will admit to knowing him.

I wake up thinking I feel Jasper's arm around me.

I've brought a couple of pairs of pointe shoes with me, one
pair nearly dead and the other brand-new. They are here as talis-
mans of a sort—I can't articulate why I packed them. I take out
my ballerina tool kit and the new pair of pointe shoes, feel their
satin against my dry hands. The ritual of breaking in pointe shoes
is a soothing compulsion, like stimming. I anoint the boxes with
rubbing alcohol to soften them and then gently crush them with
my heel. I bend the shoes back and forth to break in the shanks,
and I shave down the edges of the soles with a box cutter I picked

up at the local hardware store, and, because I am not blessed with Svetlana Zakharova's arches, I cut out a quarter of the shank from inside the shoe and file down the rough edges. I score the soles with my box cutter, cut the satin from the tips of the shoes, and darn the edges to make it easier to balance.

I put the shoes on and stand on my toes. I haven't sewn the elastics or ribbons on yet, but the shoes are already more comfortable. Still, if I were to wear these shoes onstage, I'd be clonking around like a horse. So the last step is to try and silence them. I take them out to the parking lot and viciously beat them against the concrete. My nap has deposited me into early evening, but there's still enough strength left in the sun that it slashes across my back as I brutalize my shoes. Soon, sweat beads up. I get a couple of strange looks, but I don't think about them much. Every beat of the shoes against the concrete is percussion to the cacophony of my thoughts. Kaz. Cecilia. Ryn. Irine. Anya. Jasper. The music. The music. The music.

The next day, after another lunch of fried seafood, most of which I scrape the batter off of, a man approaches me as I begin walking to my hotel. He is older—maybe mid-forties—with a smattering of gray stubble, jaundiced eyes, skin the color of a roasted chestnut. When he first calls out to me, I'm not sure what he wants, whether he's tricking me into enduring a pickup attempt, so when I pause, I pause in mid-stride, a kind of tombé, like I'm preparing to leap.

"You the one been going around asking about Paul Cordell?" he asks.

This does not sound threatening, only direct, so I relax a little. "Yes," I say. "Do you know him?"

The man looks me up and down, and I can tell he's suspicious

of me. It's in the narrowing of his jaundiced eyes, the pursing of
his dark lips. He is standing with his hands on his hips, leaning
slightly away from me. It's more than just suspicious, though. The
slightly creased brow, the chin drawn back, the chest pushed up:
I've insulted him. Sometimes, I have no idea how to act around
people; a lifetime consumed by ballet and little else will do that to
you.

I wrack my brain for what I've done, what offense I could've
given. I remember that I am no longer in New York; there is a different etiquette here.

"I'm Cece, by the way. And you are?"

Now he relaxes a bit, and I can see that I correctly identified
the problem. "Reynard. You family, then?"

I nod, my excitement growing. He knows Paul. "His sister."

Something lights up in Reynard's eyes, and I lean toward it,
eager, but then he slowly shakes his head, tsking, and something
heavy and cruel crawls up into my throat.

"Won't find him," says Reynard, still shaking his head.

"Why not? What happened? How do you know my brother?"

He takes in a long breath through long, yellowed teeth. "Paul
came down here a few years back. But he didn't stay long. Don't
nobody know where he went."

I am all of a sudden very aware of the ground under my feet
and my weight on it, the difference between my weight and that
of the large man in front of me, that of the startlingly large gull a
few feet away, its wings a perfect rain-cloud gray, its eye cocked
toward me, unnervingly cognizant, even somewhat human.

"Now, you say you Paul's sister?" Reynard asks.

I nod absently. How does the world hold it all, that incalculable
weight?

"Well," he says, "that makes me your cousin."

My attention snaps back to Reynard, his deep brown, nearly

purple skin, the silver stubble on his chin, the hands slightly too large for his body, the neat button nose, the trucker cap pulled low over his hairline. He does bear a passing resemblance to my father. A shorter, darker, fatter rendering of the man who briefly raised me.

"Then you're a . . . a Cordell or a Brown?" I ask haltingly.

"Brown," says Reynard.

I have the sudden urge to collapse into this stranger's, this distant cousin's arms and sob, but instead, I say, "And you don't know where my brother is?"

Reynard shakes his head.

"But he was here? You met him?"

Some soft thing flashes in Reynard's eyes, something between sympathy and pity. Instead of answering me, he invites me to a cookout, so I can meet my extended family, and the knowledge is as swift and merciless as a riptide. Paul will be found when he is ready to be found and not a moment sooner, and there is nothing I can do about it, even though I have missed him and worried and wondered for five years. I am not in control here. I accept Reynard's invitation.

I stuck out wildly at the Brown cookout—everyone knew everybody except me. I took endless photos with endless distant relatives. I tried not to appear stiff, hesitant. I was acting, treating this as a role.

A tutting group of women kept fixing plates for me. When a trio of little girls irresistibly begged me to perform the "Dance of the Sugar Plum Fairy" (in my goofy white Keds and yellow romper), someone posted the video to Instagram, and it quickly amassed more than fifteen hundred views. The costume of celebrity is still ill-fitting, but it is at least moderately more comfortable than trying to fit in with this family I've never known.

The children, though, frightened me. They were nearly feral—

as they ran around I could see their sharp, dry elbows and knees, their razor-like shoulder blades, the tiny white ridges of teeth. A little girl—no more than three or so—undid her overalls, baring her small brown chest, her round baby belly. I didn't know where to look, so I pretended not to notice until, to my horror, the topless girl came toddling over to me, emphatically babbling nonsense. I just smiled down at her until, thankfully, she got distracted by a patch of buttercups and wandered away.

It was like they could sense my recent rejection of motherhood. Kids can be uncanny that way. They seemed to eye me with suspicion, treating me like an excitable dog—they were curious, they wanted to get close, but they'd been told I bite when aggravated. I remember this, as a child being baffled by adults who didn't seem to find me as fascinating and charming as most other adults did. Aloof friends of my mother who discussed the prison system, affirmative action, the African diaspora in front of me, forgot themselves, swore, and then glanced at me with resentful condescension as they apologized.

I ended up spending a good amount of time in conversation with a pretty, soft-spoken woman who turned out to be an older second cousin. She invited me to her hair salon for a free styling, and I agreed to be polite, but when I wake up the next morning, I am actually excited to go. The saltwater and briny wind of Pinckney have turned my hair stiff and frizzy. I could use a touch-up. And the bustle of the cookout has left me with the realization that I have been lonely. Since joining the company, this is the longest I've gone not surrounded by at least some of my chosen family.

And I hate to admit it, even to myself, but I am sad. Ryn was right when she said that Jasper has always been an asshole, but it was a part of him I thought I understood. Both of us compulsively choose our careers first. I always assumed there'd be time later for us to choose each other first. I thought him asking me to move in with him was a step in that direction. I've always known he would occasionally disappoint me, but I didn't ever think he'd lie. I head to the Sickle to do yoga, but I find myself staring out into the ocean instead. The waves roll forward and pull back. I close my eyes and I can feel my body swaying subtly. When I open my eyes again they are damp.

My second cousin runs her hair salon out of her house, a watery blue cottage in a neighborhood full of wiry weeds and split asphalt. It is not until she ushers me inside that I realize that she only does braids. Typically, for work, my hair has to be slicked back, so I keep it straightened. I've never had extensions, and I haven't let it go natural since I was a small child. But I find myself eager for something new. As she washes my hair, working shampoo into my scalp with blunt fingers, she tells me the family lore—apparently, I have a great-grandmother who was married thirteen times—and about our family's Gullah heritage. She encourages me to check out Ebe, a section of Pinckney thick with Gullah history and culture.

The hooded hair dryer encases me in a cocoon of heat and white noise, and I feel that sadness again, the loneliness. My mind is too loud in here, so I try scrolling through Instagram to distract myself. But I can't bear the images of everyone working, everyone dancing. The photo of Jasper diving artfully into a pool. The air under the hood of the dryer is too hot, too close. I put my phone away.

I almost welcome the pain of my cousin braiding my hair. She deftly divides it into tiny sections, and then briskly braids in ombré Kanekalon hair—my cousin's recommendation, as I know jack shit about weave—pulling at my scalp to keep each braid tight. She is largely quiet now, watching television as she works—a marathon of a dance competition. I wonder if she's put this on for my benefit. I hate this kind of show, but I find myself becoming absorbed. There is a Black woman on the show, a hip-hop dancer, who, despite having no formal training, is slaying every routine they give her, and yet the judges keep finding things to disapprove of. My hair is finished in the middle of the penultimate episode, and the Black woman has not been eliminated, but I'd be surprised if she wins.

I am now crowned with long braids that are black at the roots and fade to a tawny red by the time they reach the middle of my back. They are as firm as beads, and the parts in my hair allow air to lick at my scalp. My cousin will not let me pay her, but she asks if she can take pictures of me to use on her Instagram. I agree, posing normally, and then in an arabesque. When I leave, my scalp is still vaguely throbbing, and the braids are heavy and tight. But there is a part of me that likes the pain. It is like an invisible brand. Everything it sears is mine.

[pas de caractère]

It is my last day in South Carolina. My time here has been dreamy, slow. But, already, my big, loud, real life is intruding, chipping away at the quiet illusion. I do and do not want to leave. I've enjoyed the quiet, the sleepy pace, the still-breathing hope of finding my brother. But I miss the dancing. It is an acute craving; my body aches for the long days of movement, the repetition, the stage.

I decide to follow my second cousin's advice and check out Ebe. My roots, through my father, are Gullah, and the new ballet is based on a Gullah story, so this seems a fitting way to spend my last day, a neat transition out of this interlude. I am heavy with not having found Paul. Part of me is afraid that I may have scared him deeper into hiding by coming here. In a strange way, Ebe feels like the best I'll get. Like somehow I'll be dipping into a vein Paul is also dipping into, and it'll be almost like we've reached each other at last.

Ebe is all oystershell walkways, haint blue porches to ward off evil spirits, old folks weaving sweetgrass baskets under live oaks. I buy a couple of strip quilts for myself and Ryn, a basket for Kaz. I try to relax. At every moment I feel I am on the brink of either tears or a mortal scream. We can never go back. Even if Paul were to let me find him, he'd never again be the Paul of my childhood, the Paul of his good moments. If I've found anything here in South Carolina it's this hard light: We can never go back. Even now, when I go back to New York, nothing will be the same. Because Ryn has found something she loves more than dance. Because Jasper and I are over. And because I have this overwhelming role to fill, this historic role, this bigger-than-me role. Dance is self-sacrifice for the sake of art, but this—Black ballerina—is self-immolation. I can never go back. I wouldn't want to.

I don't have any particular destination in mind as I wander around the narrow paths. I have found, in the past, that this is the best way to explore. I pass shops, a clapboard Geechee museum, a couple of nondescript restaurants. People wave to me from their stoops, their yards, their smiles open and uncomplicated. Ebe is colorful, teeming with vibrancy, and not just because of the rag quilts, the haint blue shutters and doors, the bright paintings hanging in shopwindows. But also because of the graffiti—street art, really—that covers a good number of the public buildings, the ground where there is sidewalk instead of oystershells.

I stop. The graffiti is some of the most beautiful I've seen, even in New York, or San Francisco, or Paris, Lisbon, Buenos Aires. It uses color in unexpected ways; it plays with space and dimension. And most of it has clearly been made by the same hand. I am staring at the side of a restaurant called, simply, Gullah Barbecue. The side of the plain white building bears a likeness of Botticelli's *The Birth of Venus*, only Venus's skin is a deep, rich brown, her wild, nappy hair reaches up toward the pink sky, the ocean churns, turquoise, beneath the golden shell and all around her. It stops me because it reminds me of why I love art—its complexity, its prismatic humanity. It stops me because, somehow, with only a spray can, the artist has managed to create the impression that the whole thing has emerged from a wild mass of black sketch lines.

It is tagged in the lower right-hand corner, but graffiti tags are notoriously, and deliberately, unreadable. My heart pounding, I barge into the little restaurant. For some reason, I expected the place to be empty, or nearly so, but it is actually quite busy, it being around lunchtime. Even though my stomach is far too unsettled for food now, I get in line. There is a single, harried-looking man behind the counter, and I don't want to irritate him when he's handling so many customers.

As people come in, I shoo them ahead of me in line, which is met with equal parts gratitude and suspicion. The restaurant, as it turns out, is popular, and judging by the heavenly smells coming from the kitchen, and the generous portions of delicious-looking food I see piled onto Styrofoam plates, this is not unearned. When it is finally my turn at the counter, the man behind it is sweating, his eyes hooded and somewhat amused.

"You hungry, miss? Or you just like standing in line?" He does something funny with his vowels, scoops them out so they're rounded at the bottom.

Smiling sheepishly, I order a homemade lemonade, and then I ask, "That mural outside—do you know who did it?"

For just a fraction of a second, I think I see something furtive and knowing skitter across his face, but it's gone before I can be sure I've seen it, and his features are settled into friendly neutrality.

"Not a clue, miss," he says. "Graffiti like that going up all around here. Got the old folks fired up. Some of us don't mind so much." He shrugs.

"But something like that," I point back outside, "couldn't be just thrown up overnight. It had to have taken days—somebody had to have seen him."

"Didn't say I ain't seen him. Just said I ain't know who he was."

He's smiling faintly, the look of mild amusement back, and I get the sense he's trying to give me something.

"Do you," I ask carefully, "know what he looks like?"

"No ma'am," he says.

I deflate a little. I was mistaken. He was not trying to give me anything. No one in this town is trying to give me anything. No one is going to give me my brother. I thank the man and retreat to sip my lemonade in a far corner. I drink it so quickly I give myself a brain freeze. It is saccharine. I can feel the man behind the counter watching me from the corner of his eye. I swear I even spot a couple of the kitchen workers peeking out at me. I gulp the too-sweet lemonade down and get out of there.

The street art is undoubtedly Paul's work. The sketch lines give it away. The penchant for human subjects, the emphasis on movement, the playfulness in the color, the scaling, the light and shadow all give it away. I can't read Paul's name in his tag, but I know it's him. I know his work as well as I know his face. There's the kerchiefed woman on the side of a pharmacy, the stylized line of Maasai walking with lions across the back of a bodega. A small bouquet of eyes on a low wall, a young girl stepping through the door of a brownstone into a jungle, a child climbing a bookshelf, a woman with African features and rainbow-colored skin.

There are more plays on classical paintings—*The Girl with a Pearl Earring* as a Black woman with a hoop earring; *The Creation of Adam* with God and Adam both pitch-black; a class of little Black dancers, after Degas; *The Dance of the Muses* with an African village in the background; a wildly painted, black-and-white rendition of *Little Dancer of Fourteen Years*. That one in particular speaks to me directly. I have always been Paul's little dancer. I still am, I guess. At least part of me is tucked away safe for him. A part of me that can't be consumed by my career. Paul's little dancer is a form in the midst of black chaos, her stance—hands behind her back, feet in a lazy fourth position with hips thrust forward and chin thrust up, as in the Degas—both recalcitrant and approval-seeking. Okay, Paul, I think. It's enough. It's enough for now. I place my hand on her little turned-out foot. I pull my hand away. There is black smeared on my fingertips.

VI

LE DANSEUR

It started as a normal day. All the predictability and lack of potential he rigidly clung to. Xavian woke up at 5:45 in the morning to the vibrant strings of Paganini coming from the Bluetooth alarm clock across the studio. He didn't turn it off right away—he never did. Instead, he let Caprice No. 24 play as he made his bed with military sharpness. He frowned at the little crimson smudges on his crisp, white sheets. He'd been careless the night before. He had to do a better job of washing his hands when he got home.

Paganini turned into Shostakovich as he sat on the floor with his charcoals. If he didn't do this with his hands, they itched to do other things, more destructive things. Even after four years, the longing was still bare, a stark opening within him. He could barely even remember his first year in South Carolina.

He sketched for one hour exactly, and only then did he turn the music off. In silence, he went to his freezer, retrieved the bottle of vodka he kept there. It was unopened, coated in frost, the alcohol inside thickened, nearly a syrup. He imagined what it would be like to finally open this bottle, to bring it to his mouth, to tip the cold liquid into his throat, the icy burn of it, and then the warmth, the relaxing, the heat spreading into that stark opening, shoring it up, making that place strong.

He imagined holding the ice-cold bottle in one hand and a

joint in the other, alternating between the two. The antiseptic burn of the alcohol followed by the stinging burn of the pot. The weed would make his vision do that varifocal thing, where it zoomed in and out, in and out, blurring the edges around whatever he was looking at. It made him lose his balance, made his heart race like he was constantly falling, and he wouldn't *want* to crush the Oxy between his teeth—because he would've sworn that the last time was *his* last time—but he would, and the incomparable pleasure would come rushing in like sweet, sweet water. But the euphoria would fade, and he'd have to take an Adderall just to stay awake, and it would get him through the day; he could usually make it someplace safe before the crippling anxiety came, punching the strength right out of him, leaving him sweating and gasping for breath. And there was only one way out of this, only one way to get the world to stop rising all around him like a tsunami, threatening to crush him into ashes: a pint of something strong.

And so on.

He put the vodka back in the freezer, checked the day off on the magnetic calendar. This month was all checkmarks, no gaps. It had been this way for three years, nine months.

———

Watching: The cap always felt cold against his latex-gloved fingers, and his back had felt wide open the whole time; anyone could be watching. He had to move quickly on the eyelashes so they didn't drip. The reflection of light in the irises a deft flick of his wrist. Every blink takes a split-second-size bite out of you, the curtain dropping again and again. His back felt wide open, but the eyes in front of him stared without blinking.

———

Pat usually delivered fresh seafood early in the morning, before he set up shop for the day down at the marina. But Pat had recently hurt his back, and so Rey had to go down to the marina himself to pick up the fish. This meant Xavian had to open the place up, which he hated because it meant he had to do the liquor inventory, but he would never complain to Rey. Xavian all but owed Rey his life.

The day was already hot—Xavian sweated as he took the chairs down from the tabletops, mixed the day's first batch of lemonade, which Rey insisted they sweeten to within an inch of its life. He heard Clement come in, knew it was Clement because he could hear the tinny trap music coming from the man's earphones. He stepped out so Clement could see him, and the other man smiled in greeting, his hooded eyes friendly, faintly mischievous.

"Up late painting the town red?" asked Clement.

"Rey wants you to do the liquor inventory, man."

"Damn," Clement said.

Xavian smiled to himself as he moved deeper into the kitchen, his true domain. Technically, Rey was the executive chef, but really, he let Xavian rule the back of the house. Here, he danced a dance made entirely by him, set at exactly his pace. The line cooks began to come in and he greeted them as he worked, never pausing, never slowing. He loved the sounds of the kitchen—the *skiss-thwap* of knives cutting through onions and hitting the cutting board, the pelagic whoosh of the taps, the hiss of things frying, things sautéing, things changing shape and texture, transforming, deepening. This was not the fanciest kitchen he'd ever worked in, nor the biggest or most well-known. But he was free here.

Rey arrived and beckoned to him. Xavian thought Rey was going to take him to help unload the seafood, but instead, Rey led him to the storeroom, ushering him inside and closing the door behind them, adjusting his baseball cap.

"What's up?" Xavian asked, growing a bit wary.

"Your sister, that's what," said Rey, his dark face glittering with sweat.

The room seemed to swell like a great, anaphylactic throat, the walls squeezing in. "Shit. She's here?"

Rey nodded. "Now, she's asking for Paul."

The swelling stalled. He'd been going by his middle name for years. Everyone here knew him as Xavian. Everyone except Rey, who'd figured him out right away—they'd met a few times as children, when his father used to drag him and his mother down here to see Grandma Ondine.

"But," Rey was saying, "she's got a picture. All that scruff you got now ain't going to hide you forever."

Paul was silent for a long time, trying to take in air even though there was a storm inside him.

Rey sucked his teeth. "Well?" he said. "What you going to do?"

"I don't know."

Rey sucked his teeth again. "What you mean you don't know? That poor girl is dying to find you. She's your sister."

Paul looked down at his hands, scarred and large and forever stained by charcoal and paint. How they used to shake when he didn't get what he needed. He used to try and hide it from little Cece. "Did you talk to her?"

"No. I saw her asking about you down at the marina and came to tell you about it."

Paul gnawed at a hangnail. "How did she figure out where I am?"

He was asking himself more than anything. She'd been so young the last time they came here, he didn't think she'd remember it. They didn't keep in touch with this part of the family. Even their father didn't—not since Grandma Ondine died. And he never told anyone where he was going. He'd left their mother a note, but it was vague—*Be back when I'm something better than me.* A melodramatic line pinched, in part, from Curtis Mayfield.

"Why not give all this up and go speak with her?" Rey said. "You're clean. What you still doing hiding?"

He was clean, but was he *better*? He scraped a fleck of paint from the meat of his thumb. "Look," he said, "can you take care of her, man? Make sure she's all right?"

"You really ain't going to go see her?"

"I don't know, man. I gotta think. Will you make sure she's all right?"

Rey nodded slowly. "I'll bring her to the cookout. She's family, after all."

Paul was sure that last bit was pointed, but he let it go. He thanked Rey, clapped him on the back, and returned to the kitchen, the noise he loved so well distant now, like he was hearing it from outside.

———

Color: Two of the most complicated applications of the color theory they teach you in art school are blackness and skin. Blackness absorbs the visible spectrum and does not deign to reflect it back. It is not, itself, on the visible spectrum. Most of what you think is black cannot, in fact, be so. Painting blackness is an exercise in light and shadow, value and hue. And skin is never what we call it—white, black, olive, tan. It is a cacophony of color that must be built. A rainbow is also a cacophony of color. He'd always thought it was an oversimplification to say that race is about the color of one's skin. Take that away—be a rainbow—and they'd just hate you for your nose instead. Your lips. The way you spoke. The way you danced.

———

Paul allowed himself one cigarette a day, after they closed down the restaurant, leaning against the side of the building. Today, it was not enough. His hand shook as he brought the pitiful nub to his lips and sucked at the last ashes of tobacco. The line cooks smoking with him didn't notice—they were laughing with each other about girls or something. They were kids, really. He threw the nub out and said good night.

"What you puttin' up tonight, X?" one of the line cooks asked.

"Dunno," he said, walking away. "Might hit the side of that bank."

He had no such plan. That he was the artist behind Ebe's veritable museum of street art was an open secret. Some of his pieces had even been commissioned, including his masterpiece—if he did say so himself—on the side of the restaurant. But he liked being shrouded in mystery; he liked people not knowing where his next work would pop up; and he liked privacy. He didn't need an entourage of kids following him around, thinking it was about destruction when it was really about life.

He began his walk home, going quickly, trying not to think of his sister, who was here, who had found him, who was now breathing in the same night air he was grasping at. His sister, who, despite the decade between them, sometimes felt like his twin instead of his baby sister, because he hurt when she hurt, felt her joy, her anger, always had. He could feel her now—the confusion, the loneliness. Of course she had found him.

He couldn't not think of Cece. He printed every article, clipped every ad, saved every video clip he could get his hands on. He wasn't surprised when she became the first Black ballerina at City Ballet. He'd always seen that for her. But he'd never seen himself in the picture. Where would he fit? In a shadowy corner, half faded? An invisible weight? If he had stayed, would she even be talking to him now? Would she let anyone find out that he was her brother?

———————

Consider the lion: King of the Jungle, though he lives in no jungle; King of
Beasts, though he is vulnerable; vicious, though he is tired, bedraggled, ask-
ing to survive. One can project anything onto his inscrutable face—magical
wisdom, malice. Black Man and Brother Lion walk with each other. One
body a transfiguration of the other.

He stopped in front of his building, taking big, gulping breaths.
He wanted something—another cigarette, anything. The world
was splashing up against him, violent and daunting, and the old
urge was screaming at him, the old urge to just take something—
just *take* something because this is agony you're miserable you
don't have to feel this way you could feel nothing at all.

But no. That wasn't better.

He threw his half-empty pack of cigarettes into the trash on
the curb and went up to his studio. Everything inside was in shades
of darkness. He didn't turn on a light. Nor did he linger. He
grabbed his backpack and went right back out.

Muse: When Dora Maar first met Picasso, she was so captivated by him
that she drove a penknife into her finger, her blood dampening the black
gloves she wore. Picasso kept the glove locked in a box. When he inevitably
left her for a younger woman, after nearly a decade of pitting her against
his other lover, Marie-Thérèse Walter, Maar famously broke down, and
then Picasso bought her a house to be kept in. The muse is so often broken
open by the gaze of the artist. They peel the rib cage apart and eat the
sanctity right out of them. In the end, the artist is the god, the muse trage-
dized, obscured. Let the muses dance into the foreground, let them have their
own divine hearts.

There was nothing quite like a Southern night. It smelled different, fresher somehow. It was quiet as he walked through the place
that had become his home. He avoided the residential areas,
where people might wave to him from their porches. He could go
to his sister right now. Pinckney was small; it wouldn't be hard to
find her. He could go to her and the years would all fall away.

He was sweating in his black T-shirt. He made his way to the
defunct community center on Magnolia. It used to be a museum
of Pinckney's antebellum history, and, before that, the headquar-
ters of Pinckney's first Black police force. Now they were going to
tear it down and put in a Target or something.

He climbed the fire escape up to the roof, where his garden
was. It was almost complete. When they tore this place down,
hundreds of photorealistic flowers would rain down on them,
standing out brightly amid the rubble. He'd almost entirely covered the roof. A work you could only see if you were above it or
destroying it.

He took out what he needed from his duffel bag: the cans of
paint, the latex gloves, the bandanna to cover his nose and mouth.
Every night he came out and either added to something or made
something new. He liked working with spray paint. He liked the
challenge of controlling it, liked how it managed to always get
under your gloves and onto your skin.

He listened to Tchaikovsky as he worked, with only one earbud
in so nobody could surprise him. It was the music from Aurora's
wedding in *The Sleeping Beauty*. He had such a vivid memory of
Cece dancing to this as a little girl, already so graceful, her ease of
movement so instinctual it was shocking. He'd always loved art,
but he would've never given ballet a second glance had it not been
for his sister. His little dancer. He wondered where she was now, if
she was despairing of ever finding him.

I'm here, he wanted to say.

He was a coward.

Tronie: And speaking of muses, consider the muse that is not so much a living person as a study of archetype, of expression, of physicality. The traditional canon of art history will have you believe that the default of imagination is whiteness. Even exoticism comes with a glaze of Eurocentrism—take Vermeer's imaginary girl in her Oriental turban. Expression, for him, is decidedly difficult to convey with spray paint. And he spent more time than you'd think on that hoop earring, getting the impression of light and reflection just right on that thin curve of gold.

The streets were even quieter now as he made his way to the empty beach, following the dull and steady clamor of the ocean. Of his daily rituals, this was the most sacred. He stripped down to his underwear, waded into the black water, only just now cooling from the hot day. He waded in until he was chest deep, let the next wave wash over his head.

And again. And again.

Something better than me.

Almost. Still only almost.

Birth: The first time he ever tasted the ocean the word "mother" came spontaneously into his mind. It wasn't its brine, exactly, but its complexity, its inscrutability. The habit of creation is a nihilistic act. A frank confirmation of impermanence. The fury of lines from which a figure forms will eventually collapse, the paint will fade, the canvas will crumble. The spark of life, carried to you on the tip of a finger, will eventually extinguish. If there is a God, He created you to die. Out of churning waters made with sharp, strategic swipes of deep cerulean blue, green-gold, and white, a lush figure rose; organic, fertile, dark. The sky blood-bloated pink, her hair a crown of cosmic chaos. Mother.

He'd once thought of himself as a modern Degas, that same fixation on movement and color, his sister his muse. His sister, who got the better childhood, not the one with their parents together but yelling all the time, the crying, the jealousy, the broken dishes, them pulling him back and forth between them—*He's my son! No, he's my son!*—until neither of them wanted him anymore. How could she possibly understand him? The failed artist. The lost potential. The waste. He can't do anything for her now. There are no more classes to pay for, no more tights or leotards or shoes to buy. He didn't have to stand in between her and their doggedly pragmatic mother anymore. He felt so old these days. Older than his body, older than his parents, older than the human urge to make, that destructive creativity. His ancient hands sketched the form in black paint. Something for her, something she'd recognize. The little dancer, an outrage in its time. And outrage itself not so different from terror, a great yawning blackness, opening and opening, and it's always been there, as old as the universe, or maybe older, but either way entirely unknowable except that you feel it pulling you toward it even as you arch away, arching so far back you see the sky, and the sun in it warming your face, warm, warm, though at your core you may be cold. Like that.

VII

CODA

MMay is wide awake. For the first time in a very, very long time. She and her new husband don't just jump the broom—they grand jeté over it, hand in hand, both beaming. She has reclaimed her own flight. The Hag is gone; May will never be forced into the air again. The music turns poignant as William backs away from her, giving her space. A haunting clarinet solo as she performs a series of slow balances—développé, arabesque, penché, and other side—at center stage, the ghost of her former suffering. It has not left her, even though the Hag is gone. It never will. And so it has a place at this wedding just as surely as her groom does. The music switches from minor to major, the strings come back in, every-thing picking up pace until May, pure joy again, encircles the stage with a series of saut de basques, virtuosic turning jumps, finishing back at center, breathing through her teeth as she grins through eight—*eight*—grand pas de chats.

Kaz stops me here and I stand panting as he compliments my balance. I pat the side of my head, scratching my scalp without disrupting the braids. Almost everyone has gone out of their way to exclaim over my hair. Kaz specifically asked me to keep the braids for the premiere. I'm not sure they'll last until then, but I've already found a place where I can have them redone. I refocus on my movements.

Now Kaz is comparing me to Alla Sizova's Medora. High praise indeed, I think, staring out into the mostly empty rows of seats, given he called me a drunk yeti with no extension yesterday.

"This act is the most important of the entire ballet," he is saying. "We are doing something very big here."

I try not to roll my eyes. We've all heard this many times before. It's not that what he's doing *isn't* revolutionary—making a full-length story ballet for a neoclassical company that actually celebrates diversity and pulls the classical ballet out of Europe without exoticism for once, while at the same time redefining what it means for a work to be quintessentially American. But we all wish he'd shut up about it.

"Jasper, Cece, my darling, the grand pas, please," says Kaz. He is nearly bouncing on the balls of his feet, clasping his hands together.

The wings grow silent. This is an unusually crowded stage rehearsal because Kaz has followed through on his word to turn the traditional sequence of national dances on its head. In an unprecedented move, he's partnered with an African dance troupe from Brooklyn, a Bhangra team from Queens, and a group of Oneida Nation dancers out of upstate New York. There will be a jarabe tapatío performed by a group from Houston. A trio from Hawaii will perform a hula; not the hypersexualized cliché that is an angry scar of colonization but fierce, guttural, and graceful, not all that far from the African dance. Kaz has made it so that this ballet can never truly be replicated, not even by our own company, after its opening week. All of these dancers, officially guest artists, are squeezed into the wings now, watching.

Jasper and I get into position. I keep stiffening at his touch—I won't talk to him at all outside of work. I don't want our history to taint our professional partnership, but our work is so sensual. Every time we partner, it's like I'm giving something back to him that he doesn't deserve. But then I force myself into the role. I become the dancer and the dancer alone. It helps that this pas de deux is gorgeous—it's why everyone is watching so quietly. It has notes of *Raymonda*, that complexity and strength, but with the tenderness of Odette's pas de deux with Siegfried in *Swan Lake*.

A classical grand pas de deux has a specific structure: There's an introduction, an adagio (the slow part), then the male and female variations, and a coda where the two partners come together again. This grand pas actually has two sets of variations, one slow and one fast, and the whole thing is accompanied almost entirely by piano. It is stark and breathtaking. I imagine an audience in front of me, seeing this for the first time. Despite the complaints of my body, I'm just starting to really get into it when Kaz stops us.

"Good, good," he says, waving a hand.

I shake Jasper off me.

"Your second variation, please, Jasper," Kaz says. "And, my darling, stay warm—you're next."

I escape to the back of the stage, where Sunny, as eager as ever, hands me a bottle of water and a towel. There's a dance for the SAB students in the last act, so my cygnets are around more often. I try my best to give them the mentor they want. I've been to a couple of their rehearsals, met Michelle's mom, a former dancer herself who cried when we met. I've encouraged Michelle to keep her natural, nappy hair, dissuaded Denisha from changing her name to Denise.

Little Dancers. They remind me of why I came back here, even as I struggled to pull myself from South Carolina, that black paint on my fingertips the residue directly from my brother's heart. Touching it was like touching his face. He saw me. I may never be able to see what other people see when they look at me, but for the first time, because of my little cygnets, I'm truly sensing my own importance. And not in an arrogant way—on the contrary, it's quite humbling. It's a responsibility. I feel its weight like the weight of wings.

Jasper completes his last barrel turn and I rise onto my toes. I'm back on.

Ryn has moved out of our apartment, and though with all the new endorsement deals I've agreed to and contracts I've just signed I can afford it on my own, I want a fresh start. Something closer to Lincoln Center. Something all my own. And because I recently got a few very generous checks from some of the brands I'm working with, I am doing something I never dreamed I would one day do: I am buying an apartment.

My time is limited—I want to find a place before the fall gala, when the season will really heat up for me—so I'm making Ryn tag along. But she's not particularly helpful; she makes me go to the open house of this townhouse that's so outside my price range I think the realtor can smell it on me.

"I'm not your Frenchman, you know," I tell her, my tone only slightly bitter.

"Even the Frenchman couldn't afford this," she says, running a hand over a carved fireplace. "There are *two* libraries in here."

When we leave the townhouse, though, we are both a little somber, that unique sadness of having lost something you never could've had in the first place.

"Maybe once you're a famous movie star," says Ryn.

"Please," I say. "Who knows if that's even going to happen."

"But they're coming to the gala, aren't they? And they're going to start following you around with cameras?"

"They're coming to the gala, but the surveillance doesn't start until after *Nutcracker*. And then they're going to realize I'm not that interesting, and they'll pack up their things and head back to LA."

"Oh, honey."

We have an appointment with a real estate agent to tour an apartment on Seventy-Eighth, but we get there early, so we stop at a nearby Starbucks. I get an unsweetened green tea and Ryn gets black coffee. We both have Gyrotonics later, then I have a massage, and then a photo shoot in Central Park for the promos for the new ballet. And this is my day off.

But it feels good to be really busy again, after weeks of the opposite. And I'm refreshed; I'm having more on days than off ones. I hate to admit it, but I'm starting to think Kaz was right to make me take a time out.

Ryn drops her lip balm on our way out of Starbucks and does a perfect penché on her way down to pick it up. I laugh, not loud enough for her to hear. She doesn't even realize she's dancing. A few days ago, she came to me with the announcement I'd seen coming. She is going to finish out this season and then not return. She told me she wanted to focus on being a wife. I know she wanted to say "wife and mother," and I'm touched she held back, thinking it'd hurt me. It wouldn't have hurt me. Ryn's happiness is as good as my own.

The apartment is in one of those buildings fancy enough to have a name. The building is white and gold and gleams like a natural wonder in the sunlight. It's one of those rare places that actually looks the same in person as it does in the pictures I clicked through on Zillow. Two bedrooms, one and a half bathrooms, in-unit washer and dryer, a dining room with a Juliet balcony that overlooks a grassy courtyard. There's even a decent gym in the building. The kitchen and bathrooms shine with white marble and gold, and at night, I'd be able to make out the lights of the Metropolitan Opera House from the windows in the master bedroom.

The apartment is at the top of my price range, but when the real estate agent leaves us alone in the dining room to think things over, we open the balcony doors and sink to the floor together, our bony knees touching and the outside air stroking our faces with soft fingers that smell of cut grass and exhaust, and Ryn says, "This is your place."

I nod. And for a moment I think I can't possibly be myself, can't possibly be the Celine Cordell I know, because that Celine Cordell could never so much as imagine buying an apartment in Manhattan. And then I come snapping back into myself. And find I am both quite real and quite myself; it's what's happened to me that is extraordinary, all of it. Somehow, I will simply have to learn to live with it.

I could cry. I don't, but Ryn senses it anyway, rests her head on my shoulder.

"I always thought I'd be doing this with either you or Jasper," I tell her.

"I know," she says. "I *am* here."

"For now. But after this year—"

"You'll still see me all the time. I'll be at every one of your shows."

I sigh, rest my head on top of Ryn's. Her soft hair clings to my face.

"You'll see," she says. "Nothing ever really changes."

"Until everything changes."

We are quiet. We can hear the real estate agent talking on her phone in the kitchen. We can hear the Manhattan traffic. We can hear the apartment building's noises—muted footsteps, a baby crying, someone humming, someone practicing guitar.

"Will you try it again someday?" Ryn says.

The question is a touch cryptic, but I know what she's asking me. We haven't really talked about my pregnancy or my abortion since I went down to South Carolina and came back without my brother.

"I don't know," I say.

"Maybe," I say.

"I don't think so."

The first time I sleep in my new apartment, I wake in the middle of the night feeling like a newborn. The new place looms blackly all around me; I have never lived alone before. The muted whisper of late-night traffic trickles in through my open window. I rise from my new bed—it is still without a frame—and stand before the window. There is the scent of rain. If I close my eyes, I can imagine the traffic sounds a little like the ocean. I go back to bed, sure that it will be hours before I am able to fall asleep again. The next thing I know it is morning, and I am emerging from an unsettling dream I can't quite remember. Something to do with oranges, with pulp, with blood.

I drink green tea while standing in front of the Juliet balcony and then dress in yoga pants, trainers, sports bra, vest, a visor. I'm hoping the visor will make me less recognizable—Irine has invited me and Ryn to this boot-camp class in Central Park—but I suspect this is wishful thinking. It is a pretty morning, so I sling my dance bag over my shoulder and walk to the park. I wear a pair of sunglasses and keep my head low, but I am still stopped for two selfies. I wonder if this will ever become less disconcerting, if the strange mixture of disbelief and self-reproach I experience whenever someone gushes at me will ever mature into gracious acceptance.

Irine is already there when I arrive, and I'm relieved. I've never been a fan of being the first to arrive anywhere. When Ryn shows up we collapse into a group hug. With us together like this, I can almost see our old selves superimposed on our present selves— our younger selves, our bunhead selves. Back when we all loved ballet equally, before Irine's body became unacceptable to SAB, before Ryn met the Frenchman, before I became a Black ballerina, there were only three girls who, improbably, impossibly, had something in them that made them love something enough they'd give everything to it. Novitiates. I think of my cygnets. Maybe not even one of them will make it. Danny might snap an Achilles tendon; Sunny might lose interest; Priya might gain too much weight; Denisha might be overlooked and overlooked until she just stops showing up; Michelle might develop an eating disorder and be unable to continue. It's more than just discipline—it's stone-cold luck.

The boot camp is hard. I am dripping sweat only ten minutes in. High-intensity bodyweight and agility exercises with barely any rest in between. I can see that Irine is a regular at this class. She brings a dancer's grace to the exercises, sometimes completing more reps than anyone else. There's a kind of grueling determination, a grim self-flagellation I recognize in her intensity. I wonder if she's ever forgiven her body for growing hips. Afterward, she is gracious enough to laugh at me and Ryn and make a joke about how easy we made it look. But it's not true. I, at least, am dying; Irine has forgotten how good ballerinas can be at hiding their pain. The boot-camp instructor asks to take a selfie with all three of us, but just before we gather our things and go, he pulls me aside and tells me that I am an inspiration, that he and his husband cried when they watched my interview on the news, that they named their labradoodle after me.

Irine, Ryn, and I walk shoulder to shoulder in search of a good café. I insist on finding one with outdoor seating. I do not say that this is because I would be mortified to sit at a nice, indoor table as sweaty as I am. I have redonned my sunglasses, and Irine and Ryn walk protectively with me in between them, so even though I see a couple of faces light up with recognition, no one stops us. There is a man on the corner who is playing some kind of electric violin—it is plugged into an amp. I recognize the piece: Saint-Saëns, *The Carnival of the Animals,* The Swan. The first time I saw Natalia Makarova dance this I slipped into a kind of despair, convinced I would never be able to dance that beautifully. I couldn't sleep for two days. Every now and then I revisit it on YouTube to deliberately push against that old wound of despair. It is still a little tender.

I put my last bit of cash—a $20 bill—into the musician's violin case as we pass. He blows me a kiss. Both Ryn and Irine look at me with raised eyebrows and then laugh. We find a cute, white-washed café with little wrought-iron tables set up out front, and decide to stop there. Irine orders a double shot of espresso, Ryn orders a black coffee, and I order an Americano. I also order a huge Danish if only to see if I can manage not to eat it. I find myself conducting little experiments like this, testing my body to see if it's truly over the pregnancy. I pick a small corner off of the Danish. Every now and then, I raise it to my mouth, but I never allow it in, as though I'm too distracted by gesturing with my hands to complete the motion. Eventually I crumble the corner into damp dust.

"How is your brother doing?" Ryn asks Irine.

Brother. It stings a little, snags like a hangnail.

"Oh, he's fine," says Irine. "He's a wildlife photographer, did I tell you? Always running off to who knows where. He's in Madagascar now." Her eyebrows knit together. "Or Mozambique."

"I'm surprised he never started dancing," I say. "Remember how we used to teach him adagios?"

"I think we scared him away," Irine says and laughs.

Irine is sitting with her back to the café, facing the street, and Ryn is sitting with her back to the street, facing Irine. I am in between them, and so only I spot the familiar figure just down the block. I recognize Cecilia from the shape of her long model's body, her aquiline silhouette. She is wearing a light, army-green jacket I have seen her wear many times before, her blond hair tucked under a baseball cap. She is coming out of a doughnut shop, clutching a brown paper bag to her chest. She looks nervous; she keeps glancing around. Somehow, she manages not to see me. I don't say anything to Ryn—Cecilia is bare, disrobed of her usual aristocratic and slightly disdainful polish.

I haven't seen Cecilia much since I've been back. The word is that she and Kaz are getting divorced, and she's going to move home to Spain. She looks so vulnerable now, opening her paper bag with bony fingers, almost as though she doesn't know how to do it. The bag contains a doughnut about half the size of her head. She takes a giant bite, nearly shoves the pastry into her face like she's punishing either her face or the doughnut, and I see her whole body release something. She is impossibly light; I wouldn't be shocked if she flew away. I should feel triumphant—after years of her passive-aggressive bullying, it is she, not I, who is being expelled; she, not I, who has succumbed to her own body. But all I can think about is the look on her face just after Kaz told me to take a break. Not triumphant. Perhaps commiserative? Misguidedly protective? And I feel as though what I've witnessed is immensely private, like I've walked in on her getting undressed, the bliss of releasing herself from her bra. She'd hate me if she knew I saw. I look away.

. . .

I don't have to partner with Jasper for the fall gala—I'm dancing in a world premiere that features all female dancers, and, thankfully, we get to wear sneakers—but afterward, at the Supper Ball, we feign our old offstage connection. No one tells us to do this, but we're used to feeding our donors' fantasies. And there are big names here tonight. I am wearing a dramatic gown that, I'm told, makes me look like some kind of sea goddess. I'm not that into fashion, but I did make sure my dress was from a Black designer. I happily drop her name to anyone who asks, especially to the folks from LA, even though they really only filmed me as I got ready to dance, and then as I got ready to attend the Supper Ball. It's not as strange as I thought it was going to be. I always suspect I am being watched, and now I know I am. It's oddly validating.

I put on a good show on the dance floor, but really, I'm exhausted. And not just from the show. I called my mother this morning, hoping to talk with her about South Carolina, about not finding Paul in the flesh but rather finding his voice, his message to me across a chasm. I've been back weeks, and not once has she asked me about it. In fact, we've barely spoken at all. She's been busy with school, she told me. But there's still this little-girl part of me that wants more than anything for her to get it right for me, just once. I was even willing to help her along a little. I called her this morning thinking I'd give her another chance. I thought I'd just mention my trip—just a little nudge—and she'd realize in a sudden storm of mortification and maternal guilt that she'd never even asked me about it.

But when I called, she put me on speaker. And King was there. My fury and sense of betrayal were instant, but still, I tried to temper it. I carried on one of our normal, shallow conversations, forced myself to be polite to King, who kept interjecting like it was appropriate for him to be part of the conversation at all.

Then I asked her, point-blank, if she knew Paul was in South Carolina.

She never answered me. I can't be sure she even heard me. King said something to her and she told me she had to go. I thought I'd burst into tears when I hung up. Instead, I screamed into a throw pillow.

Rohan shimmies up to me and Jasper. He's wearing a fitted suit that shimmers in the light and emphasizes the long muscles of his legs. He is drunk on champagne and probably also high—his smile is very wide and there's a faint smear of glitter on his forehead. "You guys wanna get the fuck outta here?"

I do, but I'm not up to whatever crazy after-party he's got in mind. Ryn's already left with her fiancé. It's too bad—I wanted to see if she'd spend the night at my new place. I'm still getting used to being alone.

Jasper walks me outside. The cool air is a relief.

"I'm going to call it a night," I tell him, already beginning to walk away.

"Let me walk you," says Jasper, jogging after me.

"That's okay. I'm not far."

"No, please? I'd feel better."

I pause, turn to glare up at him. "Stop it, Jasper. We're not friends."

I see him deflate a bit and feel a twinge of regret.

"I just . . . I just thought maybe you'd be ready to talk by now."

I roll my eyes, begin walking again. "We don't need to *talk*, Jasper."

I hear him following me. "Come on, Cece. We were together for four years."

"So? You think that means I owe you an exit interview? There's nothing to talk about. We both know what happened."

This isn't a hundred percent true. He only knows part of the story. But my bit wouldn't have changed the outcome—he and Anya slept together before I knew I was pregnant. But still, maybe it isn't fair that he doesn't know the full depth of my hurt.

"I know I fucked up." He's beside me now, easily keeping up with my brisk pace. "But things were off before that."

"No one told me."

"Sleeping with Anya—it was just a symptom of the bigger problem."

I laugh to myself. "Someone's been going to therapy."

"I *have* been going to therapy." He touches my arm with the tips of his fingers, like my skin might burn him. "Cece." He says my name softly, like he used to, back when we were in love. Or back when I thought he loved me. None of this is fair. "This is the most we've talked since you've been back."

I don't respond to this. Jasper closes his fingers around my arm. His hand is warm and comfortable, despite everything.

"Why were you really out?" he asks, barely above a whisper.

I could tell him the whole story. Part of me is screaming to tell him. But it's not my conscience that's screaming. It's something else, something thirsty and vindictive.

"It wasn't so I could cry over you, if that's what you're thinking."

"That wasn't what I was thinking."

We're in front of my building now. It has begun to rain. A fine, late-night mist.

"This is me," I say.

Neither of us move. Neither of us has said all we wanted to say. Even if we did, it wouldn't be enough.

"Can I come up? I just want to talk. That's all."

Obviously, I know how this ends. And there's no excuse—I'm not even drunk. Deep down, I'm already disgusted with myself, like when I say fuck it and down an entire pizza. But my apartment is a dark, empty void. As soon as I sit in that quiet it'll fill right up with noise: my brother, my mother, Paul, *Paul Paul Paul.* I invite Jasper up.

I know it's a mistake the whole time. I know it when Jasper casually slings an arm around my shoulders about ten minutes into our chat. I know it when he leans in and I don't pull away. I know it when he carries me into my dark, sparse bedroom. I know it when I insist on a condom, throw the pack at him emphatically when he balks. And I know it when I manage to get close only to have it rush away when I look down at his face. Afterward, I am sick with regret; actual nausea rolls in my gut. I slip into a T-shirt and go to the kitchen for a glass of water. Jasper follows.

"You okay?" he asks.

I down half the glass before answering. "I think maybe you should go."

"Babe—"

I hold up a hand. "Please don't call me that. This . . . was not a good idea."

"I still love you."

I set my glass down on the counter. "Jasper—"

That same, nasty thing in me wants to tell him. But what I want more than that is to not be tied to him, to not let him get in between me and ballet.

I try again. "I wish I could take it all back."

"Ouch."

"No, listen to me. I wish I could take it all back, all the way to the beginning. I wish we'd never hooked up in the first place. I think maybe we could've wound up being great partners even if we were never *together.* And maybe we could've been friends. But now—I don't know if we can ever be friends, Jasper. I mean, maybe one day. But maybe never. I just want to dance. From now on, let's just keep it to dance between us."

Jasper crosses his arms, nods slowly. "If that's what you want, Cece."

"It's what I want."

He returns to my bedroom to get dressed and I stay in the kitchen with my glass of water, full of a gut-wrenching void, a brand of terror. I'm afraid I'll never get it, what I thought Jasper and I had. Maybe it's the cost. The toll I have to pay for the dreams of mine that have come true.

Jasper reappears in my kitchen, dressed again in his evening clothes. "For what it's worth," he says, "I'm really sorry."

"I know," I say.

When he leaves, I expect a great shudder of remorse, I expect to want to run back out to him, I expect the emptiness of my apartment to crash down on me like a giant wave. But instead, I finish my water in the silence, self-disgust gradually abating. In the bedroom, the sheets are still mussed, and I find I don't want to touch them, am not ready to return to my bed. I gather my comforter from the floor and take it to the dining room. I open the double doors to the Juliet balcony, sit positioned so that only the occasional raindrop finds my face. There, wrapped in my comforter, my head resting against the doorframe, I fall asleep. I wake sometime in the dark of morning, cold and with a crick in my neck. I close the doors and trudge drowsily into the living room, where I get the rest of my sleep on the new couch.

On my day off, Kaz invites me to Mari Vanna for lunch. It's this little Russian restaurant in the Flatiron District. Because I'm inclined to appear gentile and dainty in front of my boss, I'm thinking of ordering only a salad, but Kaz knows everyone here, and he orders for both of us in Russian.

"You've lost weight," he says, eyeing me clinically. "You need your strength—our premiere is next week."

The waiters bring plates and plates of food to our table—caviar and pickled vegetables and blinis and some kind of dumpling stuffed with veal. Kaz piles food onto my plate.

"Eat, eat," he says. He eats a sliver of smoked salmon wrapped around a cornichon and closes his eyes, leans back in his chair. "So good," he says, seemingly to himself. "It's peasant food, you know? But it reminds me of my mother."

I spear a hard-boiled egg with my fork and bite into it. When I glance up, Kaz is giving me that uniquely Kaz look, the incisive, unsettling stare that goes on a little too long. I look back at him, waiting.

When he finally speaks, he speaks slowly, like English is not my native language and I don't understand it very well. "I wanted to meet with you because I wanted to ask how you were doing. We've been busy, haven't we, darling? I haven't had a chance to really speak with you."

I look at Kaz—truly look at him. He's more than just my boss. He's my mentor, my teacher. He watched me grow up. More than that, he *studied* me when I was still a student at SAB. Why? I've never asked him why.

"I'm fine, Kaz," I say. "Everything's getting better since I've been back."

This is true, I know it is. Every now and then I'll feel a twinge of revulsion at the other night with Jasper. I am working on being more forgiving of myself. When you're recovering from a bad cold, you may have a cough that lingers for a while, but it doesn't mean you're still sick. And it goes away.

I point my fork playfully at Kaz. "Just don't ever force me out again."

He laughs at this. "We'll drink to it," he says, beckoning a waiter over and speaking in Russian. He waves a dismissive hand at my objections. "We are Russian today. We will drink vodka."

He says "vodka" in his native tongue, the *v* more of a hard *w*. The vodka arrives in a flight of ten shots, and I give Kaz a look that means *Are you serious?* I'm not sure about getting day-drunk with my employer. But he laughs at this too. He hands me a shot and takes one for himself, holds it up in the air.

"*Za zhenschchin,*" he says.

I do my best to copy the syllables that seem to melt into each other—eliciting another laugh from Kaz and chuckles from a couple of nearby waiters—and we both drink. Kaz takes his shot gracefully. I take mine reluctantly, trying not to let it show on my face that the vodka is searing a fiery path down my throat.

"What does that mean?" I ask, willing my voice not to sound strangled. "The toast."

"To women," he answers. He is giving me another one of his Kaz stares.

I down a blini, hoping it will neutralize things.

"Come," he says. "Another."

"*Za zhenschchin*," I say, or try to say, and we both take another shot. This one goes down easier.

Kaz piles some more food onto my plate and I gladly oblige him by eating it all. This is clearly a lunch at which I'm going to get day-drunk with my boss, but I'm hoping to avoid getting day-*wasted* with my boss. Kaz does not seem to have the same reservation—he eats half as much as I do, and when I clean my plate, he orders more alcohol. I don't want to seem unsporting, so I drink with him. I can feel the alcohol getting to me, like someone's turned off the harsh fluorescent lights in my head and lit candles instead.

"Hey Kaz," I say, letting the vodka blur my thoughts enough to give me courage. "Why did you promote me? I mean, why did you accept me into the company in the first place? Why me out of so many others?"

He scoffs. "Survivor's guilt, eh? Don't bother with it. I kept an eye on you, because even when you were just a kid in your black leotard, I could plainly see you were something spectacular. You still are."

He takes another shot, gestures for me to do the same. I don't shoot the vodka this time. I sip. It's quite good, actually—infused with honey and black pepper.

"I know everyone is excited because I made the first Black ballerina at City Ballet," he says, waving a hand around. His accent is emerging, breaking through the vague, delicately British accent I've only ever heard from him before. "But how could I not? Even if you were green, it'd have been the same. You left me no choice. It's the dancing, it's always the dancing."

We finish our flight of vodka and Kaz orders more, this time in a carafe. He orders more food too—smoked sturgeon, potatoes with mushrooms, and some kind of tower composed of layers of chopped herring, beets, carrot, and egg. The food is homey and good. I know I'm going to feel guilty about this excessive meal later, but for now, I enjoy it and promise myself I'll squeeze in extra Pilates during the week. I am drunk, I realize. I haven't been drunk in a while.

"Yes," Kaz says suddenly, like he was just in the middle of some impassioned speech. "I'm sure you've heard: My wife and I are divorcing."

I study him closely, trying to discern how he feels about this, how I should respond. But he looks only meditative, like he's dissociated from the whole thing. "I wasn't sure if it was true," I say.

"It's true," says Kaz. He pauses. "You know she is my third wife?"

I put down my fork, surprised. "I thought you'd only been married twice."

Before Cecilia was Sandra, an heiress to whom he'd only been married for two years before leaving her for Cecilia.

He is shaking his head. "I had a wife back in Russia," he says. "Varya. We were married very young. She left me. Oh, don't give me that look—it was my own fault. Anyway, it was long ago, before I defected."

"Was she a dancer?"

"Varya? Oh yes. Beautiful dancer. But she stopped once we were married." He shakes his head, some old and undead sadness showing itself for just a moment in his eyes. He pours himself some more vodka.

"To women," I say. I'm drunk and can't remember the Russian.

"*Za lyubov,*" says Kaz.

I don't even want to look at the check when it comes. Between all the food and vodka, it's easily over five bills. But Kaz pays it without so much as blinking an eye. I remind myself that Kaz has been rich for a long time now. I'm still getting used to having money. I don't trust my new, modest wealth yet—it might sneak off in the night or evaporate like a vision in a dream ballet.

Kaz grabs my wrist once we're outside. "To the park," he says.

"What park?" I laugh.

"Gramercy Park, darling. There is no other. Not in this city."

"You have a key?" I ask, allowing him to pull me along.

He scoffs at me over his shoulder. "I am the dance chair at the National Arts Club."

The park is an impossible pocket of tranquillity. Outside, people sit on benches, enjoying the cooling fall weather. But inside the gates is another world. It is a secret garden, verdant and quiet. A little sparrow hops by, glancing at us anxiously. I wonder how it knows to peer up at our faces, as though trying to read our intent there. Remarkable, really, when you think about it.

Kaz is watching me. I can feel his scrutiny. I look up at him. His eyes are bleary but steady. It is so hard to keep your eyes still when you're trying to.

"You can never leave the company," he says. "Not until after I die."

"Why would I leave?"

This seems to please him, but that's not why I said it. I genuinely can't think of a single reason why I'd go anywhere. Even Irine has stopped trying to poach me, much to my relief. As long as I'm able to dance, I'll do it here, for this company. Kaz allows me to dance elsewhere as a guest artist, and I've always appreciated that freedom. But I will always come back home.

"Oh, Cece," he says, and sighs. "I'm becoming sentimental. It's not a good thing in an old man."

"I think you're just drunk."

He laughs. "That too." He does a quick little pirouette. Even drunk, he can't help but have his dancer's balance. "Maybe there is such a thing as magic after all. What do you think?"

I shrug.

"Don't shrug at me, darling. Dance."

"Dance what?"

"The most beautiful thing."

And even though I've had a few, even though we're in this strange and beautiful park, and I'm wearing sneakers instead of pointe shoes, I give myself some space and begin the music in my head.

This variation from Gsovsky's *Grand Pas Classique* is famous for being one of the most difficult female variations. It is technically complicated, and I have to focus my unfocused mind to remember all the steps and execute them like Kazimir Volkov is watching. For about two minutes, I make damn sure I'm on my leg, through the ballonnés and Italian fouettés, through the rapid manège of piqués and chaînés at the end.

"Good girl," Kaz says when I'm done.

I give him a reverence.

"But that was not the most beautiful thing," he says.

I wait.

Kaz pirouettes again, and this time, he holds out a hand to me. I take it.

We make up our own choreography as we go. It is undulous, organic. Our music is the wind through the trees, the birds, the sounds of cars and people, our own sequestered thoughts. We are not counting. Improvisation in dance is such a naked thing. Kaz dances with a poignancy, a kind of faded aristocracy. He is both intuitive and gentile as a partner. My movements are big and round. My spine wants to bend, my arms want to reach. I want to fly.

Kaz ends in a low arabesque, only slightly diminished because of his age and weathered knees, and I am on the cool ground, sitting with one knee bent, one arm reaching forward, our fingertips touching. We hold these final positions for a few moments—the return to earth must not be rushed. Kaz comes out of his arabesque and helps me to my feet. I am lightly sweating, and the air is cold now against my skin. Kaz pats my cheek with a cupped hand. It's very Old World European—Luca used to do it all the time.

"You know my feelings toward you, don't you?" Kaz says, his voice nearly lost underneath the hushed noise of the world around us.

"Yes," I say firmly. "I'm like a daughter to you."

Kaz nods once in resignation, looks out over the serene park. "A miraculous only child," he says.

Inside, something shatters. But it isn't painful. It's more like a release, its shivered particles tinkling through me, like the death throes of a star.

[apothéose]

Even from backstage, I can tell the theater is packed. I can feel the pressure of the audience; their anticipation is palpable. The orchestra is warming up—the inharmonious flutters of notes, the audience's garbled chatter a strange percussion. I am on my knees beside Ryn. We are kneeling next to the tray of rosin as other dancers coat their shoes in it, performing their rituals in the hopes that they won't slip and fall tonight. Ryn is shaking like a leaf.

"It's okay," I tell her, running a hand up and down the ridges of her spine. "You've done this a million times before."

"But this is the last time," she says. "This is the last premiere I'll ever dance."

Fran hops into the rosin, does a kind of running-man step while muttering "merde merde merde" to herself. She, like Ryn, has a few complicated solos in tonight's show, and Fran landed on her ankle funny in rehearsal today.

"Don't think about it like that," I tell Ryn. "It isn't making you less nervous and it may not even be true."

She gives me a look and I shrug. "In a couple of years," I say, "you might find that you miss it, and the Frenchman will start a company for you, like Irine's husband, and you'll get to do whatever you want. In the winter, you won't even bother with *Nutcracker*."

She grins. "I *am* looking forward to my last *Nutcracker* season."

"Atta girl."

We join Rohan and Adam at the portable barres and begin a rote series of movements: pliés, tendus, ronds de jambe, développés, grands battements. Staying warm. Adam is short, built more like a running back, so he holds his extensions for a long time, trying to coax his bulky muscles into loosening up. I copy him, because the long holds feel luxurious.

The audience begins to clap and our conductor—an overtly sexy man despite his graying ponytail, who is attuned to dancers' needs when we're onstage but notably aloof toward us when we're not—walks with a danseur's feline grace into the orchestra pit and up onto his rostrum, facing the audience with a bow and then turning to face the musicians, his arms raised in a kind of wide-open fifth position, the baton like a wand in his right hand. And then silence, a collective inhale before the first notes begin, a combination of strings and piano. The theme.

Townsfolk gather in the wings, patting hair into place, straightening tights, hopping up and down—preparing to dance onto the stage once the curtain goes up. I still have some time before I go on. Then I will be May, loved by all and as yet uncursed. The townsfolk are making elaborate shapes on the stage—the corps is especially in sync tonight. Ryn begins peeling off layers of clothes. It is almost her time. We look at each other. "Merde merde merde" we say.

I watch Ryn from the wings. She is beautiful, jealous June, who will curse me with the Hag. This first solo is technically complicated. Lots of long balances, lots of quick changes in tempo. Ryn takes my breath away. I'm sure my mouth is hanging open as I watch her. Because the thing is, she's not just executing the steps perfectly, she's really *feeling* them. Her emotion is tearing up the floor—I half expect to see sparks flying from her feet. She is at one moment a beam of moonlight and at the next a whirlpool; at once an invitation and a rebuke, a vulnerable young girl and a cold goddess.

If Ryn had danced like this over the last six years of our careers, she'd have made soloist a lot sooner. In fact, she'd probably be on her way to being promoted to principal by now. Ryn's talent has always been undeniable. But I've never seen her truly lose herself in a role. Until tonight. And it's because she's leaving, because she's given up on a future at the company. She is the dying swan, whose last moments before stillness are the most achingly beautiful.

I unzip my hoodie, peel off my yoga pants, my leg warmers, my down booties. In a few counts May will make her first appearance, unwittingly disrupting June's display of virtuosity simply by walking across the stage.

The first act ends with a slightly Sapphic pas de deux between Anya and me; the Hag tortures May almost tenderly. It is not just a beautiful piece of choreography, it's an inquiry into the nature of cruelty, into the complex relationship between predator and prey. But Anya mishandles the last cambré press lift and loses her grip on my hips. I slide down and she catches me, wrapping her arms tightly around my thighs.

I don't think the audience notices—I don't hear the telltale collective gasp—so, heart thundering, I whisper for Anya to keep her tight grip on my thighs and bend forward at my hips, reaching plaintively away from her. I can feel Anya shaking. We're supposed to end the pas de deux in this sort of supported fall—I'm supposed to go stiff as Anya lowers me to the floor with a hand behind my neck and then pulls me back up again, me rising back en pointe, which is the hardest part. Instead, she lowers me all the

way down and I lie flat on my back as she tilts into a penché arabesque, her hand wrapped loosely around my throat. We get
thunderous applause, several hearty cries of *Brava*. We wait a few
beats after the curtain closes to come out of it.

Kaz is waiting for us. He stares at us both for a few moments
before speaking. "I like it," he says. "We'll keep it."

"Even the slip?" Anya pants.

"*Especially* the slip."

I stuff down half a banana, some water. I dry my sweaty body,
change my costume with the help of a dresser, and fix my hair.
Jasper appears in my mirror as I'm touching up my makeup. A
nauseous bubble grows in me and then fades.

"Ready to get rescued?" he says.

"Ready as ever."

The corps gets to shine for about six minutes at the beginning
of act two, and then Fran does her solo, which is a kind of pas de
caractère—she dances the part of the town nut, who is actually
trying to tell everyone how evil June is, and accurately predicts
May's rescue. But no one pays her any mind, and June distracts
everyone with a stylized cakewalk. Ryn dances this with an as-
tounding amount of energy, and the audience shouts and whistles
when she's done. I stay warm at the barre as William, my handsome stranger, comes to town.

I take a small sip of water—I don't want to drink so much it
sloshes around in my stomach—and glance over at Kaz, who is
huddled with the Oneida dancers and a couple of girls from the
African troupe. There is the music, exotic and spirited, the sound
of my knees popping as I plié in fifth, the clack of pointe shoes on
the Marley. I wonder what the weight of all this noise is. It must
have a weight; its vibrations must be enough to move the earth. A
stagehand drops a prop—a Styrofoam planter bursting with fab-
ric flowers—and though the music covers the dull thud, Kaz

glares daggers and the poor stagehand cringes, turning scarlet from the neck up. I smile at him consolingly.

I make my way into the wings. Onstage, June is attempting to seduce William. I prepare to interrupt her yet again, this time with a wilting pas de bourrée couru across the stage. William is distracted by May, instantly smitten. I make May too exhausted to feel anything fully; William's love, her own—it is muted, only there enough to make her despair. My pointe shoes die in the middle of my sleepy pas de deux with Jasper, making the balances extremely difficult. The shoes don't support my feet anymore, so I point my toes so hard my calves cramp. It's a miracle I don't fall, though I do wobble through one arabesque, which is infuriating as I know there are several critics in the audience tonight, some of whom love to criticize my balance. When the scene ends, I run to change my shoes, throwing the dead ones at the wall in frustration.

I lie on my stomach as Ryn vigorously rubs heat into my calves and beats them with her fists. Gwen offers me a spoonful of her yogurt, which I accept not because I want it but because the offer is so kind. There isn't much time. Soon, William and May will battle the Hag, that tangled pas de trois.

Jasper crouches down next to me, patting his brow with a washcloth. "Your feet have gotten stronger," he says. "Trust me, no one saw a thing."

He rubs my back, heedless of the sweat, digs his blunt fingertips into the knots of muscle between my shoulder blades, at the base of my neck. He has done this so many times before. He knows exactly where the knots are, exactly how hard to press to get the tension to release. Ballet makes it so difficult to be more than a failing body. Even to each other. There is beauty in that, I think, in the way there is beauty in all tragic things. Jasper helps me to my feet and we jog past stretching dancers, past stagehands and idle props. Our music is starting. We count.

The Bhangra, the hula, the jarabe tapatío, the Oneidas' dance, and the African dance are all listed on the programs under "American Dances." I watch some of them from backstage, but I've just completed my grueling wedding adagio and once these dances are done, Jasper and I will have to do our equally grueling grand pas de deux. I stuff my feet into my booties to keep them warm, down the other half of my banana. It is brown and mushy now, but I don't care. I sip water and go to the barre: dégagés and frappés and relevés. Jasper is on the other side of the barre, doing much the same. I can hear the drums starting for the Oneidas' dance. We still have seven minutes before our grand pas.

Kaz approaches and holds out his hands to us. We stop our barre work and stand before him, eager to please.

"You are both doing great," he says. "If I could promote you again, I would."

Kaz lifts his chest, his signal that he's about to go into demonstration mode. He grabs both of my hands, no longer Kaz but William. I know what he wants me to do. Arabesque, promenade, attitude derrière, développé.

"Lift that leg up nice and slow," he tells me. "Slow and high. Seduce them."

I do it again.

"And Jasper," he says, wagging a finger, "remember to leave some space when you set her down from that boat lift—she's still got the fouettés. And here, before she steps up onto your leg: I want you more geometrical than classical."

He demonstrates and Jasper copies.

I hop up and down a few times to release the nervous energy roiling inside. Kaz pats my cheek, a little roughly.

"You've both done an impossible thing," he says, "breaking the curse. And there was a cost: You are inexorably bound together, not just by marriage but by the force of destruction. The intricacy of this grand pas shows how thoroughly you belong to each other now. Cece, at the end there, don't think so much about jumping into his arms—it needs to be as though he plucks you right from the air, right from that grand jeté, and *then* sweeps you down into the fish dive. You love each other, yes, but more important, he's helped you battle your way out of purgatory, and now time and space are yours again."

We nod, both of us sucking Kaz's words in, willing them into our muscles, our ligaments and bones, our very cells. The whole floor reverberates with the power of the African dance. About a minute left.

Kaz points to the stage. "Now go do it."

The audience applauds so hard I swear they must be stomping too. When the curtain finally closes on the last of our endless curtain calls, Jasper picks me up and spins me around and around. Kaz comes and kisses my sweaty face. Someone pops the cork on a bottle of champagne, and we pass it around, taking swigs straight from the bottle. I see two of my little cygnets—Denisha and Priya—sneak a couple of sips and I wink at them. They performed well tonight, and I'm surprised at how proud I am. I have a phone call this week with a woman Kaz put me in touch with who may help me set up a nonprofit to get inner-city kids to the ballet and offer free classes taught by company members—I'm already calling it the Little Dancer Foundation in my head. I hope to fill SAB with more little girls like Michelle and Denisha.

We stand and wait for Kaz's notes. He generally praises Ryn, but cautions her to be more precisely on the music in the second act.

"Anya, don't be afraid to really grab her," he says, demonstrating on me. "In all your lifts, Cece is doing most of the work by jumping, so just make sure to keep her on her leg."

Anya nods and comes over to me to practice one of the cambré presses. She takes my waist firmly, and I jump a little, arching my back as she uses her upper body strength to guide me overhead.

"Good," Kaz says. "Cece, you're beautiful, darling. Really fill up the stage in that last adagio, yes?"

When Kaz moves on to the corps, I turn and head to my dressing room. My vanity is covered with bouquets of flowers from donors I've met, balletomanes, other company members. Michelle's mom got me a dozen yellow roses with a card signed by the girls. I smile at my reflection as I scrub the makeup from my face. One of the newer corps girls walks by and catches me grinning at myself. I smile at her too and she grins back.

I reach for another makeup removal wipe and something catches my eye. One of tonight's programs, tucked under a bouquet from one of the company's celebrity board members. This month's *Playbill* features an artfully violet-tinged photo of me, standing confrontationally en pointe in a simple white leotard and white tulle skirt, hair pulled tightly back, hands at my sides, eyes staring straight into the lens. But someone has drawn over the program. Black marker. My leaping figure emerges from a writhing mass of black lines. Chaotic, invocative. Beautiful. It's a bit imprecise, like someone has sketched it in inadequate light. Adrenaline sends hot tingles into my hands and my head. I'm hungry for air, I can't get enough of it.

I clutch the program to my chest and shoot up out of my chair. I rush back out and onto the stage, startling the crew, who are in the middle of mopping up sweat. The house lights are still on, and I search the empty seats of the theater. He is not there. I run out of the theater, avoiding the stage door, where I know a crowd of people will be waiting for me. There are still people posing in front of the fountain in the plaza, waiting for cabs on Columbus. I am recognized—it is all there in the periphery of my attention. No one has the power to stop me right now. People's recognition, their desire, clings to me like cobwebs as I try to find him, try to find Paul. He is like an electrical current across my skin. A ghost. I am still wearing part of my costume under my junk clothes, and it creates a drag, like I'm trying to swim with a dress on. That subtle push back. I run up and down Columbus, and then Amsterdam, not finding him, until my body demands I stop. I have finally asked too much of it tonight. I bend forward, hands on my knees, panting. Lincoln Center pulls me back, a greater force. This place is my home.

I trudge inside, avoiding the stage door again. I shower, the water too hot and then too cold, change into my street clothes, greet my fans. The program is tucked under my tank top, held in place by the band of my bra. It is pressed against my skin, as warm as a living thing. I look for him. I wonder if he will ever let me stop looking for him. If he will ever just be here. If one day I won't have to choose. My body is beginning to cool down, my muscles twitching from fatigue. I let the crowd keep me. When they disperse it'll be just me and my brother's echo. I sign every autograph, take every picture. Stage smile, loose hug, pose. I do whatever they need me to. This is a dance, too.

When they leave me, I feel my own weight, my own lightness. When I rose onto my toes in my first pair of pointe shoes, Señora Sandy told me, *Always lift, but always be your own anchor. The shoes won't do it for you.* The evening smells like ether. I clasp it to me,

fasten it to my shoulders like a mantle. I begin my walk home, taking it with me as I go, Paul's program warmed by my warmth.

The night sky is a kaleidoscopic view of the unimaginable.
Millions of particles from the earth drift up and evaporate there.
What we understand as everything is eventually nothing. I place a
hand on my stomach, pressing the program and its drawing closer.
Big breath in.

And . . .

Acknowledgments

Thank you to Heather, my agent, who saw what I was trying to show. Thank you to Nicole, my editor, for always asking more of me and my writing. I am, as always, grateful to my parents for their unwavering support; my husband, for being my cheerleader; and my friends, for always being willing to read my drafts and always being ready to go to the ballet with me.

About the Author

Nicole Cuffy is a Brooklyn-born writer with a BA from Columbia University and an MFA from the New School. When she is not writing, she is reading, and when she is not reading, she is probably dancing. Her work can be found in *The Master's Review* 6, *The Chautauqua Review, Blue Mesa Review,* and *New England Review.* Her chapbook, *Atlas of the Body,* was an editor's choice and finalist for the Black River Chapbook Competition. She lives in Washington, D.C., with her dog and her husband.